THE WOLF DEMON;

OR,

The Queen of the Kanawha.

BY ALBERT W. AIKEN,

AUTHOR OF "INJUN DICK," "ROCKY MOUNTAIN ROB,"
"KENTUCK, THE SPORT," ETC., ETC.

THE WOLF DEMON

I0629289

1

THE PROLOGUE.

IN THE GLADE AND BY THE MOONLIGHT.

The great, round moon looked down in a flood of silver light upon the virgin forest by the banks of the Scioto, the beautiful river which winds through the richest and fairest valley in all the wide western land—the great corn valley of the Shawnee tribe—those red warriors who, in their excursions across the Ohio (the "La Belle" river of the early French adventurers) had given to the plains and valleys of Kentucky the name of "The Dark and Bloody Land."

The tree-tops were green and silver; but under the spreading branches, sable was the gloom.

The strange, odd noises of the night broke the forest stillness. One hears all noises in the night even in a civilized land; how much more wondrous then are the wild, free cries of the inhabitants of the great greenwood, untrammeled by the restraining hand of man!

The free winds surged with a mournful sound through the branches of the wood.

A ring around the moon told the coming storm.

Dark masses of clouds dashed across the sky, ever and anon vailing in the "mistress of the night," as though some unquiet spirit was envious of the pale moonbeams, and wished to cover, with its mantle, the earth, and cloak an evil deed.

A frightened deer came dashing through the aisles of the forest—a noble buck with branching horns that told of many a year spent under the greenwood tree.

Across a little open glade, whereon the moonbeams fell—kissing the earth as though they loved it—dashed the deer, and then, entering again the dark recesses of the forest, the brown coat of the wood-prince was lost in the inky gloom.

Then in the trail of the buck, guided by the noise of the rustling branches, came a dark form.

As the form stole, with noiseless tread, across the moonlit glade, it displayed the person of an Indian warrior.

A red brave, decked out in deer-skin garb, stained with the pigments of the earth in many colors, and fringed in fanciful fashion.

The warrior was a tall and muscular savage, one of Nature's noblemen. A son of the wilderness untrammeled by the taint of civilization—a brave of the great Shawnee tribe, the lords of the Ohio valley from the oil "licks" of the Alleghany stream to the level prairies where the Wabash and the White pour their muddy tide into the great river of the New World, the winding, smiling Ohio.

Fast on the trail of the deer he followed, although the chase was almost hopeless.

Hardly had the warrior crossed the glade and entered the thicket, when, on his track—following him as he was following the deer—came another form through the forest.

A form that moved with noiseless steps; a form that cast behind it a shadow gigantic in its hight.

The form did not pass across the glade, but skulked around it in the shadow, as though it feared the moonlight.

The warrior penetrated into the thicket beyond the glade, but a hundred yards or so. Then satisfied that the deer was thoroughly alarmed and had sought safety in flight, the warrior began to retrace his steps. The Shawnee brave dreamed not of the dark and fearful form—that seemed neither man nor beast—that lurked in his track.

He had hunted the deer, but little thought that he, too, in turn was hunted.

The red chief guessed not that the dread demon of his nation—the terrible foe who had left his red "totem" on the breast of many a stout Shawnee brave—was even now on his track, eager for that blood which was necessary to its existence.

With careless steps the warrior retraced his way.

From behind a tree-trunk came the terrible form. One single blow, and a tomahawk crashed through the brain of the red-man.

With a groan the Shawnee chief sunk lifeless to the earth.

The dark form bent over him for a moment. Three rapid knife-slashes, and the mark of the destroyer was blazoned on the breast of the victim, reddened with blood.

Then through the aisles of the forest stole the dark form.

All living things—the insects of the earth—the birds of the night—shrunk from its path.

It crossed the glade full in the soft light of the moon.

The rays of the orb of night fell upon a huge gray wolf, who walked erect like a man! The face of the wolf was that of a human. In the paw of the beast glistened the tomahawk of the red-man, the edge now scarlet with the blood of the Shawnee chief.

For a moment the moon looked upon the huge and terrible figure, and then, as if struck with deadly fear at the awful sight, hid itself behind a dark cloud.

When it again came forth, the strange and terrible being, that wore the figure of a wolf and the face of a man, had disappeared, swallowed up in the gloom of the forest.

Once again the creatures of the night came forth. Again the shrill cries broke the stillness of the wood.

THE MARK ON THE TREE.

Two rifle-"cracks" broke the stillness of the wilderness, that stretched in one almost unbroken line from the Alleghany and Blue Ridge peaks to the Ohio river. The reports re-echoed over the broad expanse of the Kanawha and Ohio rivers, for the shots were fired near the junction of the two streams—fired so nearly at the same time that the two seemed almost like one report.

Then, before the smoke of the rifles had curled lazily upward in spiral rings on the air, came a crash in the tangled underbrush, and forth into a little open glade—the work of Nature's master hand—dashed a noble buck. The red stream bursting from a wound just behind the shoulder and staining crimson the glossy brown coat of the forest lord, told plainly that he was stricken unto death.

The buck gained the center of the glade, then his stride weakened; the dash through the thicket was the last despairing effort of the poor brute to escape from the invisible foes whose death-dealing balls had pierced his side.

With a moan of pain, almost human in its expression, the buck fell upon his knees, then rolled over on his side, dead.

The brute had fallen near the trunk of a large oak tree—a tree distinguished from its neighbors by a blazon upon its side, whereon, in rude characters, some solitary hunter had cut his name.

Scarcely had the death-bleat of the buck pierced the silence of the glen, when two men came dashing through the woods, each eager to be the first to secure the game.

One of the two was some twenty yards in advance of the other, and reached the body of the dead buck just as his rival emerged from the thicket.

Placing his foot upon the buck, and rifle in hand, he prepared to dispute the quarry with the second hunter, for both men—strangers to each other—had fired at the same deer.

The hunter who stood with his foot upon the buck, in an attitude of proud defiance, had reloaded his rifle as he ran and was prepared to defend his right to the game to the bitter end.

In person, the hunter was a muscular, well-built man, standing some six feet in hight. Not a clumsy, overgrown giant, hardly able to bear his own weight, but a man as supple and as active as a panther. He was clad in buck-skin hunting-shirt and leggins, made in the Indian fashion, but unlike that fashion in one respect, and that was that no gaudy ornaments decorated the garments. Upon the feet of the hunter were a pair of moccasins. A cap rudely fashioned from a piece of deer-skin, and with the little flat tail of the animal as an ornament, completed the dress of the hunter.

The face of the man was singular to look upon. The features were large and clearly cut. The cold gray eye, broad forehead, and massive, squarely-chiseled chin, told of dauntless courage and of an iron will. A terrible scar extended from the temple to the chin on the left side of the face.

The hunter was quite young—not over twenty-five, though deep lines of care were upon the face.

The second hunter, who came from the tangled thicket, but paused on the edge of the little glen on beholding the threatening attitude of the hunter who stood with his foot on the deer, was a man who had probably seen forty years. He, too, like the other, was of powerful build, and his muscular frame gave promise of great strength.

He was dressed, like the first, in the forest garb of deer-skin, but his dress was gayly fringed and ornamented.

In his hand he bore one of the long rifles so common to the frontier set-tler of that time, for our story is of the year 1780.

The clear blue eye of the second hunter took in the situation at a glance. He readily saw that the man who stood so defiantly by the deer was not dis-posed to yield his claim to the animal without a struggle. So the second hunter determined upon a parley.

"Hello, stranger! I reckon we're both after the same critter," said the hunter who stood on the edge of the little glade.

"Yes; it 'pears so," replied the other, who stood by the deer.

There was something apparently in the voice of the last comer that im-pressed the first favorably, for he dropped the butt of his rifle to the ground, though he still kept his foot upon the deer's carcass.

"Well, stranger, we can't both have the game. I think I hit him, an' of course, as it is but nat'ral, you think so, too. So I reckon we'd better find out which one of us he belongs to; 'cause I don't want him if my ball didn't finish him, an' of course, you don't want him if he's mine by right," said the second hunter, approaching the other fearlessly.

"You're right, by hookey!" cried the other, yielding to the influence of the good-humored tone of the other.

"Let me introduce myself, stranger, 'cos you seem to be a new-comer round hyer," said the old hunter. "My name's Daniel Boone; mayhap you've heard of me."

"Well, I reckon I have!" exclaimed the other, in astonishment. "Thar's few men on the border but what have heard on you. I'm right glad to see you, kurnel."

"How may I call your name?" asked Boone, who had taken a fancy to the brawny stranger.

"Thar's my mark—my handle," said the stranger, pointing as he spoke to the name carved on the tree-trunk by which the deer had fallen; "that's me."

Boone cast his eye upon the tree.

Such was the inscription blazoned upon the trunk of the oak.

"You see, kurnel, the buck evidently thought that it was a ball from my rifle that ended him, 'cos he laid down to die right under my name," said the hunter, with a laugh.

"Abe Lark!" Boone read the inscription upon the tree aloud.

"Yes, that's me, kurnel; your'n to command," replied the hunter.

"Stranger in these parts?" questioned Boone.

"Yes," replied the other; "I've jest come down from the north. I camped hyar last night, an' this morning I jest put my mark onto the tree, so that folks might know that I was round."

"I'm right glad to meet you," and Boone shook hands warmly with the stranger hunter. "And while you're in these parts, just take up your quarters with me. I'm stopping down yonder, at Point Pleasant, on a visit to some friends of mine."

"Well, I don't mind, kurnel; I'll take your invitation in the same good spirit that you offer it," said Lark.

"Now for the deer; let's see who the animal belongs to," cried Boone, kneeling down by the carcass.

"Why, kurnel, I resign all claim. It ain't for me to dispute with Kurnel Boone!" exclaimed Lark.

"Resign your claim?" cried Boone, in astonishment. "Not by a jugful. I'll wager my rifle ag'in' a popgun that you're as good a hand at the rifle as myself. It's just as likely to be your deer as mine."

Then the two carefully examined the carcass. They found the marks of the two bullets easily; both had struck the animal just behind the shoulder, but on opposite sides. It was difficult to determine which had inflicted the death-wound.

"Well, now, this would puzzle a lawyer," muttered Boone.

"S'pose we divide the animal, share and share alike," said Lark.

"That's squar'," replied Boone. "We'll take the buck in to the station. By the way, what's the news from the upper settlements?"

"Well, nothing particular, 'cept that the red devils are on the war-path ag'in," replied Lark.

Boone was astonished at the news.

"On the war-path ag'in, eh? What tribe?"

"The Shawnees and the Wyandots."

"The Shawnees and the Wyandots!" cried Boone: "then we'll see fire and smell gunpowder round these parts before long."

"I shouldn't wonder," said the other.

"Well, I'm glad that you have brought the news. We'll be able to prepare for the imps."

"You can depend upon it," said Lark; "a friend of mine has been right through the Shawnee country. They are coming down onto the settlements in greater force than was ever known before. They've been stirred up by the British on the border. I did heer say that the British Governor agrees to give so much apiece for white scalps to the red savages."

"The eternal villain!" cried Boone, indignantly.

"The Injuns are a-goin' to try to wipe out all the settlements on the Ohio. It will be a blood-time while it lasts," said Lark, soberly.

"We'll have to face it," replied Boone. "Did your friend hear what chief was goin' to lead the expedition ag'in' us on the south?"

"Yes; Ke-ne-ha-ha."

"The-man-that-walks," said Boone, thoughtfully. "He's one of the best warriors in all the Shawnee nation. Blood will run like water along our borders, I'm afeard."

"Yes, and the renegade, Simon Girty, is to guide the Injuns."

"If I had him within reach of my rifle once, he'd never guide another Injun expedition ag'in' his own flesh and blood," said Boone, and his hand closed tightly around the rifle-barrel.

"I was jest on my way to the settlement at Point Pleasant when I started up the buck this morning," said Lark.

"Well, I'm right glad that it happened as it did, 'cos I shouldn't have had the pleasure of meetin' you," said Boone. "Now, s'pose we swing the buck on a pole an' tote it in to the station. I reasonably expect that there'll be some white faces over yonder when they hear that Ke-ne-ha-ha an' his Shawnees, to say nothin' of Girty, are on the war-path."

"There ought to be good men enough along the Ohio to whip any force these red devils can bring," said Lark.

"Well, they're awful scattered, but I reckon that now that we know what's goin' on, we can get men enough to give the Shawnees all the fighting that they want."

Then the two slung the buck on a pole and started to the station known as Point Pleasant.

CHAPTER II.

THE SECRET FOE.

In the pleasant valley of the Scioto, near what is now the town of Chillicothe, stood the principal village of the great Shawnee nation—the Indian tribe that could bring ten thousand warriors into the field—deadly enemies of the pale-faced intruder.

All was bustle within the Indian village. To one used to the Indian customs, it would have been plain that the red-skins were preparing for the war-path.

The village was alive with warriors. Gayly-painted savages, decked with ocher and vermilion, strutted proudly up and down, eagerly waiting for the time to come when, like tigers, they could spring upon the pale-faces and redden their weapons with the blood of their hated foes.

Over the village ruled the great chief, Ke-ne-ha-ha, or "The-man-that-walks"—so termed, first, because he was reputed to be the fastest runner of any red braves in the Ohio valley, Shawnee, Wyandot or Mingo; second, that when a youth, on his first war-path against the Hurons, he had stolen by night into the midst of a Huron village, literally walked among the sleeping warriors, and brought back to his comrades the scalp of a great Huron chief, whom he had dispatched without alarming the sleepers—the greatest warrior in all the Shawnee nation—a chief wise in council, brave on the war-path, and wily as the red fox.

In the village of the red-men were two whose skins were white, though they were Indians at heart. The two were renegades from their country and their kin.

These two stood together by the river's bank, and idly watched the daring and howling warriors. They were dressed in the Indian fashion, and were sinewy, powerful men in build.

The taller of the two, whose hair and eyes were dark, was called Simon Girty. At one time he had been reputed to be one of the best scouts on the border, but, for some reason, he had forsaken the settlements and found a home with the fierce red-men of the forest-wild, giving up home, country, friends, every thing. He had been adopted into the Indian tribe, and none of his red-skinned brothers seemed to bear as deadly a hatred to the whites as this renegade, Simon Girty.

His companion was not quite so tall, or as stoutly built. He was called David Kendrick, and was an adopted son of the Shawnees, as Girty was of the Wyandots.

"This is going to be a bloody business," said Girty, as he surveyed the yelling Indians, who were busy in the "scalp-dance."

"Yes, our chief, Ke-ne-ha-ha, has sworn to break the power of the whites along the Ohio. The braves are well provided with arms by the British Governor. Kentucky never saw such a force upon her border as this will be," replied the other.

"The more the better," said the renegade, Girty, moodily.

Then a howl of anguish rung through the Indian village. The braves stopped their sports to listen. They knew the signal well: it was the wail for the dead. It told that some Shawnee warrior had gone to the spirit-land.

The cry of anguish came from a party of braves entering the village from the south. In their midst they bore what seemed, to the eyes of the renegades, a human body.

The warriors deposited their burden before the door of the council-lodge.

Attracted by the death-note, Ke-ne-ha-ha, the great chief of the Shawnees, came from his lodge.

The chief was a splendid specimen of a man. He stood nearly six feet in hight, and was as straight as an arrow. He was quite light in hue for an Indian, and his features were intelligent and finely cut.

Astonishment flashed from his eyes as he gazed upon the face of the dead Indian, around whom, at a respectful distance, were grouped the Shawnee warriors.

The chief recognized the features of the brave known as Little Crow, a stout warrior, and reputed to be one of the best fighting-men in all the Shawnee nation.

"Wah!" said the chief, in a tone that betrayed deep astonishment, "the soul of the Little Crow has gone to the spirit-land—he rests in Manitou's bosom. Let my braves speak—who has taken the life of the Shawnee warrior?"

"Let the chief open his ears and he shall hear," replied one of the braves, a tall, muscular warrior, known as Watega. "Little Crow went forth, last night, to hunt the deer in the woods of the Scioto. He was a great warrior; his arm was strong—his feet swift on the trail. He told his brothers that he would return before the spirit-lights (stars) died. He did not come. His brothers sought for him. By the banks of the Scioto they found him, but the hatchet of a foe had taken the life of the Little Crow."

Then the chief knelt by the side of the body and examined the wound in the head; the clotted blood marked the spot.

The head of the chief had been split open by a single blow, and that dealt by a giant's hand. The wound had apparently been made by a tomahawk, and, as the chief guessed, the dead man had been attacked suddenly, and from the rear.

"Did my warriors find no trail of the enemy who took the life of their brother?" asked the chief, still keeping his position by the body, and with a puzzled look upon his face.

"Wah!—the Shawnee braves have eyes—they are not blind, like owls in the light. When they found the Little Crow dead, they looked for the track of the foe. They found footprints by the body, but the trail came from nowhere and went nowhere."

"And the footprints—Indian or pale-face?"

"Pale-face, but the moccasins of the red-man," answered the brave.

The brow of the chief grew dark. A white foe so near the village of the Shawnee, and so daring as to attack and kill one of the best warriors of the tribe, apparently without a struggle, must needs be looked after.

"My braves must hunt down the pale-face that wears the moccasin of the Indian and uses the tomahawk," said the chief, gravely.

Then Ke-ne-ha-ha drew aside the blanket that was wrapt around the body of the dead brave. A cry of horror broke from the lips of the great chief, and was re-echoed by the surrounding Indians when they gazed upon the naked breast of the dead warrior.

"*The totem of the Wolf Demon!*" exclaimed the chief.

The circle of friends gazed upon the mysterious mark in silent consternation. Their staring eyes and fear-stricken countenances showed plainly how deeply they were interested.

And what was the totem of the Wolf Demon?

On the naked breast of the brawny dead chief were three slashes, apparently made by a knife, thus:

And the blood, congealing on the skin, formed a Red Arrow.

It was the totem of the Wolf Demon—the invisible and fatal scourge of the great Shawnee nation. Thus he marked his victims.

The chief arose with a troubled look upon his haughty face.

"Let my people sing the death-song, for a brave warrior has gone to the spirit-land. Ke-ne-ha-ha will seek the counsel of the Great Medicine Man, so that he may learn how to fight the Wolf Demon, who has stricken unto death the great braves of the Shawnee nation, and put the totem of the Red Arrow upon their breast."

Sorrowfully the warriors obeyed the words of the chief, and soon the sound of lamentation wailed out loud on the air, which, but a moment before, had resounded with the glad shouts of triumph.

Slowly and with knitted brows Ke-ne-ha-ha betook himself to the lodge of the old Indian who was the Great Medicine Man of the Shawnee tribe.

The death of one of the principal warriors of his tribe by the dreaded hand of the Wolf Demon, almost within the very precincts of his village, and at the moment when he was preparing to set out on his expedition against the whites, seemed like an omen of evil. A dark cloud descended upon his soul, despite all his efforts to remove it.

The two renegades had joined the circle around the dead Indian, and had listened to the story of how he met his death. Then, when the circle had broken up, they had slowly walked back again to their former position by the bank of the river.

A puzzled look was upon Girty's face. After they had resumed their former station, he spoke:

"Dave, the words of the chief are a mystery to me, though the Indians seem to understand them well enough. What did he mean when he spoke of the Wolf Demon? and what did that mark of a Red Arrow, cut on the breast of the dead Indian, mean?"

"Why, don't you know?" asked the other, in astonishment.

"No; you forget that for the past six months I have been at upper Sandusky, with the Wyandots."

"Yes; and it is just about six months since the Wolf Demon first appeared."

"Explain," said Girty, unable to guess the mystery.

"I will. For the past six months some mysterious being has singled out the warriors of the Shawnee tribe for his victims. He always seems to take them by surprise; single warriors alone he attacks. And on the breast of those he kills he leaves, as his mark, three slashes with a knife forming a Red Arrow, like the one you saw on this fellow."

"But the name of the Wolf Demon?"

"I will explain. One Indian alone has lived to tell of an encounter with this mysterious slayer. He was only stunned, and recovered. He reported that he was attacked by a huge gray wolf, with a man's head—the face painted black and white. The wolf stood on its hind legs like a man, but in hight far out-topping any human. He caught a glimpse of the monster as it struck him down with a tomahawk that the beast held in its paws. And that's the story of the Wolf Demon, who has killed some of the bravest warriors of the Shawnee nation."

"But what do you think it is?"

"I reckon it's the devil," said the renegade, solemnly.

CHAPTER III.

A TIMELY SHOT.

From one of the largest of the dwellings that composed the little frontier settlement of Point Pleasant came a young girl.

She was about sixteen, and was as pretty as one of the wild flowers that bloom unseen amid the rocky ravines through which ran the tumultuous Kanawha.

Dark-brown hair rippled in wavy masses back from her olive-tinged brow, browned by exposure to the free winds of the wilderness and the sunbeams that danced so merrily over the surface of the rolling river.

The bright color in the cheeks of the girl, her free step, that possessed all the grace and lightness of the bounding fawn, told of perfect health, as also did the sparkling brown eyes and rose-red lips that seemed to hold such dewy sweetness in their graceful curves.

The maiden was known as Virginia Treveling. She was the daughter of General Lemuel Treveling, a man who had great experience as an Indian-fighter on the Western border, and who had settled down in Point Pleasant, and was reputed to be by far the wealthiest man in all the country around.

So, by virtue of her father's wealth, as well as by the aid of her own beauty, Virginia Treveling was the belle of the station known as Point Pleasant.

Her right to the title was not disputed, and few envied her, for Virginia was as good as she was beautiful.

Many of the young men of Point Pleasant and of the neighboring stations had sought to gain the favor of the winsome maid, but to all she said, *nay*!

The man to whom the fair girl would freely give her heart had not yet met her eye; but Virginia was young—scarcely old enough to be wooed and won.

The maid was clad in simple homespun garments, the work of her own hands, for she was a true American girl, a daughter of the frontier, and looked not with favor upon the gaudy trappings of fashion.

The little tin pail that she carried in her hand told her mission.

The great blackberries were shining in huge purple clusters in the rocky passes that surrounded Point Pleasant, and, like the fortifications of the olden time, seemed to forbid approach.

With her light, graceful step, the girl passed through the village, and taking the trail that led to the south, along the bank of the stream, soon left the settlement behind.

There was little danger in this incursion into the deep woods, for the Indians were on the northern bank of the Ohio; and then, too, there had been peace between the settlements and their red neighbors for some time.

The girl followed the trail for about half a mile, then, turning abruptly to the east, entered a little defile, where the blackberries grew thick and rank.

Picking the berries as she went slowly along, she soon lost sight of the trail leading from the town.

The maiden had not been gone from the path many minutes when the hoof-stroke of a horse rung out with a dull "thud" on the still air of the forest.

A horseman was approaching from the south. A traveler, probably, from Virginia.

Then the horseman came into sight. He was a young man, dressed plainly in a homespun suit of blue. Upon his head he wore a broad-leafed felt hat, that shaded the sun from his eyes. A short, German rifle, carrying a ball of forty to the pound, and richly ornamented on the stock with silver, was resting across his saddle in front of him. A keen-edged hunting-knife, the blade some eighteen inches in length, was thrust through the leather belt that girded in his waist.

The face of the young horseman was a frank and honest one. The full, steel-blue eyes showed plainly both courage and firmness. The handsome, resolute mouth confirmed this.

In figure, the rider was about the medium size, but his well-built, sinewy form gave promise of great muscular power.

The rider was named Harvey Winthrop. A descendant was he of one of the staunch old Puritan fathers. And now he was seeking his fortune in the far Western wilds, for the fickle goddess had not smiled upon the young man. A student at a foreign university, he had been hurriedly called home by the sickness of his father, his only parent. He arrived just in time to close that father's eyes. And when he came to settle up his parent's estate, instead of finding himself—as he had expected—the possessor of a goodly fortune, he discovered that some few hundred dollars was all in the world that he could call his own.

Young Harvey Winthrop, though, had the right stuff in his nature. Bidding his friends adieu, he set forth to make new ones, and to carve out for himself a fortune by the banks of the "Beautiful River" the Ohio.

So it is that, on that pleasant summer's day, the young Bostonian found himself on the trail leading to Point Pleasant, and was fast approaching that station.

"The settlement can not be far off now," he said, musing to himself as he rode along, and, rising in his stirrups, he strove with his gaze to penetrate through the mazes of the almost trackless forest before him.

Then, to the astonished ears of the young man came a woman's scream, evidently given under great alarm.

The traveler checked his horse and snatched the rifle from the saddle.

Again on the still air rung out the scream, shrilly, coupled with a cry for help. The cry came from the ravine on the right.

In a second he leaped from the saddle, and, rifle in hand, plunged into the ravine. His horse—a well-trained beast—remained motionless on the spot where his rider had left him.

The young man dashed up the steep ascent at break-neck speed.

The noise made by his steps fell upon the ears of the woman who uttered the scream. She knew that help was near.

A few steps more and the young man beheld a scene which nearly froze his blood with horror.

Fleeing down the ravine came a young girl—who, even at this moment of excitement, he noticed was beautiful, almost beyond expression; and behind her, in full pursuit, was a huge black bear.

The girl was Virginia Treveling. In her search for berries she had stumbled upon the bear, who was busily engaged feasting upon the luscious fruit.

But Bruin, in a twinkling, forsook the berries for the human.

Then from the lips of the girl came the shrill screams that had brought the traveler to her rescue.

The girl reached the young man.

"Keep on, Miss," he cried, quickly; "fly for your life! I'll keep the brute at bay."

Small time was there for conversation, for the bear, at his lumbering trot, was coming rapidly onward.

"He will kill you!" cried the terrified girl.

"Yes, and you, too, if you don't run," said the young man, coolly. "One life is enough; so save yours."

"I will not go!" exclaimed the girl. "Give me your powder flask and a bullet. After you fire, if you miss him, I can load."

The hunter threw a glance of admiration at the heroic maid who seemed so cool at this moment of danger; but he did as she requested. Then, as the bear came on, he leveled his rifle at the brute, and sighting one of his eyes, fired. But the bear swerving in its course at the moment, the ball glanced across his bony head and shot off as if it had been but a boy's marble.

The beast paused for an instant, shook its head as if annoyed, then, with an angry growl, he came straight upon the young man.

Winthrop had handed his rifle to the girl, and, drawing his knife, awaited the onset. His only hope of escape was to close in with the animal, and stab him in some vital part before he could use the terrible claws and teeth.

The bear reared on its hind legs and prepared to seize the young man with open mouth.

Winthrop felt that the crisis had come.

The young man raised his knife to plunge it into the shaggy breast before him, while, with eager but trembling hands, the girl reloaded the rifle.

But the sharp crack of a rifle came quick on the air.

Winthrop heard the "hiss" of a bullet that whirled past, close to his ear. Then, with a grunt of agony, the bear fell over on its side, clawed the air wildly for a moment—growled in pain, and sunk into the silence of death.

The rifle-ball which had passed so near to the ear of the young man had entered the body of the bear between the fore-legs and buried itself in the great red heart.

Winthrop could hardly believe his eyes when he beheld the grim king of the forest lying in death at his feet; when he saw the huge paws motionless that he had expected to feel tearing his own flesh.

He had been saved almost by a miracle.

A timely shot, and a good one, for an inch either way would have missed the heart of the bear or killed the young hunter.

Winthrop felt that both he and the beautiful girl had been saved by the shot of the, as yet, hidden friend.

The young man looked for his preserver. Judge of his astonishment when forth from the bushes that fringed the rocks, with a rifle in hand—a very forest queen—came a young girl!

CHAPTER IV.

THE GIRL THAT FIRED THE SHOT.

Winthrop looked with amazed eyes upon his preserver, for that the girl had saved his life by coming so timely to his rescue, there was hardly a doubt.

The young man saw a beautiful girl, clad in the Indian fashion, her garb gayly fringed and decorated with colored beads. But though clad in the garb of the Indian, more white blood than red leaped in the veins of the forest child.

Her skin was of a rich olive tinge; a peculiar skin—so thin, despite its darkness, that it showed the quick play of the surging blood in the veins beneath.

Dark-brown hair floated in tangled masses from the fillet of deer-skin, adorned with eagle-plumes, that encircled her head. Her eyes were dark brown in their hue, and large and full as the eyes of the deer.

Grace was in every motion, yet one could easily see that the graceful limbs were strong and sinewy—muscles of steel beneath the silken skin.

Lightly the girl bounded down, from rock to rock, until she reached the bottom of the defile wherein stood the two by the carcass of the dead bear who had fallen by the rifle of this forest fay.

Nor was Virginia less astonished at the sudden appearance of the dark-hued maiden than the young stranger.

She gazed with amazement on the girl who was so unlike all of her sex in looks and dress.

"A lucky shot!" exclaimed the wood nymph, kneeling by the side of dead Bruin, and examining the wound that had given him his death.

"I owe you my life!" cried Winthrop, impulsively; "for had I once got into the grim hug of the brute, I'm afraid he would have made sad work of me."

"No, not to me," replied the girl, "but to the great One above who first sent me to your aid, and then gave me the skill to send the ball home to the heart of the bear."

"I shall thank you, though, all the same," replied the young man. "You have saved my life, and, while I live, I shall never forget it."

"Don't speak of it any more, please," said the girl, a blush mantling to her cheeks at the earnest gaze of the young forester. "You threw yourself into danger to save this young lady; Heaven sent me to your aid, for it was not right that you should be sacrificed while acting so nobly."

"Yes; and I must thank you, sir, for periling your life in my behalf," said Virginia, in her low, sweet voice, that thrilled like pleasant music through the heart of the young adventurer.

"You make me ashamed of my simple service," replied Winthrop. "I would have done the same for any one in peril. It is our duty in this life to help our fellow-creatures, and I would be unworthy of the name of man had I stood by and witnessed your peril without making an effort to save you."

The forest maiden watched the girl's face while the young man was speaking, with a peculiar expression in her dark eyes.

"I am Virginia, daughter of General Treveling, of Point Pleasant; if you are going thither, I am sure my father will thank you heartily for the service you have this day rendered his only child."

"I *am* going to Point Pleasant, and shall be pleased to meet your father, whom I have heard highly spoken of many times on my way here," said Winthrop. Then he turned to the girl in the Indian garb, who stood leaning upon her rifle, with her eyes intently fixed upon the two. "Lady, may I not know the name of her whose well-directed shot saved me? There may come a time when I can repay the service."

"Do not ask my name," said the girl, in a mournful tone; "it is better, perhaps, that you should *not* know it."

Winthrop looked his astonishment at this strange speech.

"I really do not see how that can be, lady," he said, after a moment's pause. "I am sure I shall never forget the service, nor your name, if once I hear it."

"I repeat that it is better that you should not know it," said the girl, slowly.

"Why so?" demanded the young man, while on the face of Virginia was written strong curiosity to know the meaning of the girl's words.

"You think you owe me a debt of gratitude," said the dark-hued maiden. "It is a pleasant thought for me to know that *some* one thinks well of me. If I tell you my name, perhaps the gratitude that you now think you owe will vanish, and in its place will come loathing."

"You speak in riddles," said Winthrop, unable to guess her meaning, but plainly seeing that some mystery was concealed in her words. "I do not see how the knowledge of your name will change my sentiments in any way whatsoever. I beseech you, tell me what it is. I can never forget the name of the one who saved my life."

"And you, Virginia Treveling," said the girl, turning abruptly to the General's daughter. "Do you not know who I am?"

"No," replied Virginia, "but I should like very much to know, for I feel that, in part, I owe you my life too."

"Blame yourself, then, if, after I have told you my name, you shrink from me, and gratitude dies in loathing. *I am Kanawha Kate!*"

Virginia started when the name fell upon her ears. The quick eye of Kate noticed the start. Winthrop did not manifest any emotion whatever. It was the first time he had ever heard the name, and though he wondered somewhat at the strange appellation, still he saw nothing in it to alarm him in any way.

"You shrink from me," said Kate, with a bitter smile—she was referring to the almost unconscious start that Virginia had made when she heard the name. "You know who I am. You have heard evil tongues talk of me, and you are not so grateful now as you were a moment ago."

"Nay, you wrong me," said Virginia, gently. "In all my life I have never heard evil spoken of Kanawha Kate. I have heard you called wild and way-ward—spoken of as one more like a boy than a girl—who liked to roam about the forest better than to sit at home. But when I heard the tongues of the settlers speak lightly of you, I have always remembered that you were an orphan—without mother or father—with no one to tell you what you should do."

"You are right. I have grown up like a weed, uncared for by all"—there was great bitterness in the tone of the girl's voice—"my only relative a renegade from his country and his race—a white Indian, far worse than the dusky savages. Why should I not be an outcast, despised by all, when my unhappy fate dooms me to such a life?"

"No, not despised by all," said Virginia, firmly. "I do not despise you; I love you—that is, if you will let me." And the girl placed her hand gently on the shoulder of the other.

"Oh, I thank you so much!" The words came in a half-sob from the lips of the forest child.

"Let me be your sister. Come and see me at my home at the station. Few will be bold enough to say aught against the sister of Virginia Trevel-ing." Proudly the young girl drew up her form as she uttered the words.

"Yes, and for want of a better, take me for your brother," said Winthrop, impulsively, "and the man who dares to breathe a word against you will have to face the muzzle of my rifle."

"It is many a long day since such kind words have fallen upon my ears," said Kate, sadly. "Perhaps I should not be so wild if my parents had lived. But, Miss Virginia, I will come and see you."

"Do, and I promise you a hearty welcome!" exclaimed Virginia.

"Oh, I *will* come!" cried Kate, her eyes gleaming.

"Good-by, then," and the rescued girl turned to Winthrop. "If you are going to Point Pleasant, I will be your guide, and I am sure that my father will be very glad to see you, particularly when he learns that you have saved the life of his only child!"

Virginia embraced Kate heartily, and kissed her as if she had been a sister; Winthrop shook her warmly by the hand, and then the two, leaving the forest maid standing by the body of the dead brute, retraced their way to the little trail that led to Point Pleasant.

Kate, leaning on her rifle, remained in a deep reverie, gazing absently upon their departing figures.

Winthrop found his horse exactly where he had left him. Passing the bridle over his arm, he walked by the side of Virginia toward the station.

"What a strange creature that girl is," he said, as they walked onward.

"Yes; I have often heard of her, though I have never happened to meet her before. The settlers tell a great many stories about her. They say that she can ride better than any man on the border. That she knows every foot of the country for miles around, even to the Indian villages on the other side of the Ohio. Then, too, they say she is a splendid shot with the rifle, and can use the hunting-knife like a woodman."

"We can vouch for her skill in marksmanship," said Winthrop, and a half-shiver came over him when he thought of the huge bear, with its fierce eyes and shining teeth.

"Yes; poor girl, she is a niece of the renegade, Simon Girty, and that, I think, makes the settlers dislike her—as if she should answer for the misdeeds of her wicked uncle!" Virginia spoke with feeling; her face lighted up, and Winthrop thought that he had never looked upon a prettier maiden.

CHAPTER V.

VIRGINIA'S SUITOR.

In the best room of Treveling's house sat the old General and a young man, known as Clement Murdock. He was a relative of Treveling, and was much esteemed by the old General.

General Treveling was a man of fifty. Years had whitened the hair of the old soldier and bent the once stalwart form.

Murdock was some thirty years old—a dark, sallow-faced man, with a piercing black eye and a haughty bearing.

The young man had just entered, and returning the General's cordial greeting, had taken a seat by his side.

"What's the news?" asked Treveling.

"Nothing particular, General," replied the other.

"Nothing fresh from the red-skins? It's about time for them to be on the war-path against us again."

"They have not forgotten the thrashing they got last year, I suppose," said the young man. "But I want to speak with you on a subject which I have thought a great deal of lately."

The old General looked astonished at this beginning.

"Very well, what is it?" he asked.

"In regard to your daughter, Virginia, General," said Murdock, slowly. "I would like your permission to pay my addresses to her. I have long loved your daughter, and I should like to make her my wife."

"Well, Clement, you know that you have my best wishes. There isn't a man in the settlement that I would rather give my child to. But, win her consent: *that* comes first, of course. If she is willing, I shall not object."

The joy of Murdock plainly showed itself in his face.

"That is all I ask, General," he said, quickly. "I thought it but right that you should know my intentions first."

"Well, you have my good will, Clement," said the old soldier, "and I do not doubt but that you will find favor in the eyes of Virginia. She will be home soon. She has gone for blackberries down the river."

And as the father spoke the door opened and Virginia entered, followed by the young adventurer, Harvey Winthrop.

"Oh, father, I have had such an escape," said the maiden, quickly; then she gave an account of her adventure in the forest with the bear.

"Why, sir, I owe you the life of my child!" cried the General, earnestly, when the girl had finished her story. "How may I call your name?"

"Winthrop—Harvey Winthrop, an adventurer seeking his fortune on the border," replied the young man.

"You must drive your stakes with us, for a short time, at least, if we can not induce you to make Point Pleasant your permanent home," said the old soldier, heartily. "I am General Treveling, sir; this, my daughter, Virginia, and this gentleman a relative of ours, Clement Murdock."

Although Murdock shook hands in a friendly way with the stranger who had rescued his fair cousin from the bear, yet, in his heart, he wished him at the bottom of the Ohio. Was Clement afraid that the handsome stranger would interfere with his plans regarding the gentle Virginia?

Frankly—in the same spirit that it was given—Winthrop accepted the invitation of the old soldier. Perhaps, too, the thought that he should enjoy the society of the fair girl, whose life he had saved, had something to do with his ready acceptance of the hospitality of the old General.

Leaving her father and Winthrop engaged in busy conversation, Virginia withdrew into the inner room. Murdock, seizing the opportunity, followed. He had resolved to declare his passion at once. He had been an open and avowed lover of Virginia's for some time. In fact, all the settlers thought it would be a match. And Murdock, though he did not openly say that he was the accepted suitor of the General's daughter, yet by many a sly hint he contrived to impress all with that belief. So, one by one, his rivals for the girl's favor had withdrawn from the contest, and left the field clear to the scheming lover.

Yet now, even at the eleventh hour, when he had thought the hand of the girl was his beyond a doubt, this young stranger had stepped into the field, and that under such circumstances that the girl's gratitude if not her love must be surely his.

Murdock was sorely annoyed at the accident which had given the young man such a claim to the girl's esteem. He determined, however, to ask for the hand of the girl at once.

Virginia turned in some little astonishment when she discovered that she was followed by Clement.

He carefully closed the door behind him and approached the young girl.

"Virginia," he said, in his softest and smoothest tones, "I have long wished for an opportunity to tell you how much I love you. I have spoken to your father, and he approves my suit. Virginia, can you give me the priceless treasure of your love? Will you be my wife?"

The girl flushed to the temples at the words of Murdock. She had suspected that he sought her, but had carefully avoided leading him to think that she favored his suit. For, to tell the truth, the young girl did not love but rather feared him. There was a bad look in the fierce black eyes, and ugly lines about the sensual mouth, and these things she had noticed. In her heart Virginia thought that Murdock was far from being a good man.

"I am sorry, Mr. Murdock, that you have spoken in this way to me," said the girl, slowly, and with evident embarrassment. "It grieves me that I must pain you with a refusal. I can not accept the love that you offer."

Murdock started in anger, and the frown that knit his brows showed plainly his deep displeasure.

"Are you in earnest?" he asked, in amazement.

"Surely I am," replied the girl. She did not like the tone in which the question was put.

"Had you not better take time to think over the matter?" he said. "You may change your mind."

"That is not likely," she answered, coldly. "I can decide now as well as any time in the future. I feel that I can not love you."

"Do you love any one else?" he asked, quickly.

A faint flush came to the cheeks of the girl, which did not escape the jealous eyes of the rejected lover.

"You have no right to ask that question," she cried.

"Will you answer it?"

"No!"

"No?"

"No!" repeated Virginia, all the fire of her nature roused by the insolent manner of the man who stood lowering before her.

"You do not dare to answer it."

"It is no business of yours what my motive is," replied Virginia, proudly.

"You fancy yourself in love with some one. You can not deceive me. Let your lover look to himself. If you can not be my wife, I swear that you shall not be the wife of any other man. You are a beautiful girl, Virginia, but your beauty will be fatal to the mortal that dares to cross my path!" Murdock spoke in heat, and the angry glare of a demon shot from his fierce black eyes.

"If I have a lover, he will be able to defend himself from the coward who only dares to threaten a woman!" And with these words Virginia swept proudly from the room.

"By all the powers of darkness, I swear that I will find means to bend your haughty spirit, and on your knees you will be glad to ask my pardon for those proud words!" cried the baffled lover, his voice hoarse with rage.

Then he left the house by the back door and gained the street. He did not care to meet the eyes of the old General, for he readily guessed that his discomfiture would easily be perceived.

"Who can this lover be?" he mused, as he walked slowly down the street. "Can it be this young stranger who saved her from the bear in the ravine? It may be. I am sure that there isn't a lad on the border that is favored by her, for I have watched her closely. Is the prize then that I have toiled so to gain to be snatched from my hand by this adventurer? She must marry me, or—*she must die*! She is the only obstacle between me and the fortune of the old General. That fortune I am determined to have, and the silly caprice of a weak girl shall not keep me from it."

Stern and frowning was the brow of Clement Murdock as he strode along. Dark and gloomy thoughts were passing rapidly through his mind.

"The die is cast—I have decided," he muttered, as he walked onward. "First to find *who* this lover is, that has crossed my path—for that the girl has a lover or is in love with some one, I am certain. I marked the slight flush that crimsoned her cheek when I charged her with loving another; that blush revealed to me the truth. I have a rival, and a dangerous one, for she loves him. I *must* discover who it is. If the young adventurer is the man, let him look to himself, for the fortune that he comes to seek by the banks of the Ohio, may resolve itself into a grave in the forest with the gaunt gray wolves as mourners. True, the acquaintanceship is but a few hours old, but love comes at first sight, sometimes. The fortune of my relative shall be mine, either with Virginia or without her. I must find some willing tools to aid me, for I feel a presentiment that I shall have need of strong arms and reckless hearts, ere long."

Then the eyes of Murdock caught sight of a little group of settlers at the lower end of the station near the bank of the Kanawha.

"Hallo! what's the meaning of that I wonder?" he exclaimed; "there's evidently some trouble afloat. Another Indian attack, perhaps. I must see what it is." And he advanced to the group.

26

CHAPTER VI.

ANOTHER VICTIM.

As Murdock approached the group, he saw that Colonel Boone and a strange hunter were in the center of the party.

Another strange face also met the eye of the new-comer. It was that of a man attired in the homespun dress of the emigrant. His hair was jet-black, and his skin tanned almost as dark as the hue of a red-skin. He stood on the outer edge of the group, leaning on a long rifle. The keen, dark eyes of this stranger had a restless look, and wandered continually about him.

Murdock felt sure, the moment he beheld the face of the stranger that he had seen him before somewhere, but, for the life of him, he could not guess when or where. Slowly he drew nigh, keeping a wary eye upon the hunter-emigrant.

Boone had been telling the settlers the news imparted to him by the solitary hunter whom he had encountered in the forest in such a peculiar manner, and who was called Abe Lark.

"The Shawnees again on the war-path!" cried a stalwart settler, known as Jacob Jackson, and renowned as an Indian-fighter.

As Boone had predicted, there were white faces among the settlers when they heard the terrible news.

"True as shootin'!" cried Boone, "an' comin' ag'in' us in bigger numbers than has ever been seen on the border since we licked 'em right hyer in the Dunmore war."

A heavy frown came over the face of the stranger, who stood a little apart from the others, as Boone mentioned the battle of Point Pleasant. It was evident that the mention of that bloody fight brought back some unpleasant recollections to the mind of the stranger.

Murdock was watching the man closely, but he was careful not to betray to the stranger that he was being watched.

"Who leads the red-skins?" asked Jackson.

"Ke-ne-ha-ha," replied Boone.

"The-man-that-walks!" said Jackson.

And at the name the faces of the whites grew serious. They knew full well that a better chieftain than the Shawnee never donned the war-paint, and that the whites had no abler or more deadly foe than Ke-ne-ha-ha.

"Thar'll be lightnin' all round then, for sure," said Jackson, in a tone of conviction. "We've got to fight doggoned well to whip the Shawnees this time. Who fetched the news, kurnel?"

"This stranger, hyer," replied Boone, pointing to Abe Lark, who stood by his side.

"Glad to see you, stranger," said Jackson, tendering his huge paws and receiving a grip that made him wince with pain, muscular and hard as his horny palm was.

"Same to you, ole hoss," returned Lark, with a grin on his disfigured face at the expression of astonishment that came over the features of burly Jake Jackson, when he received the powerful squeeze of Lark's hand.

"Jerusalem!" muttered Jake, looking at his hand in amazement, "that's a reg'lar b'ar-hug an' no mistake."

"Wal, I reckon the man that gits a grip from me knows it," replied Lark.

"Well, 'bout this news. Are you sartin, stranger, that the red devils are a-comin' ag'in' us?"

"If you don't hear the Shawnee war-whoop inside of ten days you kin jist chaw one of my fingers off, an' I don't keer which you take," replied Lark, with another grin.

"Then it will be fight, and no mistake."

"You kin bet your moccasins on that, an' you'll lose 'em every time. The Shawnees have sworn to wipe out every white settlement along the Ohio. Thar'll be nigh onto ten thousand Injuns in the field. They are hot arter blood. You'll have to fight for your top-knots or lose 'em."

A bitter look was on the face of the dark-skinned stranger as he listened to the words of Lark.

"Curses on this meddling hunter!" he muttered, between his teeth; "how could he have learned of Ke-ne-ha-ha's plan to surprise this station. Now, thanks to him, they'll be on their guard, and the Shawnees will have to fight for what scalps they take."

Not an expression on the face of this stranger was unnoticed by Murdock, who still watched him keenly, but with a puzzled look.

"Can it be possible that it is he?" Murdock mused. "*Would* he dare to venture here in the midst of his foes? To venture into the presence of the men who, if they penetrated his disguise, would hang him up to the first tree without troubling either judge or jury? Yet I am sure it is he, though his face is darkened by some means, and his hair is black. He comes as a spy, probably. Ah!" and a brilliant thought occurred to the mind of Murdock. "Suppose I get him to aid my plans. He is in my power, if he be the man I think he is, for a single word uttered by my lips, and the settlers would almost tear him to pieces. I'll watch him closely." And with this resolution in his mind, Murdock did not remove his eyes from the stranger. The dark-skinned hunter was so occupied in watching the group of settlers and listening to their conversation that he did not notice that he in turn was watched.

"Well, neighbors," said Jake Jackson, after thinking for a moment, "if the Injuns are a-comin' we've got for to fight 'em, an' I am ready for one."

"And I for another!" cried a loud, clear voice.

All turned to look at the speaker, who had approached unobserved. He was a tall, muscular fellow, dressed in the forest garb of deer-skin.

"Sim Kenton, by the Eternal!" said Boone, taking him warmly by the hand.

It was indeed the famous scout, whose reputation as an Indian-fighter was second to none on the border.

"Glad to see you, Sim!" continued Boone, and the group of settlers eagerly echoed the welcome. "What's the news?"

"Thar's a thunder-storm a-comin'," replied the scout. "I s'pect from what I heerd, as I come up, that you know the Shawnees are on the war-path."

"Yes, yes!" cried a dozen voices.

"I've just come down from the Muskingum, whar I've been on a hunt, and not five miles from this hyer station, I come across a big Injun lyin' dead in the woods with a clean dig right through the skull. A powerful fellow he war, too; looked as if he mought have given Old Nick himself a sharp tussle."

All wondered at the news brought by the scout. That a red-skin should be killed so near the station, and yet no one in the station know of it, was strange.

"What tribe was he? could you tell, Sim?" asked Boone.

"Shawnee," replied Kenton. "A big brave he was in the tribe, too. I knowed him well. He was called Watega."

The dark stranger, who had pressed forward eagerly to listen with the rest, could hardly prevent an oath escaping from his lips. This movement on his part did not escape the searching eyes of Murdock.

"I know the chief," said Boone; "he was one of the principal warriors of the tribe. A clean dig through the skull, you say?"

"Yes; the man that made it must be a hurricane, for he split the Injun's head clean open."

"Who could have done it?" said Jackson, in wonder.

"That's what I'd like to know," said Kenton, with a puzzled air. "Thar ain't any man along the border, that I know of, that is powerful enough for to do it. Thar warn't any marks of a struggle, neither. The Injun had been taken by surprise, an' settled with one blow. Why, it looks as if the devil himself had had a hand in it."

"Nothing but one clean dig, eh?" said Boone, reflectively.

"Nothing else," replied Kenton, "'cept some knife-cuts on the breast, as if the slayer cut his totem thar, arter finishing the brute."

29

Boone gave a slight start—a start that was imitated by the dark-skinned stranger who was listening to the conversation so eagerly.

"And them marks—three knife-cuts, making a red arrow?" asked Boone.

"Right to an iota!" cried Kenton, astonished at the knowledge of the other.

"The Wolf Demon, by hookey!" exclaimed Boone, in a tone of wonder. And at the name of the dreaded foe of the Shawnee nation, the dark stranger shuddered.

"What in creation do you mean by the Wolf Demon?" asked Kenton, who had never heard the story of the mysterious scourge of the Shawnees, which was well known to Boone.

Then the old hunter told the wondering crowd the story of the Wolf Demon. Told of the incomprehensible being in the shape of a huge gray wolf, but with the face of a man, who seemed to be an avenging angel destined to hunt down to his death any solitary Shawnee brave who strayed from his brethren in the forest.

Wonder-stricken, the stout borderers listened to the tale; deeply superstitious, they accepted the legend of the Indians without question; one and all were convinced that the Wolf Demon was, as the Shawnees asserted, proof against either steel or ball, and was no human, but a denizen of another world.

"Whar was the body?" asked Jackson.

"Just beyond a tree where some hunter had cut his name—Abe Lark," answered Kenton.

"Wal, we were nigh it this mornin'!" cried Abe, in astonishment.

The dark-skinned stranger, having apparently heard all he wanted, strolled leisurely away.

Murdock, convinced now that he was not mistaken as to the identity of the stranger, followed him slowly.

"Let this Wolf Demon come within range of my rifle, I'll quickly prove whether he is man or devil," said the unknown, as he walked onward. "Watega dead? That interferes with my plans, but I can do without him, since it must be so." And with these strange words on his tongue, he was suddenly astonished by being hailed by Murdock.

CHAPTER VII.

THE SCHEME OF CLEMENT MURDOCK.

The stranger turned in no little surprise at being accosted by the young man.

"Did you speak to me, stranger?" he asked.

"Yes," answered Murdock; "I should like to have a few minutes' conversation with you if it is agreeable."

The stranger shot a rapid glance at the face of the young man, but he saw nothing therein to alarm him.

"Certainly," he replied, after thinking for a moment.

"This is my shanty," said Murdock, referring to the log-house before whose door they stood. "Come in; we can talk inside without being overheard."

There was a strange expression upon the face of the other. He cast a rapid glance around him, and laid his hand upon the handle of the hunting-knife at his girdle, as if he had half a mind to stab the young man—who was fumbling with the rude fastenings of the door—and then make a bold break for freedom and the woods. But the momentary glance around convinced him—that is, if he had such an idea—that to carry it out would be hopeless, for a dozen or more of the settlers were between him and the forest. So, with a muttered curse upon his ill luck, he followed Murdock into the cabin.

Murdock produced a flask of whisky and a couple of tin cups, and motioning his rather unwilling guest to draw near the table, he pledged him with the fragrant corn-juice.

The stranger tossed off the fiery liquor with a moody brow. He suspected that he was in a trap, and he felt far from being easy.

"Do you know that your face is strangely familiar to me?" asked Murdock, with a meaning smile.

"Indeed! that is strange," responded the other, half inclined to spring upon the young man, for he felt a strong apprehension that his disguise was penetrated.

"I think we have met before," said Murdock, with another look full of meaning.

"I don't remember ever meeting you," replied the stranger, who now almost repented that he hadn't made a bold dash for freedom when at the door.

31

"I feel sure that we have met," said Murdock. "How may I call your name?"

"James Benton," replied the other.

"From Virginia?"

"Yes."

"Well, I have never met a Mr. Benton," said Murdock.

"I was sure that you were in error when you said that you knew me," said the stranger, with an air of relief.

"Not as Benton, but under another name, I have met you."

"Ah!" The hand of the stranger sought the handle of his knife. The movement was not unnoticed by the keen eye of Murdock.

"Don't be alarmed; I mean you no harm," he said, quickly. "If I had wished to denounce you, there wouldn't have been any need of bringing you into my house. All that would be necessary would be to speak your name in the middle of this station. Why, the very sticks themselves that form the stockade would rise out of the ground to seize you, to say nothing of the men."

"For whom do you take me?" asked the stranger, in a hoarse voice.

"For the man for whose body, dead or alive, the settlers on the border would give more than they would for any other man that walks upon earth, be his skin white or red," replied Murdock.

The stranger glanced at him with sullen eyes.

"Be assured, however," continued the young man, "that I mean you no harm. On the contrary, I need your aid, and I'm willing to pay you well for it. Come, is it a bargain?"

"You know my name?" said the stranger, slowly, without replying to the question.

"Yes, you are—" and Murdock, bending over, whispered a name in the ear of the stranger. "Am I right?" he asked.

"Yes," said the stranger, sullenly. "But I cannot understand how you penetrated my disguise."

"Particularly when it deceived Boone and a half-score of your deadly foes, who would be almost willing to give ten years of their lives to draw a bead on you at fair rifle range."

"That is possible," replied the other; "but the bullet is not yet run that will take my life."

"If I were to call out your name from that door, a long rope and a short shrift would save the bullet the trouble," said Murdock.

The stranger winced at the words.

"Don't be alarmed; I don't mean to betray you," continued Murdock. "It was an astonishing thing that I alone should penetrate your disguise and guess who you were. I never saw you but once before, either, and that was years ago. But now to business. As I said before, I need your aid, and I am willing to pay you well for it."

"What is it you want me to do?"

"There's a girl in the settlement that has rejected my advances. I don't care so much for her, but she's the heiress to a large fortune. Now, if the girl marries me, of course I get the fortune, or if she dies, I get the fortune, for I am the next heir. Now, I don't want to take the life of the girl if I can help it. I had much rather marry her; but, unfortunately, she has taken a fancy to some one else, and won't listen to my suit. Now, my plan is to carry the girl off. I know a lonely cabin, now deserted, some ten miles from the station, on the other bank of the Kanawha. I want the girl carried there, and the impression given to her that she is a prisoner in the hands of the Indians. Then I'll pretend to follow on the trail—gain access to the cabin; offer to assist her to escape, if in reward she'll marry me. Of course she'll feel grateful for the risk I run for her sake, and consent. Then I'll escape with her, take her back to the settlement, and the thing is done."

"But suppose she refuses to marry you?"

"Then she won't escape from the hands of the red-skins, but they'll kill her," said Murdock, coolly.

"And in that case, you'll come in for the property?"

"Exactly."

"The plan ought to work," said Benton, thoughtfully.

"I don't see how it can fail. I want your assistance, and I've got a fellow in the station that will help me. You two will be enough to play Indian. It won't be much trouble and very little risk, and I'll pay well for it."

"When do you want it done?" asked the stranger.

"The sooner the better," replied Murdock. "I suppose that will suit you."

"Yes, for I'll soon have other fish to fry along the border," said the other, and a demon light gleamed from his fierce eyes.

"Do you expect to drive the whites from the Ohio?" asked Murdock.

"No, but I'll raise such a blaze along the river, and strike such a blow that it shall be felt, even to Virginia!" cried the other, in a tone of fierce menace.

"It will be a bloody time," said Murdock, thoughtfully.

"Yes, blood will run like water," replied the stranger. "But what is the name of the girl that is to be carried off?"

"Virginia Treveling."

The stranger started as though he had trodden upon a snake.

"What, the daughter of General Treveling?" he cried.

"Yes," replied Murdock, wondering at the look of fierce delight that swept over the face of the other.

"Satan's fires!" cried the other, in triumph. "I'll do the job for you. I owe the father a bitter grudge. I struck him one blow, some twelve years ago, just after he wronged me. I doubt if he's forgotten or forgiven it to this day. It's about time for me to strike him another."

"Why, how did General Treveling ever wrong you?" asked Murdock, in wonder.

"I was a scout under him in Dunmore's campaign. One day he told me openly, and before a dozen others, that I lied. I gave the lie back in his teeth, for I never took insult from mortal man. Then he struck me. I didn't think even for a moment that he was my superior officer; all that I knew was that I was struck—degraded by a blow. I measured him with my eye and felled him to my feet with a single stroke. Then I was seized—tried by a drumhead court-martial, and sentenced to be publicly whipped in presence of the whole army, and I *was* whipped, too. As the lashes fell upon my naked back, and cut long, quivering lines in the yielding flesh, with every lash I swore a bitter oath of vengeance. Then, my punishment done—a whipped, degraded slave, a man no longer—they untied me. I sunk down at their feet almost helpless. They raised me up; I was covered with my own gore. This General Treveling—then only a colonel—looked on me, his victim, with a scornful smile—ten thousand curses on him! I was maddened with rage. I shook my fist defiantly in his face, and before all I said: 'Your quarters shall swim in blood for this!' I kept my word. I have shed white blood enough along the Ohio for me to swim in. My vengeance, too, against this man was fearful. I stole his eldest child—left it to die in the forest. I tore his heart as his lashes had torn my back. And now, I strike him a second time."

Murdock gazed at the rage-inflamed countenance of the dark-skinned man with a feeling akin to awe.

"It is a bargain, then, between us?" the young man said.

"Yes; to get another chance at him, I'd go through the fires of Hades!" the other replied.

And so the compact was made.

34

CHAPTER VIII

BOONE IN A TIGHT PLACE.

Earnestly and with anxious faces the settlers discussed the chances of the coming war.

With one voice Colonel Boone was selected as the commander of the station.

Messengers were dispatched to warn the neighboring settlements.

Then Boone, taking Kenton and Lark aside, suggested that they should make a scout into the Shawnee country and discover, if possible, against which settlement the Indian attack would be directed.

The suggestion suited well with the bold and daring spirit of the border, and both Kenton and Lark gladly expressed their willingness to accompany the skillful and daring woodman.

Boone gave Jackson a hint as to his intention, and then the three left the settlement and entered the forest, heading toward the Ohio.

Reaching the river, Lark drew from a little tangled thicket near the river's bank a canoe. He had previously hidden it there when he had crossed the Ohio on his way from the Shawnee country to Point Pleasant.

By means of the canoe the three crossed the river. On the northern bank they concealed the canoe in the thicket, and then, striking to the north-west toward the Scioto river, they plunged into the wilderness and took the trail leading to the villages of the Shawnee nation.

On through the tangled thickets went the three rangers, all their senses on the alert to discover traces of the hostile red-skins.

After many a weary hour's march, the three came near to the village of Ke-ne-ha-ha.

Then they proceeded with increased caution. As yet they had not seen a single trace that denoted the presence of the Shawnees.

The scouts were now within some two miles of Chillicothe, where Ke-ne-ha-ha's village was located.

Then Boone called a halt.

"Now, boys," said the leader, "we are nigh to the red devils, an' we must be careful or we'll stumble upon some of 'em afore we knows it. I think our best plan is to find some hiding place to serve for a head-quarters, and then, separately, after dark, we'll scout into the village, an' maybe we'll be able to discover some of the plans of the red varmints."

"I know just the place for us," said Lark. "We're nigh to it, too."

Then Lark piloted the way through the forest—the three had been standing by the bank of the Scioto—and at last halted by a huge oak tree, at the base of which grew a tangled mass of bushes.

"Hyer's the spot," said Lark, pointing to the tree.

"Whar?" asked Boone, who could not perceive any hiding-place except it was in the branches of the oak.

"Hyer."

Then Lark parted the tangled bushes with his hand. Boone and Kenton saw that the trunk of the oak was hollow. It contained a cavity, fully large enough to afford a secret refuge to the three, and the bushes closing behind them after they had entered the hollow oak completely concealed them from sight.

"This hyer is an old hidin'-place o' mine," said Lark, as they stood within the hollow. "I diskivered it one day when I shot a b'ar nigh hyer. The b'ar made for this bit of bush. He had his den in this very tree-trunk. I followed him up an' that's the way I diskivered it."

The shade of night was now fast descending upon the earth, and darkness was vailing in the forest and river with its inky mantle.

"Now, we'll scout into the village," said Boone; "we'll meet hyer ag'in in the morning—that is, if the savages don't captivate us."

"Agreed," responded the two others, and then all three left the hollow oak.

With a silent pressure of the hand they separated, each one picking out a path for himself, but all tending in the direction of the village of Ke-ne-ha-ha.

The three hunters had been gone some ten or fifteen minutes when a dark form stood by the oak.

He plunged his eyes carefully into the darkness that surrounded him, as if fearful of being watched.

At last, apparently satisfied that no human eye looked upon his movements, carefully and cautiously he separated the bushes in front of the oak, and entered the hollow space within the tree. The bushes closed with scarce a rustle behind him.

The insects of the night who had been disturbed and awed to silence by the tread of the light foot, that prowled so cautiously along the dim aisles of the forest, began again their nocturnal cries.

The tree-toads cried, and the crickets chirruped. The air seemed full of life. The owl—the minion of the night—came forth from his perch in the tree-trunk. The young moon, too, rising, cast its silver sheen over the forest.

Then again, suddenly, the voices of the night sunk into silence, for, forth from the hollow of the oak, that the three daring scouts had selected for their rendezvous, came the dark figure that but a few minutes before with stealthy steps had stolen beneath the leafy branches. It was evident that the secret of the hollow tree was known to another than the scouts.

Cautiously through the forest stole the dark form. The tree-toad hushed its cries; the cricket noiselessly crept to his hole; the owl peered forth from its cavity in the tree-trunk, and then with its great eyes shining with fear, shrunk back within the darkness of its lair, when it caught sight of the dark form that so silently glided amid the trees.

On went the dark form through the forest. All living things seemed to shrink from it in horror.

The moonbeams, slanting down and tinging the green of the forest top with rays of silvery light, fell upon the figure as it glided through a little opening in the woods.

The moonbeams defined the figure of a huge gray wolf, who walked erect like a man, and who had the face of a human. The dark form held in its paw an Indian tomahawk.

The moonbeams were gleaming upon the Wolf Demon, the terrible scourge of the Shawnee tribe.

On through the forest went the hideous form, almost following in the footsteps of the scout, Kenton, who had little idea of the terrible creature that lurked behind him.

Boone had selected the bank of the river as his pathway to the village of the Indians.

Carefully the ranger proceeded onward.

As he approached near to the Shawnee village, he could hear the sound of the Indian drums and the war-cries of the warriors.

From the sounds Boone easily guessed that the Indians were preparing for the war-path.

Boone reached the edge of the timber. Before him lay the village of his deadly foes.

A huge fire was burning before the council-lodge in the center of the village, and the warriors were dancing around it.

"Look at the red devils!" muttered Boone, who from the convenient shelter afforded by a fallen tree, just on the edge of the timber, could easily watch the scene before him. "They're pantin' to redden their knives in the blood of the whites."

Then the scout counted the Indians who were dancing around the fire, and the others who were either watching the scalp-dance, or lounging leisurely around the village. The number of the red-men astonished the borderer.

"Jerusalem!" he muttered, "thar's a tarnal heap of them. I judge they'll take the war-path soon."

Then a squaw, with a gourd in her hand, evidently going to the river for water, left the village and came directly toward the spot where Boone was concealed.

The alarm of the hunter was great.

"Dod rot the luck!" he muttered, in disgust, "why on yearth don't she go straight to the drink, cuss her! She'll come plumb down on me if she keeps on, an' then she'll raise the village with her squalls."

The squaw, who was quite a young girl, and very handsome, came directly on toward the ambush of the spy.

Then Boone saw that she was followed by one of the Indian braves.

The great hunter began to feel extremely nervous. In truth, unless the squaw changed her course, his position was one of real peril.

"They'll lift my ha'r if that blamed squaw diskivers me, sure," he muttered, in consternation.

The girl paused for a moment.

The heart of the hunter beat quick with hope.

"Now go to the river, you durned red-skin," he said. It is hardly necessary to remark that the observation was not intended to reach the ears of the girl.

But the squaw hadn't any intention of going to the river. The gourd carried in her hand was simply an excuse to leave her wigwam.

When the girl found that the young brave—whom in reality she had stolen forth to meet—was following her, she continued on her course, which led directly to the fallen tree, behind which Boone was concealed.

"Oh, cuss the luck!" he muttered, in despair. "I wish she was at the bottom of the Scioto. If she diskivers me thar'll be a row. I'm in for it like a treed coon."

The girl, now satisfied that her lover had seen her leave the wigwam, and conscious that he understood her motive, approached the tree and sat down upon the trunk.

The young brave carelessly, so as not to excite the attention of the other Indians, if any of them had chanced to see him, strolled toward the thicket. Reaching it, concealed by the shadow cast by the forest line, he took a seat upon the fallen tree by the side of the squaw.

Boone hardly dared to breathe, lest he should betray his presence to the twain. The scout was in a trap from which he saw no escape.

CHAPTER IX.

LOVE AND HATE.

Harvey Winthrop had been the guest of the old General some three days, and during those three days he had discovered that he loved the fair girl, Virginia, whose life he had saved, and he had reason to believe from her manner toward him that she was not indifferent to that love.

Our hero determined to learn the truth. He was not one of those who believed that it needed years to foster and ripen love. Within his heart he felt that he loved Virginia with a pure and holy passion. He was sure that he could not have loved her any better if he had known her all his life.

Virginia guessed that she was loved by the young man—what girl does not guess when she is loved?—and, perhaps, willing to give him a chance to declare that love, she suggested an excursion to the ravine where she had been rescued from the bear by him.

Gladly Winthrop announced his willingness to accompany her.

So the two set out for the ravine.

They passed down through the station and took the trail leading up the Kanawha.

As they walked onward, chatting gayly together, they had no suspicion that they were closely followed by three men, who, holding a consultation together on the edge of the timber, had noticed them as they passed.

Leaving the trail, the girl and the young man walked into the ravine.

The three men, who had followed him so closely, paused at the entrance to the gorge, apparently to consult together.

"The fellow is her lover, as I guessed," said the foremost of the three, the one who had been the most eager to follow the two.

"It looks like it," said the taller of the two others, who was the dark skinned stranger, who had called himself Benton. The third one of the party was a worthless fellow who hung about the station, ready to drink "corn-juice" when he could get it, and fit for but little else. He was known as Bob Tierson.

"I'd gi'n him a load of buckshot ef he came arter my gal!" said Bob, who was somewhat given to boasting.

"Perhaps I may," replied Murdock, who was the leader of the party. He spoke with an angry voice, and a lowering cloud was upon his sallow face.

"If the young fellow was out of the way, this would be a good opportunity to try the Indian game," said Benton, suggestively.

39

"Ef it was me, I'd put him out of the way mighty doggoned quick!" exclaimed Bob, who seldom lost an opportunity of telling what he would do.

"For the first time in your life, Bob, you've said a wise thing," said Murdock.

"Fur the first time!" cried Bob, in indignation. "Wal, I reckon now, I don't take a back seat to any man in the station—"

"In drinking whisky? No, you don't, to do you justice," said Murdock, sarcastically. "But, Benton, can you fix up for the Indian now?"

"Yes, easily enough," replied the one addressed. "I've got the pigment to paint our faces with in my pouch. Just lend me your hunting-shirt, and take my coat."

"How about your hair?"

"Tie a handkerchief over it, nigger-fashion," suggested Bob.

"Yes, that will do," said Murdock. "The girl will be so frightened that she won't be apt to notice you much. Tie a handkerchief over her eyes the moment you grab her."

"And the young feller?" asked Bob.

"Leave him to me," and Murdock tapped the butt of his rifle significantly.

"And you'll leave him to the wolves, eh?" said Bob, with a grin.

"I shouldn't wonder," replied Murdock, dryly.

"But the report of the rifle—if it should be heard at the station—"

"A hunter after game, that's all," said Murdock. "But come, let's tree our game; I've an idea that there'll be a love-scene between the two up the ravine, and I'd like to be a looker on." Murdock ground his teeth at the very thought.

So, cautiously and slowly, the three left the little trail by the banks of the Kanawha, and followed in the footsteps of Virginia and Winthrop up the ravine.

The girl and the young man reached the spot where the encounter with the bear had taken place, and there they halted.

The quick eye of the girl caught sight of the drops of blood dried upon the rock, where the bear had fallen and died.

"See," she said, pointing to the spots upon the rock; "but for you my blood would have stained the stone instead of the brute's."

"And but for that strange girl who came so aptly to my rescue, my blood might have been there, too," said Winthrop.

"It was a moment of terrible peril," and Virginia half-shuddered at the bare remembrance.

"Yes; but it was evidently not your fate to die by the claws and teeth of the bear."

"What will my fate be?" said the girl, reflectively.

"A bright and happy one, I hope," replied Winthrop. "I am sure that you deserve none other."

"Ah!" said the girl; "but we do not get our deservings in this world." As she spoke she sat down upon a rock that cropped out of the ground, and looked up into the face of the young man with her clear, bright eyes. In his heart Winthrop thought that he had never seen such clear, innocent eyes before.

"You should get yours," replied Winthrop, "or else there isn't any justice in this world."

"I hope so," said Virginia, half-sadly.

"How beautiful the forest is!" said the young man, glancing around him; but in his heart he thought the fair girl at his side was far more beautiful than any of her surroundings.

"How do you like our home by the banks of the Ohio?" asked Virginia.

"So well that I think the rest of my life will be spent in yonder settlement," replied Winthrop, quickly.

"Oh, I'm so glad of that!" The tone of the girl showed that the words came directly from her heart. A warm flush came over the face of the young man as the words fell upon his ears.

"I am so glad to hear you say that!" The earnest tone of Winthrop told the girl that her suspicion was truth. She was loved.

"You are?" murmured Virginia, in a low tone. She felt that the words that she wished to hear—for she loved the man that had risked his life so nobly—would soon be spoken.

"Yes, I am! can you guess why?" The voice of Winthrop trembled as he spoke.

Virginia glanced up shyly in the face of the young man, then dropped her eyes to the earth again. She did not answer.

Encouraged by her silence, Winthrop spoke:

"Virginia, I have known you but a few days, but I feel as if I had known you all my life. I have never met any one in the world that I have liked as I do you—that I love as I do you; for, Virginia, I love you with all my whole heart."

Virginia hung her head; her glances shyly swept the ground. She did not reply.

"You are not offended at my words, Virginia?" he said, earnestly.

"No—no," she replied, slowly, looking up in his face with a half-smile.

Winthrop guessed the truth in the soft eyes that looked so lovingly into his own.

"Virginia, may I hope that some day you will learn to love me?" Winthrop asked, with eager hope patent in his voice.

Virginia Treveling was a truthful woman, and so she answered truthfully:

"No, not learn to love you, Harvey, for I *do* love you already!"

A moment more, and the head of the fair young girl was pillowed on the manly bosom of her lover.

Oh! the flood of joy that came over the young man when he discovered that the love that he wished so to gain was all his own. That the heart now beating so fondly against his breast was devoted to him, and to him alone.

"Virginia, do you love me, then?" he asked.

"Yes," she murmured, softly.

"You will be my wife?"

"Yes."

"You will be mine, then, forever and forever?"

The young man gently raised the little head that nestled so snugly on his breast. Virginia understood the movement, and anticipated the wish of her lover. With a shy smile upon her face, and a coy look in her dark-brown eyes, she gave her lips up to her lover's caress.

The lips of the lovers met in a long, lingering kiss—the first proof of love, so dear to all hearts. Lip to lip and soul to soul.

Virginia Treveling gave herself to Harvey Winthrop.

A moment only the lovers remained in each other's arms.

Then the sharp crack of a rifle broke the stillness of the summer air.

With a groan of anguish Winthrop reeled from the fond embrace of the young girl. He clutched wildly at the air, and then fell heavily on his side upon the rocky surface.

With a shriek of terror Virginia knelt by the side of her lover.

The shriek of the young girl was answered by the shrill war-whoop of the Indian.

Forth from their covert in the thicket sprung two painted braves, and rushed with eager haste toward the young girl.

Virginia did not try to fly. Her senses were chilled to numbness by the fall of the man who but a moment before had pressed the warm love-kiss upon her willing lips.

Eagerly the two that came from the thicket seized the girl. With a moan of anguish she fell fainting into their arms.

The bird was in the net.

CHAPTER X.

THE CABIN IN THE FOREST.

One of the white red-skins—for the two who had seized Virginia were the dark-skinned stranger, Benton, and the tool of Murdock, Bob Tierson, painted and disguised as Indians—tied a handkerchief tightly over the eyes of the senseless girl, completely blindfolding her.

When this had been accomplished, Murdock came from his covert in the bushes, and approached the two.

The blackened muzzle of Murdock's rifle told plainly that it was he who had fired the shot which had stricken the young stranger, Harvey Winthrop, to the earth, even while the kisses of the girl he loved were fresh upon his lips.

"The girl has fainted," said Benton, who supported the light form of the hapless Virginia in his arms.

"So much the better!" exclaimed Murdock; "it aids our purpose. We must convey her at once to the lonely cabin of the Kanawha."

"And this critter?" said Bob, kicking the motionless form of Winthrop with his foot, carelessly, as he spoke.

"Is he dead?" asked Murdock.

Bob knelt down by the side of the young man.

"Yes, he's gone dead," replied the borderer, after a slight examination.

"I did not think it likely that he lived," said Murdock, with a grim smile. "I seldom have to fire twice."

"Well, you've settled him, for sure," observed Bob, with a grin.

"Leave him alone, then; the crows and wolves will finish him before the morrow," said Murdock.

"He ought to have known better than to fool round this piece of calico," observed Bob, with another grin.

"He won't be apt to do it again."

"No, dog my cats if he will!" cried Bob, expressively.

"Can you carry the girl, Benton?" asked Murdock.

"Yes, easily," replied the one addressed, raising the motionless form of the young girl in his arms, apparently without an effort.

"Let us be going, then. If we can reach the cabin before she recovers, so much the better for my plan."

Murdock led the way, followed closely by Benton carrying the girl while Bob brought up the rear.

Swiftly through the forest they went.

A half-hour's march up the Kanawha and Murdock halted by the bank of the river. Drawing a dug-out from its concealment in some bushes that overhung the water, by its aid the party crossed the river.

On the other bank of the stream, they again plunged into the forest—first, however, carefully concealing the dug-out in a similar hiding-place to that in which they found it.

After a three hours' tramp through the thicket, they came to a little log-cabin in the center of a little clearing. The cabin bore the marks of decay, and the long grass that grew thick over the threshold told that the builder had long since abandoned the dwelling.

Virginia had recovered from her faint some time before the party had reached the solitary cabin.

Terrible indeed were the feelings of the young girl. A prisoner in the hands of the merciless red-men—for she had no suspicions that her captors were white—she shrunk from the thought of what her fate would be. Then, too, when she remembered that she had seen her lover fall before her eyes, perhaps mortally wounded, she felt as if her heart would break.

The two disguised men placed the girl in the cabin; then Bob left Benton alone with the maid. Murdock was afraid that Virginia might recognize the borderer in spite of his disguise; but as Benton was a stranger there was but little danger that the girl would suspect her captors to be of her own race and blood.

Benton removed the bandage from the eyes of the girl.

"Squaw—prisoner to Shawnee," said the disguised white, imitating the manner and speech of the red-skin. "No try to run or warrior take scalp."

Then Benton joined the other two on the outside of the cabin, closing the door carefully behind him.

"Well, the game is treed," said Bob, with a chuckle.

"Yes," replied Murdock, a grim smile of satisfaction upon his sallow face. "Now you two keep watch here and be sure that the girl does not escape. I will return to the station. Her absence will be discovered before long and search will probably be made. If they discover the body of the stranger, this Winthrop, in the ravine, which they will be sure to do if any saw them leave the settlement together, which is probable, it will lead all to suspect that the man was murdered by some strolling red-skins and the girl carried off by them."

"But may they not trace us?" asked Benton, shrewdly. "There are keen scouts in the station. If they once strike our trail, they'll be apt to run us to earth."

"There is little danger in that," replied Murdock. "After we left the ravine we struck the regular trail leading up the river. There are many fresh footprints on the trail; it will be difficult for even the best Indian scout on the border to pick out the marks left by us from the others. Besides, crossing the river would be apt to throw the keenest trailer off the scent. I do not think that any one will discover or even suspect our agency in the girl's disappearance."

"'Tain't likely," observed Bob.

"No, I think that you are right, and that you will succeed in your plan regarding the girl," said Benton. There was a strange sound in the voice of the man as he uttered the simple sentence, and a peculiar expression in his dark, snake-like eyes. Murdock did not notice the strangeness of the tone nor the look.

"I can not fail," said Murdock, decidedly. "You will need food for the girl. Here in the hollow of this tree," and Murdock led the way to a small white oak, some dozen paces from where they stood, "is some dried deer-meat. I think I shall rescue the girl to-morrow," and Murdock laughed slightly, at the idea, as he spoke. "There is a small hole under the logs in the back of the cabin, by which I can creep inside and appear to the girl in my new character of a saving angel, periling all to rescue her from the hands of the red-skins."

"Yes, but may she not discover this hole and escape through it?" asked Benton.

"No, a heavy log on the outside, that can not be stirred from the inside of the cabin, prevents that."

"To-morrow, then, you'll return?"

"Yes, to-morrow."

Then Murdock left the twain to watch the cabin and the prisoner, and plunging into the forest took his way back to Point Pleasant. And in his heart, as he walked along, he gloated over the success of the plan that had struck a hated rival from his path and given entirely into his power the girl whose fortune he craved.

We will now return to the little ravine wherein, stark and ghastly, lay the form of the young stranger, Harvey Winthrop; the man who had left home and friends to carve out a future by the banks of the Ohio, and who had fallen by the ball of the assassin, without even a chance to struggle for his life.

The little ravine looked bright and beautiful; the rays of the fast-dying sun glinted down, gayly, through the tree-tops, and played in beams of lambent light upon the pale face, whose open eyes glared, as if in mockery, on all around.

The rocky glade was as fair to look upon with the dreadful evidence of man's crime lying in its center, as when, but a short hour before, its leafy branches had formed a living frame to a picture of true love.

A huge black crow flying high and lazily in the air caught sight of the white face that so steadily stared with its stony and fixed eyes at the sky.

The bird of evil omen swooped round in circling flight above the motionless figure.

Each circle was smaller than the previous one, each second brought the bird nearer to its destined prey.

Still stared the eyes upward—still on the white face played the flickering sunbeams.

With a downward swoop, the carrion-bird alighted on the breast of the stricken man.

The blood that stained the hunting-shirt of the silent figure crimsoned the talons of the disgusting bird.

With a hoarse note the crow flapped its sable wings as if in gloating triumph over the coming feast.

One short minute more and the great eyes would stare no more at the sky above. The beak of the carrion crow would be scarlet with human gore.

But, ere ten seconds of that minute passed away, a slight rustle came from the tangled thicket that fringed the ravine. The crow, with a hoarse note of anger, spread its wings and, cheated of its prey—cheated of the great eyes and the banquet of blood—soared lazily upward.

Then from the thicket, with stealthy tread, came a gaunt wolf.

A moment later the beast stood upon the edge of the ravine. Then it scented the blood that had trickled from the breast of the man who lay motionless upon the rocks.

With noiseless steps the gaunt beast came onward. It halted by the side of the motionless figure.

The fierce eyes of the wolf peered into the face of the human, and the huge jaws opened and shut with an ominous clash.

Then from the tree-top the carrion bird stooped again to earth.

Alarmed for a moment by the flap of the wings, the wolf lifted its huge jowl and displayed its white tusks in anger. The prowling beast was willing to fight for the human banquet.

But the carrion crow and the huge gray wolf were comrades of old in the great greenwood, and many a banquet had they shared together.

The crow opened its beak and the wolf licked its jaws as they stood by the side of the fallen man.

CHAPTER XI.

THE SURPRISE.

Boone, concealed in the bushes behind the fallen tree, on which sat the Indian girl and the red warrior, cursed the unlucky star that led the twain to select the place of his concealment for a stolen interview.

The scout hardly dared to breathe lest he should betray his presence to the two.

They, however, looking with eyes full of love upon each other, thought only of the happiness that they enjoyed when thus together.

The girl was the daughter of the great chief, Ke-ne-ha-ha; her lover was a young brave known as the "White Dog." A warrior young in years, but who had already distinguished himself on the war-path against the foes of the great Shawnee nation.

The children of the wilderness, wrapped in the joy of the stolen meeting, had little thought of aught else, and never for a moment suspected that within arm's length, a listener to their conversation, lay the great ranger and scout, Daniel Boone—the man whose death-dealing rifle was destined to tumble many a plumed and painted warrior to the earth.

The scout, who fully realized the danger of his position, could see no possible way to escape. He knew full well that the slightest movement on his part would inevitably betray his presence to the two who sat on the trunk of the fallen tree. Once discovered, every warrior in the Shawnee village would be quick on his trail.

One thought only consoled Boone. From the conversation of the squaw and chief—Boone understood enough of the Shawnee tongue to comprehend what was said—he might learn something concerning the Indian expedition. If he could gain important information, and manage to escape without betraying his presence to the Indians, then his mission would be accomplished.

"Is the chief satisfied?" asked the girl, with a smile, gazing full into the dark eyes of her lover as she spoke.

"Yes," replied the warrior. "Le-a-pah has kept her word. She is the singing-bird of the Shawnee nation. The White Dog will love her till the great lamp in the sky grows old and the spirit-lights fade and die forever."

"Le-a-pah is the daughter of a great chief; he would be angry if he knew that his child met the young brave by the forest," said the girl, sadly.

"The White Dog is a young warrior, but the scalps of the Delaware already hang and dry in the smoke of his wigwam." The tone of the young chief was proud as he uttered the words that told of his prowess.

"The chief speaks with a straight tongue," and the girl looked with pride into the manly face of her lover. "Le-a-pah loves the White Dog, but the great chief, her father, has said that she must be the wife of the warrior who is called Black Cloud. The heart of Le-a-pah is sad, for she can not love the Black Cloud."

"The Black Cloud is old—the singing-bird is young. Would her father mate the bounding spring with the chill autumn? It is bad!" and the young brave shook his head sadly.

"The Black Cloud is a great chief," said the girl.

"When the White Dog comes back from the war-path against the white-skins on the Ohio, *he* will be a great chief, too. Many white scalps will hang at his belt, and his tomahawk will be red with the blood of the long-rifles," said the chief, proudly.

Boone, from his hiding-place, listened intently when the warrior spoke of the expedition to Ohio. This was the very information he was after.

"The white-skins are many; the Shawnee chief may fall by their hands," and a shadow of apprehension passed across the face of the Indian maiden as she spoke.

"Then his spirit will go to the long home beyond the skies, and in the spirit-land will chase the red deer. But, if the White Dog comes back to the banks of the Scioto, then Le-a-pah must be his wife and dwell forevermore in his wigwam."

"The Shawnee girl will be the wife of the young chief whom she loves as the sun loves the earth, or she will never sing in the wigwam of a chief."

"Good!"

The young brave drew the slight form of the unresisting girl to his heart.

"The chief will love the singing-bird while he lives; when he dies, her face will be in his heart," said the warrior, fondly.

"When does the chief go on the war-path?" asked the girl.

"Three sleeps more and the Shawnees will burst like a thunder-cloud on the pale-faces," replied the Indian.

"On the Ohio?"

"Yes," answered the chief.

"Now, if the heathen would only say whar," muttered Boone, listening eagerly.

"The white-skins will fight hard." The girl was thinking of the peril that her lover was about to encounter.

"The red-men will fight as they have never fought before," said the warrior. "The tomahawk and brand shall scourge the pale-face from the ground that the Great Spirit gave to the Indian. The waters of the Kanawha shall run red with blood. The Shawnees have not forgotten the many braves that fell by the deadly leaden hail of the white-skins many moons ago, by the Ohio and Kanawha."

The chief referred to the defeat sustained by the Indians at the hands of the border-men commanded by Lewis, which took place some years before the time of the action of our story.

"It is against Point Pleasant, then," said Boone, to himself, as the words of the Indian fell upon his ear. "Well, let 'em come! I reckon we can blaze 'em as bad the second time as we did the first. Now, if these young critters would only make tracks out o' this, how quick I'd make a bee-line for the Ohio. But—dog-gone their copper-colored hides!—they don't seem at all in a hurry to go."

The scout was right in his thought. The two lovers were in no hurry to bring their love-meeting to a close. It was probably the last chance that they would have of being together, and they were anxious to improve the opportunity. Love is the same the world over, whether it springs in the heart of the savage, beneath the spreading branches of the oak in the forest wilderness, or in the breast of fashion's votary in the crowded city.

Warmly the warrior pressed his suit and told of the deathless flame that burned within his heart. Coyly listened the girl to the avowal that she loved to hear.

The lover eagerly pleaded for a farewell kiss from the lips that he had ne'er touched. Shyly the Indian maid refused the favor, though in her heart she consented.

The chief clasped the girl in his arms. She, with assumed anger, freed herself from his embrace and pushed him away. The chief, losing his balance in the struggle, tumbled over backward from the log, coming down plump on top of the scout concealed in the bushes behind the tree.

Quick from the throat of the Indian came the note of alarm. He realized instantly that the form concealed in the bushes must be the form of a foe.

With a mighty effort, Boone rolled the chief to one side, then sprung to his feet, prepared to fly for his life.

The Indian girl shrieked with terror when she beheld a pale-face spring up amid the bushes.

Her cry attracted the attention of the Indians in the village, and, with hasty steps, they rushed toward the line of timber, anxious to learn the cause of the alarm.

Boone felt that desperate effort alone would save him. A foot-race through the forest with a score of Shawnees was the only chance, but to escape the vengeance of the Indians would require a fearful effort.

As the scout started, his foot caught in a clinging vine, and over he went on his face. Before he could recover, the young chief, the White Dog, was upon him.

The Indian was sinewy and stout of limb, yet he was no match for the stalwart scout. With a grasp of steel, Boone grappled with the red warrior.

For a moment they swayed to and fro over the earth; the scout trying to break the grip of the Indian, and he striving to hold the unknown foe until his brethren should come to his aid.

The Shawnees were approaching fast. Their shouts rung out on the air like a death-knell.

Thus nerved to redouble his exertions, the iron-limbed scout swung the red-skin from the ground, and essayed to cast him from him; but, like a snake, the supple savage twined himself around the body of the white.

The cries of the Indian girl, alarmed for the safety of her lover, were answered by the angry shouts of the approaching crowd, who could plainly see that there was a struggle going on in the borders of the thicket.

"Help! help!" cried the girl: "this way! a white-skin!"

"Let go your hold, you cussed red imp!" cried Boone, between his teeth, as he vainly tried to break the grip of the red chief.

The Indian now was merely trying to hold the white foe till assistance should come to his aid.

Desperate, Boone's hand sought the handle of his knife. The bright blade flashed in the air; a second more, and it would have been buried to the haft in the body of the White Dog, but the Indian girl perceived her lover's peril, and sprung to his aid, grasping the hand of the scout just as he was about to plunge the knife in the red-man's breast.

The red chief, taking advantage of the girl's aid, twisted his leg around that of the scout, bore Boone backward to the earth, upon which the combatants fell with a heavy shock. A second more, and the Shawnee warriors surrounded the contending men.

With many a cry of triumph they bound the daring pale-face who had lurked so near to the Shawnee village.

CHAPTER XII.

KENTON SEES THE WOLF DEMON.

After having secured with tough thongs of deer-skin the stalwart limbs of their prisoner, they bore him forward to where the fire burned in their village.

All the inhabitants, attracted by the noise of the capture, had left their lodges and now pressed forward to look upon the prisoner.

Great was the astonishment of the Shawnees when the flickering light of the flames, falling upon their captive, revealed to them the well-known face of Daniel Boone, the great scout of the border.

A howl of delight resounded through the Indian village at this discovery. The red-skins had no foe whom they dreaded more than the man they now held, bound and helpless, a prisoner in their midst.

A grim smile was upon the features of Ke-ne-ha-ha, the Shawnee chief, as he looked upon the face of the man who had so often escaped him on the war-path.

"The white-skin is no longer an eagle, but a fox; he creeps into the shadow of the Shawnee village, to use his ears," said the chief, mockingly.

"The Shawnees have already had proof that I can use my hands," replied the scout, nettled by the words as well as the tone of the savage. "A chief that is not fox as well as eagle, is not worthy to go upon the war-path. His scalp should be taken by squaws."

The Indians could not dispute the words of Boone.

"What seeks the white chief in the village of the Shawnees?" asked Ke-ne-ha-ha.

"Guess, and maybe you'll find out," replied the captive coolly.

"The white-skin comes as a spy—a foe into the village of the Shawnee," said the Indian.

"When did any of your nation, chief, ever come except as a spy or a foe to the houses of the whites?" asked Boone.

"Ugh! the white-skin has stolen the land of the red-man. Cheated him with lies. Ke-ne-ha-ha is a great warrior—he will take the scalps of the long-knives and burn their wigwams," said the Indian, proudly.

"You'll have to fight afore you accomplish *that*, Injun, I reckon," replied Boone, whose coolness and courage astonished the red warriors.

"The white-skin shall die!" said the chief, fiercely.

51

"I reckon we've all got to die, sometime, Injun," answered Boone, not in the least terrified by the threat.

"Let my warriors take the prisoner to the wigwam of Ke-ne-ha-ha," said the chief.

The order was instantly obeyed. The prisoner was carried to the wigwam—one of the largest in the village. In the center of the lodge a little fire was burning.

The scout was laid upon a little couch of skins within the lodge; then, in obedience to an order from the great chief, the Indians withdrew and left the captive alone with Ke-ne-ha-ha.

The chief's wigwam stood only a few paces from the banks of the Scioto, that stream running close behind the Indian lodge.

After the Indians had placed the helpless prisoner within the lodge, they returned again to their scalp-dance around the fire, excepting a few warriors, who, under the leadership of the White Dog—who suddenly found himself famous by his capture of the great scout—made a circuit of the forest surrounding the Shawnee village to discover if there were any more white foes lurking within the wood.

The search was fruitless. No trace could they find of the presence of a white-skin; and so, finally, they came to the conclusion that the daring ranger was alone. The Indians then returned to the village.

The escape of Kenton from the search of the Indians is easily explained. He had approached the village on the west, and, skillfully taking advantage of the cover afforded by the bushes, had, like Boone, reached the edge of the timber. From his position he commanded a view of the village, and from his concealment beheld the capture of his friend. Guessing shrewdly that the presence of one white man might lead them to suspect that there were others in the neighborhood, he determined to withdraw from his dangerous position. He had seen no sign of Lark since he had parted with him at the hollow oak, and he came to the conclusion that Lark had not yet reached the village.

Kenton retreated from his exposed position. Slowly making his way through the wood, his eyes fell upon a large oak tree. The thought suggested itself to him that in the branches of the oak, he might find shelter.

So up the tree he mounted.

Once more in his hiding-place, vailed in as he was by the leafy branches, he felt that he could bid defiance to any search that the Indians might make.

Hardly had Kenton adjusted himself comfortably in the tree, when he heard a slight rustling in the bushes to the right of the oak. The keen ear of the alert scout instantly knew that some one was moving cautiously through the thicket. The sound came from the direction of the village.

Kenton thought that, possibly, it was Lark, who, like himself, had scouted into the Shawnee village, and was retreating to safer quarters.

Then, through the dim aisles of the forest came a dark form gliding onward with stealthy steps. In the uncertain light Kenton thought he recognized the figure of Abe Lark, the scout. Bending down from his hiding-place, Kenton was about to warn him that a friend was near, when the dark form crossed a little opening upon which the moonbeams cast their rays of silvery light, and Kenton caught a glimpse of the form as it glided through the moonlit opening.

The lion-hearted scout almost dropped from the tree when his eyes fell upon that form. The hair upon his head rose in absolute fright. His eyeballs were distended, and cold drops of sweat stood like waxen beads upon his bronzed forehead.

Well might he feel a sense of terror, for there below him glided—what?

The vast proportions of a huge gray wolf, walking erect upon hind legs, but the wolf possessed the face of a human!

A moment only the wolf—man or phantom—whatever it was—was beheld by the astonished scout, then it disappeared in the gloom of the thicket.

With the back of his hand Kenton wiped the perspiration—cold as the night-dew—from his brow.

"I've seen it!" he muttered, to himself. "It's the Wolf Demon. Jerusalem! I'd rather fight forty Shawnees than have a tussle with a monster like that. I always thought that the Injun story 'bout the Wolf Demon was all bosh, but now I've seen it; so near the Shawnee village, too. Thar'll be a hurricane soon, or I'm a Dutchman."

Leaving the scout to his meditations, we will follow the course of the terrible figure that had so affrighted the stout Simon Kenton, who was one of the bravest hearts on the border.

Cautiously and carefully through the thicket the creature glided. It was making its way to the Scioto river.

Suddenly the figure paused, and apparently listened for a moment.

The sound of footsteps of the Indian warriors, headed by the White Dog, scouting through the forest, broke the stillness of the night.

But for a moment the mysterious Wolf Demon listened; then as the Indians came nearer and nearer, with a leap, as agile as that of the squirrel, the terrible form seized hold of a branch of the oak beneath which it was standing, and swung itself up into the concealment of the leaves of the tree.

The Indian braves came on and paused for consultation under the branches of the very tree that concealed, in its leafy recesses, the terrible scourge of their race.

"Wah! The pale chief is alone," said one of the warriors; "no other pale-face is within the woods."

"He is a brave chief to come alone to the lodges of the Shawnee nation," said another of the warriors.

"Boone is a great brave," said the White Dog, who felt a natural pride in extolling the bravery of the prisoner whose capture was placed to his credit.

"He will never take the war-path against the Shawnees again," said one of the braves, with on accent of satisfaction.

"No; his scalp shall blacken and dry in the smoke of a Shawnee's lodge," said the White Dog.

"It is good," responded another, with a grunt of satisfaction.

"The great white-skin will die by the fire, and the red braves will dance around him with joy," said the Indian who had first spoken, with a fierce expression of delight in his voice.

"The long-knife was alone—no more are within the wood; let us return to the village," said the White Dog.

The other warriors grunted their assent, and the party, turning upon their heel, took the way leading back to the village.

Hardly had the figure of the rearmost savage disappeared in the gloom of the wood, when forth from the tree came the terrible figure.

Lightly it bounded to the ground, and, with a glittering tomahawk clutched in its paw, followed swiftly but cautiously on the track of the red-men.

The Indians, however, kept together. Had one remained behind the other, he would never have lived to have told what struck him.

The terrible form followed to the edge of the timber, and ground its teeth in rage at the escape of its foe.

Then it headed again for the river, keeping within the shelter of the timber. The river reached, the mysterious prowler took advantage of the stream's bank, which had been hollowed out by the washing of the water, to reach the wigwam of Ke-ne-ha-ha in which Boone was confined.

There, in the very shadow of the wigwam, the terrible figure lay upon the ground concealed by the darkness, and listened intently.

CHAPTER XIII.

THE OFFER OF THE SHAWNEE CHIEF.

Boone and the chief of the Shawnees were alone together in the Indian wigwam.

The white man wondered why the Indian had dismissed his warriors. He guessed that the chief had probably something to say to him privately, and which he did not wish the others to hear; but of the nature of that communication he could not form the least idea.

Ke-ne-ha-ha surveyed the prisoner for a moment in silence.

The dim light of the fire illuminated the interior of the wigwam, so that each could plainly distinguish the face of the other.

At length the chief spoke.

"The pale-face is a great warrior in his nation—many red chiefs have fallen by his hand."

"Yes, but it was in fair fight, man to man," replied the scout.

"The squaws of the slain braves mourn their loss—they call upon the chief of the Shawnees to give them the blood of the white-skin who has stained his hand red with the blood of the Shawnee. The tears of the widowed wives fall thick upon the ground. The heart of Ke-ne-ha-ha is sad when he thinks of the brave warriors that the pale-face has sent to the happy hunting-grounds. Why should not the Long Rifle die by the hand of the redman?"

"What on yearth is the use of askin' any such foolish questions?" cried Boone, impatiently. "You know very well that you're going to put an end to me, if you can. As for the blood that I've shed of your nation, I've always struck in self-defense. If any of your warriors feel aggrieved, I'm ready to meet 'em—even two to one—and give 'em all the satisfaction that they want."

Ke-ne-ha-ha looked at the white keenly as he uttered the bold defiance.

"Ugh! When the hunters catch the bear they do not let him go free again, nor do they let the Long Rifle go free now that they have caught him. The red chiefs will punish the warrior who has killed their brothers, without risking their lives against him. The fire is burning now before the council-lodge of the Shawnee. When it burns to-morrow the white hunter will be in its center, and the angry flames shall lap up his blood. The ashes of the Long Rifle alone shall remain to tell of the vengeance of the red chiefs."

The Indian still looked with searching eyes into the face of the prisoner as he told of the manner of his death. But if the Shawnee chief expected to see there the signs of fear, he was disappointed, for the iron-like muscles of Boone's face never moved.

"Why in thunder do you want to tell a fellow that he's a-goin' to be roasted?" asked Boone, coolly. "Won't it be time enough for me to find out when you tie me to the stake, and I see the smoke a-rising around me?"

The Indian was evidently annoyed that his words had not made more impression upon the scout.

"The white skin does not fear death, then?" the chief asked.

"Yes, I do," answered Boone; "I fear it like thunder. Just you let me loose once, and see how I'll run from it. Lightning will be a fool to my heels."

The joking manner of the scout puzzled the red warrior. He knitted his brows for a moment, as if in deep thought. Then again he spoke.

"The white chief is a great warrior. What would he give to escape the fire-death of the Shawnees?"

Boone couldn't exactly understand the meaning of the chief's words, though the question that he asked seemed plain enough.

"Well, chief," Boone said, after pausing for a moment, as if deliberating upon his answer, "life is sweet; a man would give almost anything for life. But the question with me now is, what can I give?"

"Yourself," said the chief, laconically.

"Eh?" Boone could not understand

"The white chief is a great brave; he has put to death many great chiefs. If he will become a son of the Shawnee nation, the warriors will forget what he *has* done, and will look forward to what he *will* do."

Boone was considerably astonished at the words of the chief, although this was not the first time in the course of his eventful life that the Indians had endeavored to get him to join with them.

"Become a Shawnee, eh?"

"Yes," answered the chief.

"Then the Shawnees will not burn me?"

"No."

"But if I refuse?"

"To-morrow's sun will rise upon your death."

"If I become one of your tribe, what am I expected to do?"

"Take the war-path with the Shawnee braves against the white-skins," answered the chief.

"That is, betray the men who speak my tongue—who are my brothers—into the hands of your people?"

"Yes," replied the chief; "my brother speaks with a straight tongue."

"I'll see you hanged first," muttered Boone, indignantly, to himself, but he was careful not to let the speech reach the ears of the Indian. He fully understood the dangerous position that fate had placed him in, and the thought flashed through his mind that if he could deceive the savages by pretending to accept their offer, he might delay his execution—gain time, and possibly, through some lucky chance, contrive to effect his escape.

Boone had been fully as near to death before, and yet escaped to tell of it. He did not despair even now, though a prisoner in the midst of the great Shawnee tribe.

"How long will you give me to think over this proposal that you make me?" Boone asked. "You know a man can't change his country and his color as easily as to pull off a coat and put on a hunting-shirt."

The Indian thought for a moment over the question of the scout. Bound securely as he was; surrounded, too, by the Shawnee warriors, escape was impossible. There was little danger in delaying the sentence of the white-skin.

"Will until to-morrow suit my brother?" asked the chief.

"To-morrow?" said Boone; then to his mind came the thought that, before that morrow came, something might transpire to aid him to escape. "Well, until to-morrow will do, though it's mighty short time for a man to make up his mind on such a ticklish question as this is."

"To-morrow then my brother will say whether he will become a Shawnee or be burnt at the stake to appease the unquiet souls of the brave warriors that his hand has sent to the happy hunting-grounds?"

"Yes," answered Boone, "to-morrow you shall have my answer." But, even as he spoke, in his heart he prayed that some lucky accident might aid him ere the night was over.

"It is good," replied the chief, gravely. "Let my brother open his ears. The chief of the Shawnees would talk more."

"Go ahead, chief," said Boone, who wondered what was coming next.

"My brother is a great warrior; he has fought the Shawnees many times —fought also the Mingoes, the Delawares and the Wyandots. Many a red chief has leveled his rifle full at the heart of the white brave, but the bullet was turned aside by the 'medicine' of my brother. Is the chief a medicine-man?"

Boone understood the superstition of the Indians. He saw, too, that possibly he might use the belief of being invulnerable against rifle-ball to aid him in his desperate strait.

"The chief will be silent if I speak?" Boone asked, mysteriously.

"The heart of Ke-ne-ha-ha is like the pools of the Scioto—cast a stone into them, it sinks to the bottom and remains there. So shall the words of my brother sink into my heart."

"I am a medicine-man."

"And bullet can not harm my brother?"

"No," said Boone, impressively; "not if I keep out of its way," he added, to himself.

The Indian looked at Boone for a moment in silence; a slight expression of awe was in his face. Then the chief came nearer to the old scout, and in a solemn tone, spoke:

"Has the white-skin ever heard of the Wolf Demon of the Shawnees?"

"Yes," answered the scout, somewhat surprised at the question.

"The Wolf Demon is the scourge of the Shawnee tribe. Many brave warriors have fallen by the tomahawk of the monster, and on their breasts he leaves his totem—a Red Arrow. Ke-ne-ha-ha is the great chief of the Shawnee nation; scalps hang thick in the smoke of his wigwam; he is not afraid of man or demon. But the scourge of the Shawnees fears to meet a warrior unless he is alone in the forest. Ke-ne-ha-ha has sought for the Wolf Demon, but he can not find him. The red chief would kill the monster that uses the totem of the Red Arrow. If my brother is a medicine-man, can he not tell me where I may find the Wolf Demon?"

"I can not," answered Boone.

The chief looked disappointed.

"The red-man is sorry. He will see his brother in the morning." Then the chief stalked, moodily, from the lodge.

For an hour or more Boone remained in silence. The fire in the center of the lodge burnt out and darkness surrounded the scout.

Then to the keen ear of the woodman came the sound of a knife cutting through the skins that formed the walls of the wigwam.

A few minutes more and Boone, despite the gloom of the wigwam, could see that a dark form stood by his side.

The scout knew in an instant that it was a friend. He thought it either Lark or Kenton that had so aptly come to his assistance.

CHAPTER XIV.

A MYSTERIOUS DISAPPEARANCE.

On the morning following the day on which the young stranger, Harvey Winthrop, had been shot down in the little ravine by the Kanawha river, and Virginia was carried off by the villainous tools of Clement Murdock, to the lonely cabin on the other bank of the stream to that on which the settlement of Point Pleasant was located, Murdock again stood before the cabin. The stranger, Benton, and the drunken vagabond, Bob Tierson, had remained by the cabin, still wearing their Indian disguises.

"How does the girl bear it?" Murdock asked, on joining the others. The three stood within the wood just beyond the little clearing.

"Oh, well enough," answered Benton. "I took her in some breakfast this morning. She's been crying all night, I reckon. I spoke Injun-fashion to her. She implored me to take her back to the settlement and promised all sorts of rewards."

"She'll be quite ready then to look upon me in the light of a deliverer, I suppose," said Murdock, a smile lighting up his sallow features.

"All you've got to do is to go in and win," said Bob, with a grin.

"That is just what I intend to do," replied Murdock, enjoying his triumph in anticipation.

"By the way, are they making any row in the settlement over the girl's disappearance?" asked Benton, carelessly.

"Yes, all the settlers have been scouring the forest since last night when her absence was discovered," answered Murdock.

"And her father—the old General—what does he say about it?"

"He is nearly crazy over the disappearance of his daughter. I nearly felt pity for the old man, but I consoled myself by thinking how great his joy would be, when I brought his daughter back to him, and how glad he would be to receive as his son-in-law the man who, at the peril of his life, rescued her from the murdering red-skins."

Murdock smiled grimly as he spoke.

"Well, dog my cats if it ain't as good as a show," said Bob, with a laugh all over his huge, ugly face at the idea. "I shall have to be 'round to witness the interesting meeting."

"Yes; you must make yourself scarce as soon as I take the girl off, for you'll have the whole country on your trail. Of course I shall have to describe where I found her."

"But, s'pose they do come arter us, how kin we kiver up the trail?" asked Bob.

"Oh, easy enough," replied Murdock; "the moment you strike the trail on the other bank of the Kanawha, who can tell whether you go up or down? There's too many fresh marks on it for any one to be able to pick out ours."

"There isn't any danger," said Benton, calmly.

"Well, I'm glad of that, for I don't like any more danger than I've got to scratch through," observed Bob, and to do him justice he spoke the truth. Bob's reputation for bravery was not particularly good among the settlers of Point Pleasant.

"Did they discover the body of the young man that you knocked over with your rifle?" asked Benton.

"No," replied Murdock, and a slight bit of uneasiness was plainly perceptible in his tone.

"No?" said Benton, astonished.

"No," again said Murdock, "and I am somewhat puzzled to account for it, too. The searching parties must have passed through the ravine, it is so near the settlement. I can not understand it at all. I am sure that he was dead when we left him. You examined him, Bob. Did he show any signs of life?"

"Nary sign," replied Bob, emphatically. But Bob's examination of the body of the man who had fallen by the bullet of Murdock's rifle, had been but a slight one, and Bob was not likely to be a very close observer or be able to decide between life and death in a doubtful case.

"I can not understand it," said Murdock, absently. He was indeed sorely puzzled by the strange circumstance. The thought had occurred to him that, possibly, the shot that he had aimed with such deadly intent at the heart of his rival might have failed to accomplish the death of the young stranger. Perhaps his rival still lived and might attempt to wrest from him the prize he had toiled so to gain. The thought was wormwood to him, yet he had brooded over it all the way through the forest, thought of little else from the time he left the settlement at Point Pleasant till he stood before the lonely cabin by the Kanawha. "He may have escaped death, but yet I do not see how it can possibly be. I am sure I hit him fairly, and I do not often have to fire twice at one mark."

"Why, thar ain't a doubt but what he's gone under," cried Bob.

"But I do not understand how it is that the settlers in searching for the girl did not come upon his body," said Murdock.

"It is strange," observed Benton.

"Jist as easy as rollin' off a log," said Bob.

"What is?" questioned Murdock.

"The reason why they didn't find him."

"Is there a reason?"

"Of course," replied Bob, confidently. "Didn't you tumble him over just before nightfall?"

"Yes."

"Well, do you s'pose the wolves would let him lay there all night? No, sir."

"The wolves, possibly, may have made away with the body, but yet the bones would remain," Murdock said, thoughtfully.

"Why, no," said Bob, "the wolves would naturally drag the body off into the woods and the bones would be left thar!"

Murdock breathed easier after this possible solution of the mystery. He had had a dreadful suspicion that he might see again in the flesh the man whose life he had tried to take.

"Now to put my plan in execution," Murdock said. "I shall enter the cabin by the hole in the ground at the back of the shanty, and represent to the girl that, at the peril of my life, I have come to save her."

"Oh, it will work easy enough," said Bob.

"I hope so; you had better wait till I get out of sight with the girl; then make your way back to the settlement," said Murdock.

"All right," replied Bob, while Benton silently nodded his head.

Then Murdock left the two and took a circle through the wood which would bring him to the back of the cabin.

Bob watched Murdock until he was out of sight; then he turned, abruptly, to Benton.

"Say, got any more corn-juice?" he asked.

"No," replied Benton, in a surly way.

"That's a pity," said Bob, reflectively.

"What did you want to go and drink it all up for?" asked Benton, indignantly.

Benton that morning had produced a large flask of whisky, and left it with Bob while he went off to shoot a squirrel for breakfast. On his return he found that Bob had drank up the entire contents of the flask and was in a drunken slumber. He had just awakened out of it when Murdock came.

"It was 'tarnal good corn-juice," said Bob, smacking his lips at the remembrance.

"Well, you didn't leave any for me to taste, so I don't know whether it was or not," said Benton, in ill-humor.

"You didn't come back, an' I make a p'int never to let whisky spile when I'm 'round to drink it up," exclaimed Bob.

"The next time you get any of my whisky to drink, I reckon you'll know it," said Benton, significantly.

"Well, you needn't get riled at a feller," replied Bob.

From where the two stood they commanded a view of the cabin. Their astonishment was great when they beheld Murdock come from behind the cabin in evident agitation. He stopped before the door of the log-house, which was fastened on the outside by a rude bar—Murdock's device to prevent the escape of the prisoner. Then he beckoned for the two to come to him.

Astonished, they obeyed the gesture. Evidently something was the matter.

"Who saw the girl this morning?" demanded Murdock, when they approached.

"I did," responded Benton.

"At what time?"

"Just after sunrise."

"And you have watched the cabin since then?"

"No, I was off in the woods for a little while."

"But *you* remained," Murdock said, turning to Bob; "you watched the cabin in his absence?"

"Of course I did," responded Bob, stoutly. "I never took my eyes off of it." Considering that he had been fast asleep for about two hours, of which time Benton had been away, Bob told his story with a good grace.

"I can not understand it," muttered Murdock, an angry cloud upon his brow. "The door is secure; the log behind, just as I left it."

"Why, what's the matter, Clem?" asked Bob, who saw plainly that something had gone wrong, though what it was, he could not guess.

"Look for yourselves," cried Murdock, angrily, throwing open the door of the cabin as he spoke.

Eagerly the two looked in.

The cabin was empty! The girl was gone!

With blank faces the three looked at each other.

The girl had been spirited out of their hands by some means, but how, they could not tell. There was no possible solution to this mystery. No way by which the girl could escape, and yet she was gone. Vanished without a trace of the manner of her escape. Murdock was beaten, but how or by whom he could not even guess.

CHAPTER XV.

THE RENEGADE'S DAUGHTER.

By the northern bank of the Kanawha, some five miles from the settlement of Point Pleasant, stood a lonely cabin. A little clearing surrounded it.

The cabin was situated about half a mile from the broad trail leading from Point Pleasant to the Virginia settlements.

A narrow foot-path led from the broad trail to the lonely cabin, but so little was it used and so dense had grown the weeds and rank grass of the forest about it, that it would almost have required the practiced eye of the savage, or his rival in woodcraft, the white borderer, to have discovered the existence of the path.

The cabin itself, though situated far from the line of civilization, showed evident signs of human occupation.

The wild vines of the forest, transplanted from their native fastness, twined and bloomed about the rough logs that formed the walls of the cabin. And with the wild children of the wood grew red and white roses, the floral gems that art had plucked from nature.

A little garden patch, that showed plainly the traces of careful tending, was on the further side of the cabin and extended down near to the bank of the Kanawha.

This lonely cabin, far off in the wild woods, remote from civilization, was the home of the strange, wayward girl whom the settlers at Point Pleasant called Kanawha Kate, and whom the red chiefs, in their fanciful way, termed the "Queen of the Kanawha."

In the interior of the lonely cabin a strange scene presented itself to view.

On a rude couch of deer-skins lay a man. He was moaning, helplessly, as if in great pain.

The shirt that covered his manly breast was stained with blood.

From the position in which the wounded man lay—on his side, with his face buried in the folds of the deer-skin—his features were concealed from view, yet from the pallor of the little part of his face that was visible, it was evident that the man had been stricken nigh to death.

By the side of the suffering man knelt the brown-cheeked beauty, Kanawha Kate.

Anxiously she bent over the stricken man. A little cup of the muddy water from the Kanawha was by her side, and with her hands, wet with the discolored drops, she bathed the feverish temples of the wounded man.

Tender as a mother nursing her first-born, the girl laved the hot flesh.

As the cooling touch of the wet, brown hand passed softly over his temples, it seemed to ease the pain that racked the muscular limbs.

The rigid lines of the face, distorted by the agony of pain, grew soft. The moans of anguish were stilled. The simple treatment of the girl was relieving the torture felt by the stranger.

Eagerly the girl watched the face, and smiled when she saw the muscles relax and the painful breathing become low and regular.

"He will not die!" she cried, in joy, but barely speaking above a whisper for fear of disturbing her patient.

"He will live and owe that life to me. Oh! what joy in the thought!" Then a few moments she remained silent, watching the pale face before her with many a long, loving look.

Few of the settlers at Point Pleasant who had seen Kanawha Kate roaming the forest, rifle in hand—as good a woodman as any one among them— would have guessed that, within the heart of the forest-queen was a world of tenderness and love.

They had seen her bring down the brown deer with a single shot, wing an eagle in his airy circle in the sky and bring the kingly bird tumbling to earth; had seen her when the Ohio, lashed into white, crested waves by the mad winds, bid defiance to the boldest boatman to dare to cross it, launch her dug-out and fearlessly commit herself to the mercy of the dashing waters.

How could they guess that with the dauntless courage of a lion, she also possessed the tender and loving heart of a woman? But so it was.

"It was Heaven that sent me to his aid," she murmured, gazing fondly on the white face. "How beautiful he is; how unlike the rough fellows in yonder settlement," and the girl's lip curled contemptuously as she spoke.

"He is a king to them. Oh! what would I not give to win his love; but that thought is folly. I am despised by all; but no, there is one who speaks fairly to and thinks kindly of me—Virginia Treveling. She has a noble heart. She is the only one in yonder settlement who has not treated me with scorn and yet fate has decreed that we shall stand in each other's way." Mournful was the voice of the girl as the words came from her lips; sorrowful was the look upon her face.

"It is a hopeless passion that I am nourishing in my heart. I must not love him, for I can never hope to win a return of that love."

Sadly she looked upon the wounded man.

A footfall outside the cabin attracted her attention. Quickly she bounded to her feet and seized the rifle that hung over the rude fire-place. Then she stood still and listened.

"Who can it be that seeks the home of the outcast girl?" she murmured, as with eager ears, every sense on the alert, she listened.

"Can it be one of the settlers from Point Pleasant? No; but few of them know of my dwelling-place, and fewer still would care to seek it. Is it a red-skin? No; I would not have heard his footfall if he comes in malice."

Then the girl heard the sound of footsteps approaching the house.

"Ah!" exclaimed the girl, suddenly, as a thought flashed through her mind; "perhaps it is his foes coming to seek him," and her glance was on the wounded man as she spoke. "If so they had better have sought the den of the wolf, or the nest of the rattlesnake than my cabin. They must kill me before they shall harm him."

Hardly had the speech come from her lips when a bold knock sounded on the door.

"Who is there?" cried Kate.

The door—a heavy one, braced strongly—was barred on the inside and was fully stout enough to defy the strength of a dozen men, let alone one.

"Open and you will see," responded a hoarse voice.

The girl started when the tones fell upon her ear.

"Can it be he?" she muttered, and wonder was in her voice.

"Why don't you answer, gal?" exclaimed the voice of the stranger. "Don't you know me, or have you forgotten your own flesh and blood?"

"It is my father," she murmured, but there was little love in the tones.

Then, without further parley, she unbarred the door. It swung back slowly on its rusty hinges and a tall, powerfully built man, clad in a deer-skin garb fashioned after the Indian style, entered the room.

The stranger was the same man whom we have seen in the Shawnee village, Girty's companion, by name David Kendrick.

He, too, like Girty was execrated by the settlers. An adopted son of the great Shawnee nation, with his red brothers he had stained his hands in the blood of the men whose skins were white like his own.

There was little love expressed in the face of Kate as she looked upon her father, for the renegade Kendrick bore that relation to her, though by the inhabitants of Point Pleasant it was generally supposed that she was some relation to Girty; but that was not the truth.

"Well, gal, how are you?" questioned the new-comer, roughly. But before the girl could reply, the eyes of Kendrick fell upon the figure of the wounded man stretched upon the couch of skins.

"Hullo! who's this, eh? Hain't been getting a husband since I've been up in the Shawnee country, have you?"

"No," answered the girl, scornfully and quickly.

"Needn't get riled 'bout it," said the father, bluntly. "Who is he, any-way?"

"A wounded stranger whose life I have been trying to save."

"I s'pose you're in love with him, eh?" asked Kendrick, with a covert glance from under his heavy brows at the girl.

"In love with him! What good would it do me to fall in love with any decent white man? Am I not *your* daughter? the child of a renegade?" exclaimed the girl, bitterly.

"Better come with me and I'll find you a husband in some of the great chiefs of the Shawnee nation."

"I'd blow out my brains with my own rifle first," cried the girl, angrily.

"Don't get your back up; I only suggested it. You've got the temper of an angel, you have. If you ever *do* get a husband, you'll comb his hair with a three-legged stool, I reckon, whether his skin is white or red."

The girl made no reply, but turned away her head with a look of scorn.

"Seein' as how I was 'round the clearing I thought I'd call in and see how you was. I didn't expect to find the old cabin turned into a hospital."

"Would you have had me leave this poor fellow to die in the wood, like a dog?" asked the girl, spiritedly.

"Life ain't worth much, anyway," said the renegade, contemptuously. "One man ain't missed in this hyer big world."

"What brings you so near to the station?" asked Kate.

"Ain't it natural that a white man should want to see some of his own color, once in awhile?" asked Kendrick, with a grin.

"Your color!" said the girl, in scorn, "though your face is white yet your heart is red! yes, as red as your hand has been with blood. In yonder settlement they call you the white Indian, and they would tear you to pieces if they could get their hands upon you—show you as little mercy as they would show a wolf."

"That's true, gal, true as preachin'; but do you suppose the hate's all on one side? I reckon not," and the renegade laughed discordantly. "I've seen many a white man dance while the red flames were burning his life away, and I've laughed at the sight."

"And the guilt and shame that belongs to you clings to me also. I am your daughter, and that I am so is a curse upon my life. It has made me an outcast—forced me to seek a home far from the bounds of civilization. It has deadened all the good in my nature. It is a wonder that I am not thoroughly bad, for all think me so." The tone in which the girl spoke showed plainly how deeply she felt the cruel truth.

"Inside of a month the settlers at Point Pleasant won't jeer at you," said Kendrick, meaningly.

"What will keep them from it?" asked Kate, in wonder.

"Ke-ne-ha-ha and his Shawnees. There's a hurricane coming, gal, and Point Pleasant will be the first to feel it. Let 'em laugh now, they'll cry tears of blood soon."

CHAPTER XVI.

THE WOUNDED MAN.

"Within a week every red brave in the Shawnee nation will be on the war-path, and with the Shawnees are the Wyandots and the Mingoes. Thar's a bloody time ahead, gal."

"And you are leagued with the red fiends," said Kate, indignantly.

"And ar'n't I red now, too?" returned Kendrick, with a frown—"red at heart, although my skin may be white. But, gal, I've come to give you warning of this attack, so that you can look out for yourself in your expeditions in the forest. The Indians will be as thick as bees between here and the Ohio. And if they should come across you in the forest your scalp might adorn the belt of some one of my red brothers. Not that I think that any of the Shawnee tribe would harm a hair of your head, that is, if they knew who you was. But in the wood they won't be apt to examine very closely, till they put a bullet through you."

"I am not afraid," said the girl, scornfully. "I do not think there are many of the Shawnee warriors that are a match for me in woodcraft."

"That's so, gal; I'll back you ag'in' 'lifting a trail' with any red-man that ever stepped."

"Do not fear for me; I can take care of myself."

"By the way, gal, thar's one thing I want to ask you," said the renegade, suddenly. "In your wanderings about in the forest, did you ever see a strange-looking creature with the body of a wolf and the face of a human?"

"No," said the girl, in wonder.

"I don't know what to think of it, gal. Thar's something—whether man, beast, or demon, no one knows—a-hunting the Shawnee nation. It attacks the warriors, singly, in the forest. Kills them with a single lick of a tomahawk, and then cuts on their breasts three knife-slashes, making a red arrow."

"Have you ever seen it?" asked the girl.

"Me? no," replied the renegade.

"It is probably but an Indian fable; such a creature as you describe can not exist."

"But I've seen the dead Indians, though, with the red arrow cut on their breasts; thar's no mistake about that," said Kendrick.

"I have never met any such figure as you describe in the forest."

"Well, I reckon it's the devil, after all."

"Father, you understand the treatment of wounds, do you not?"

"Yes, a little."

"Can you not extract the ball from this stranger's wound?"

"Well, I kin try."

And then the renegade bent over the sleeping man. With his keen-edged hunting-knife he ripped open the stranger's shirt.

Silently, for a few moments, Kendrick examined the wound; then with his strong arms he turned the stranger over, gently.

"It's all right, gal; 'tain't nothing but a flesh wound. The ball has passed right through the side just under the shoulder. He's suffering more from loss of blood than any thing else. A few days will fix him all right. Just bind up the wound. Put on a bandage and a poultice of these leaves," and the renegade drew a handful of leaves from the Indian pouch that hung by his side, and gave them to the girl. "It's a Shawnee medicine and powerful healing. Just chew the leaves up and apply them wet to the wound. And now, I must be going. It ain't much use for you to waste your time curing this young fellow, because, if he stays round hyer, the savages will have his scalp afore he's a week older. Look out for yourself, now." And, with this parting injunction, the renegade left the house.

"And to think that this man, a renegade to his country and his kin, a consort with the red Indians, is my father," the girl muttered, bitterly.

Then she proceeded to dress the wound of the stranger. She applied the leaves as directed by the renegade. Then bound them tightly in their place with strips of cotton.

The cooling influence of the simple savage remedy seemed to give almost instant relief to the wounded man.

Anxiously she watched the expression of his face.

A few minutes of silence ensued. Then the stranger, with a sigh, turned, restlessly, on the deer-skin couch and awoke.

The wounded man was Harvey Winthrop.

Wolf and carrion-bird alike had been cheated of their banquet of blood by the timely arrival of the Kanawha Queen.

In astonishment, Winthrop looked around him.

"Where am I?" he muttered, in a haze.

"In safety, in my poor cabin," said Kate, softly.

Winthrop gave a slight start as the tone of her voice fell upon his ear.

He turned his glance upon the girl, and in a moment recognized her.

"Kate!" he exclaimed, in astonishment.

A warm blush, accompanied by a look of delight, swept over the girl's face as Winthrop pronounced her name.

"You remember me, then?" she said, in joy.

"Yes, of course. Am I likely to forget one who saved my life? and now I suppose I owe a double debt, another life; for, as I guess, to you again I owe my existence."

"I found you in the forest, wounded and senseless," said the girl, simply.

"In the same ravine where I met you, was it not?"

"Yes."

"Strange that twice in that one spot I should have come so near to death and yet escaped it."

"It was Providence that sent me to your aid. I know not why I directed my steps to that spot," and a half blush was on her face as she spoke, for, to speak truthfully, she should have said that it was a secret but earnest wish to look again upon the scene where she had met the handsome stranger, that led her to the ravine. But that truth she would not own even to herself.

"I thank both Heaven and yourself for the timely rescue," said Winthrop, earnestly.

"How did you receive your wound?" asked the girl.

"I do not know," replied Winthrop, with a puzzled air.

"You do not know!" exclaimed Kate, in astonishment.

"No, I was shot down without warning. I heard the sharp report of the rifle, then felt the burning sensation of the bullet tearing through my side, and then—I knew no more, until I awoke from my swoon a moment ago."

"I can not understand it," said Kate, thoughtfully.

"Nor can I. I have not an enemy in the world, that I know of, and here too in the West I am a stranger; have only been here a few days; hardly time enough to make acquaintances, let alone enemies. Perhaps, though, it was one of the savages that attacked me; to them all white men are foes."

"No Indian bullet stretched you on the earth," said Kate, decidedly. "Had it been an Indian that shot you, he would have taken your scalp instantly, as a trophy of victory; such is the custom of the red-men. You must have been insensible for some time when I reached your side, for quite a little pool of blood, that had flowed from your wound, was on the ground, and, as I came up, a huge gray wolf stole away into the thicket, and a crow winged its flight up through the tree-tops. Had there been Indians near, the wolf and crow would not have been by your side."

Winthrop shuddered when he thought of what his fate would have been but for the timely arrival of the girl.

"It is all a mystery to me," Winthrop said, absently. "I can not understand why any one should desire my death."

"And whoever attempted your life has a white skin, and not a red one; of that you may be sure," said Kate, decidedly.

"I can not guess the riddle."

Then for the first time to Winthrop's mind came the thought of Virginia Treveling.

"And Miss Treveling?" he exclaimed.

Kate looked at him in wonder. She could not understand the meaning of the exclamation.

"Miss Treveling?" she said.

"Yes; was she not with me, when you discovered me helpless?"

"No," said Kate, in utter astonishment.

"Why, this is a greater mystery than even the attack on me. Miss Treveling was with me in the ravine when I was shot."

"She was?"

"Yes; what could have become of her?"

"I can not guess."

"Could she have returned to Point Pleasant for assistance?"

"She would not have left you to bleed to death."

"You did not see her?"

"No."

"Would you have met had she gone to the station? Did you come from that direction?"

"No, I entered the ravine from the east by an old Indian trail."

"And my rifle, my knife?" exclaimed Winthrop, glancing around the room, as though he expected to see his weapons in some corner.

"There were no weapons near you."

"I have it at last—a clue to this mysterious attack," exclaimed Winthrop, excitedly. "Miss Treveling has been carried off. The ruffians, whoever they are, shot me down that they might secure her."

As he spoke, in Kate's mind came the dreadful suspicion that her father, the renegade, might have had something to do with the attack on Winthrop; but then in an instant she dismissed the thought as unworthy of belief, for her father had not acted toward the wounded man as if he had been his assassin.

"There are many wild and dangerous characters on the borders of the Ohio. Men whose lawless lives have driven them from civilization to the forest wilds; yet I should not think that there would be any one of them desperate enough to seize upon General Treveling's daughter, nor can I understand what they would gain by so doing."

"You are sure that the attacking party were not Indians?"

"Yes; first, because they would have taken your scalp; second, there is now peace along the Ohio border between the white men and the red, although no one can tell how soon the tomahawk will be again uplifted." The words of her father, the renegade, relative to the Indian expedition, were fresh in her mind as she spoke.

"I am certain that I was shot down like a dog, without mercy, that she might be carried away. The pain of my wound is nothing now to the pain in my heart when I think of what may be her fate."

Deep with anguish were the tones that came from the lips of the young man, and sorrowful was the cloud that darkened his face.

Mournfully Kate gazed upon him, but she spoke not.

"Lady, you can judge of my sufferings when I tell you that Virginia Treveling is my plighted wife. The words binding her life to mine had just passed her lips when the shot of the assassin struck me to her feet."

Each word that he spoke was like a dagger-thrust to Kate. She felt a deathlike faintness come over her, but with an effort that tried all her powers, she repressed the agony that was tearing her heart.

"She is to be your wife?" she said, rising.

"Yes."

"I will find her. If she is within a hundred miles of the Ohio, wood, swamp or village shall not hide her from me."

She snatched her rifle from the wall, and in a moment was gone.

CHAPTER XVII.

VIRGINIA'S ESCAPE.

Alone, a helpless captive in the hands of the dreaded red-men, Virginia felt that her situation was indeed a terrible one. Then, too, she had seen her lover fall helpless at her feet, struck down by the fatal shot of the ambushed foe. What his fate had been, even if he had not been killed outright by the ball that tore him from her arms and laid him prostrate on the earth, it was not difficult to guess. The red warriors rarely spared a fallen foe, and, in imagination, she saw the fair-haired scalp of the man she loved so well, dangling at the girdle of some brawny Indian chief.

With such thoughts as these passing rapidly through her mind, the terror of her situation was doubly increased.

On a rude bench that stood in a corner of the cabin, Virginia sat motionless as a statue, and wept many a bitter tear.

What her fate was to be, she understood only too well. A girl reared on the border, she understood the customs of the savages that claimed the valley of the Ohio as their own. And over her soul crept a sickening fear when she thought of the life that was in store for her, a slave to some Indian brave.

There was little chance of rescue. A miracle alone could save her.

A low knock at the door roused her from her abstraction.

How long she remained in the cabin she could not tell, but she knew that some hours must have passed away.

The cabin door opened slowly, and a man dressed in frontier fashion entered, cautiously.

It was the man who had called himself Benton. Of course he was unknown to the girl. Benton had washed off the war-paint, and appeared a white man, as he was.

A cry of joy rose to Virginia's lips and she sprung to her feet, but at a sign of caution from him she restrained herself.

To her the face of a white man gave hope of deliverance. She had little suspicion that all her captors were of her own color, and not of the dusky hue of the savage.

"Be silent and cautious," said Benton, in a whisper; "a word above a breath may cost both of us our lives."

"You will save me from the hands of these terrible savages?" murmured the girl.

"Yes, I will try to," replied Benton, "but it will be a task of danger. You must follow my instructions to the letter or we will never escape the toils that surround us."

"I will do so," replied Virginia, quickly.

"Come, then; tread cautiously. The savages have left but one man to guard the house, and he has fallen asleep in the thicket."

Then Benton led the way from the house, and the girl followed, cautiously.

The two passed close to where Bob Tierson lay in the bushes, fast asleep.

Benton, in leaving the flask of potent corn-juice with the worthy Bob, had rightly calculated that Bob would speedily dispose of the contents, and get gloriously drunk on the same.

The trap that the swarthy-skinned stranger had laid had caught the redoubtable Bob, and once he had fallen into deep and heavy slumber, it was an easy task for Benton to remove the prisoner from the log cabin.

Benton had fastened the bar again across the door of the house, so that it seemed all secure, and left no trace of the prisoner's escape.

When they had crossed the little clearing, and gained the shelter of the wood, Benton halted.

"Now, young lady, I must take you in my arms and carry you for a little while, so that the ground shall bear no traces by which you may be tracked and recaptured. These red-skins have the scent of a bloodhound, and the moment they discover your escape they will scour the country for miles around in search of you. Therefore, for your safety as well as for my own, we must leave, in border parlance, a blind trail."

"Adopt any method that you please to secure my escape from these terrible savages and I will bless you for it," said Virginia, earnestly.

Benton raised the light figure of the girl in his strong arms as though she had been a child, and then rapidly threaded his way through the forest.

The course that Benton followed led toward the Ohio, and ran parallel with the Kanawha.

For some thirty minutes, with rapid steps, Benton went onward, making his way through the thicket without doubt or hesitation, as if he were perfectly familiar with the country.

At the end of the thirty minutes he halted on the edge of a little clearing, close by the banks of the Kanawha. In the center of the clearing stood a log-cabin, something like the one which had held Virginia a prisoner.

The cabin, too, like the other, was deserted. The perpetual danger existing of Indian attacks had caused the settlers to seek the protection of the station.

"There, young lady, this must be your home for a little while," said Benton, as he strode into the cabin and placed Virginia upon her feet.

"Must I remain here?" asked the girl, in wonder.

"Yes, for a short time," replied Benton.

"But why not take me at once to Point Pleasant?"

"Why it would probably cost both of us our lives should we attempt to reach the station at present," replied Benton. "The woods between here and the mouth of the river are swarming with red-skins. You can judge how bold they are, when they dared attack and carry you off from so near the station."

Virginia had little idea that one of her captors, one of the "red-men," was even then speaking to her.

"Did you see my capture in the ravine?"

"Yes; I was concealed in the bushes. I did not dare to show myself, for the Indians were too strong. But I followed, hoping to get the chance by cunning to get you out of their hands."

"And the young man that was with me?" Virginia asked, tremblingly. She wished to learn the truth, yet feared to.

"He was killed by the shot that struck him, fired by one of the Indians," and Benton spoke what he believed to be the truth. He did not believe it possible that Winthrop could have survived his wound.

Virginia's heart sunk within her at the fatal news. Her lover dead, she felt almost willing to die too.

"You remain here and I will go at once to Point Pleasant, find your father, tell him where you are, and then with a party strong enough to cope with the red-skins, he can come and rescue you."

The plan was reasonable enough, and Virginia could find no fault with it, though she trembled to remain alone in the cabin while the woods around swarmed with hostile Indians.

"Suppose the savages should discover my retreat while you are absent?" Virginia asked.

"There is very little danger of that. All the Indians, with the exception of the party that captured you, have kept on the other side of the Kanawha. There is nothing to bring them on this side of the river. Keep within the shelter of the house. I will return by nightfall with your father and his friends."

"Heaven will reward you, sir, I am sure, for this kindness to a helpless girl," said Virginia, earnestly.

"I hope so," replied Benton, with a grim smile upon his sallow face. Then he left the house, crossed the clearing, and disappeared in the thicket.

Virginia sunk upon her knees and poured out her heartfelt thanks to the Great Power that was, apparently, watching so carefully over her life, and had brought a stranger to rescue her from the terrible danger that had menaced her well-being.

Poor, innocent girl, she knew not that as she was thanking Heaven for her rescue, the snare was still close around her; that the man whom she looked upon as a friend and deliverer was a more deadly foe than any painted warrior that roamed the forests of the Ohio valley.

No Indian is so terrible as the renegade to his country and his kin, the white-faced savage.

Once within the thicket, Benton gave vent to a grim laugh of triumph.

"The bird is in the net, and yet she imagines she is free! Oh, this will be a glorious vengeance. Once before, years ago, I made the heart of my enemy writhe with anguish, and now again I tear it. And this cunning plotter, Murdock, would use me as his tool. In yonder settlement for the moment I was in his power. Had he but spoken my name aloud, the settlers would have torn me to pieces with as little mercy as the wolves show to the wounded deer. But here, in the free woods, the tide of affairs is changed. Here I own no man as master."

On through the forest, retracing his steps toward the cabin where Virginia had been confined, he went.

"Watega's death I can not understand," he said, musingly, communing with himself as he walked onward. "Can it be possible that there is a spirit-form that haunts the woods and marks the Indians for his prey? It is almost beyond belief, and yet there is no disputing the terrible evidence of his hand. Watega was a great brave; few warriors in the Shawnee tribe as good as he, and yet he falls by the hand of this Wolf Demon, apparently without even a struggle for his life, if the words of Kenton can be believed, and he always speaks the truth. Can it be that it is some borderer in disguise that is doing this terrible work? No, that is improbable. Is it then a fiend from below that walks the earth in this dreadful shape? It is beyond my comprehension. I'd like to have him within rifle range once more, though; I'd soon prove whether the Wolf Demon be a demon indeed, or a mortal in a wolf's skin."

Proceeding rapidly onward with his swinging stride, Benton soon reached the cabin again. Bob was, as he had left him, fast asleep in the bushes.

The events that followed the arrival of Clement Murdock—how he found the cabin deserted and his prisoner gone—we have already related.

"Well, dog-gone my cats, if 'tain't funny," said Bob, scratching his head in wonder.

"I can not account for it!" cried Murdock, angrily.

"I wonder if this 'ere clearin's got any spooks 'round it?" said Bob, with a nervous glance about him.

"One thing is certain, the girl is gone," observed Benton.

"Yes, but how?" exclaimed Murdock.

"Maybe she clumb out of the roof," suggested Bob.

"The roof is tight, you fool!" said Murdock, angrily.

"You needn't bite a feller's head off 'cos he opened it," growled Bob.

"Let us search the forest; she may be concealed near here," Murdock said.

We have omitted to state that Benton had replaced the war-paint upon his face before coming again to the little clearing.

"That will be your best plan," observed Benton. "I wish you luck," and as he spoke he turned upon his heel to depart.

"You are not going?" Murdock asked.

"Yes, I have kept my word with you and did what I promised, and now my way lies different from yours."

"Well, I'll keep your secret."

"What do I care, now that I am out of the stockade of Point Pleasant, whether you do or not? Here, in the woods I fear no man," and, with the haughty speech, the stranger departed. His form was soon lost to view among the foliage of the forest.

"Well, he's a cuss, now, anyway," said Bob, looking after the stranger in astonishment.

"A man better to have for a friend than an enemy," said Murdock, quietly; "but, come, let us see if we can not discover some traces of the girl."

At the end of an hour the two were no wiser than when they began.

CHAPTER XVIII.

A TERRIBLE FRIEND.

Boone gazed in astonishment at the tall figure that, in spite of the gloom that enshrouded the interior of the Indian wigwam, he could distinguish standing in the center of the lodge.

With noiseless steps the dark form moved to the door of the wigwam and listened for a moment. Then it lifted the skin that served for a door and peered out into the gloom of the night.

"Who the deuce can it be?" mused Boone, as, a helpless prisoner on the couch of skins, he watched the movements of the unknown.

"It ain't Kenton or Lark, I'm putty sure, 'cos it's too big for either of 'em. Who on yearth can it be? A friend, anyway, and friends are allers welcome, particularly when a feller's in sich a 'tarnal tight place as I am now. I s'pect they'll roast me to-morrow, and eat me, too, for that matter, if I wasn't so 'tarnal tough."

Swelling on the night-air came the distant whoops of the savages.

Apparently satisfied with his scrutiny, the unknown let fall the skin that served as the wigwam door, and again advanced to Boone.

"Say, stranger, this is a pesky fix," said Boone, in a low and cautious tone.

The unknown answered not, but knelt by the side of the prostrate man.

Then Boone felt two powerful arms seize him, and roll him over on his side. As the hands of the mysterious stranger touched him, Boone felt a cold shiver creep all over him. The hands of the stranger seemed to be armed with claws like the paws of a beast.

"Jerusalem, stranger!" muttered Boone, "you ought to cut your finger-nails; they stick right into a feller; and why didn't you tell me to turn over? I kin do that well enough, although I'm in a pesky fix hyer."

Then Boone heard the slight grating noise that a knife makes cutting through leather.

The old hunter guessed the truth in an instant. The mysterious unknown was cutting the thongs that bound his arms.

"Go ahead, stranger!" cried Boone, cautiously; "you don't say much, but you work well."

A moment more and the bonds that bound Boone's arms loosened. The tension gone, the stout deer-skin severed by the keen-edged steel, and the arms of the hunter were free.

With a grunt of relief, Boone stretched his arms in the air. Confined as they had been, the sensation of freedom was a pleasant one.

As carelessly the hunter extended his arms in the air, one of his hands touched the arm of the stranger. Again a cold shiver came over Boone.

"By hookey!" he muttered, to himself; "either your hunting-shirt's made of bear-skin, or else you've more hair on your arm than I have on my head. I don't understand this riffle a bit; but it's a friend, anyway, whoever he is."

Then the stranger cut the thongs that bound Boone's feet.

Again the hand of the stranger touched the hunter, and again it seemed to him as if that hand was armed with the claws of an animal.

"I wish the derned critter *would* say something," muttered Boone, slightly uneasy. "If he wasn't acting so much like a human I should think that it was a pet b'ar that had got hold on me."

The stranger rose to his feet.

Boone followed his example.

"It's a pleasant thing to be free, stranger," Boone said, trying to look into the face of the strange being who had come so aptly to his rescue. But the gloom of the wigwam hid the face and form of the unknown with an ebon mask.

Besides, too, the unknown had taken a couple of blankets from a lot that lay in the corner of the wigwam, and wrapped one around his waist and the other over his head, when he had first entered the lodge.

The stranger stooped, took up another blanket, and gave it into Boone's hands. The unknown seemed to possess the cat-like faculty of seeing in the dark.

As he gave the blanket into Boone's grasp, again his hand touched that of the hunter.

"By jingo! his finger nails are awful," muttered the hunter, to himself. "If his toe-nails are as long, I shouldn't like to have him for a bedfellow. If he kicked any, he'd scratch a man half to death."

The unknown took hold of a corner of Boone's blanket and raised it a little in the air.

Boone understood what the unknown meant in an instant.

"You want me to put it round my head, eh, so as to kiver up my face?"

A vigorous tug at the blanket answered the hunter.

"I s'pose you mean yes by that, hey?"

Then a second tug came.

"All right, I understand," said Boone; "but why in thunder can't you speak and let a feller know what you mean?"

The stranger moved to the door of the wigwam, still keeping his hold on the corner of Boone's blanket. The old hunter followed him.

At the door the unknown paused for a moment, as if to listen.

"Goin' right through the Injin village?" said Boone, in astonishment.

The stranger answered as before by a vigorous tug at the blanket.

"Why in thunder don't you answer a feller?" asked the hunter, thoroughly puzzled at the strange silence of the unknown who had come so timely to his rescue.

The stranger replied not, but raised the skin that hung at the door and passed out into the darkness of the night.

"I'll see who it is, or what it is when we get outside," muttered Boone, to himself. "He acts more like a brute than a human. Derned if I like a man that can't answer a civil question. There's a moon, so I can see what sort of a critter he is; but, by jingo! the same light that shows him to me will also show us to the Injins. This is goin' to be a narrow squeeze."

But the unknown had no idea of issuing from the door of the wigwam into the Indian village.

A single glance had shown the stranger that three stalwart warriors, seated a few paces from the lodge, kept vigilant watch upon it.

Still keeping his hold upon the blanket, the mysterious being who had so astonished the old hunter by his silence, moved with noiseless step across the wigwam to the back of it, where he, by aid of his knife, had gained entrance to it. Boone, guided by the movement of the blanket—for it was almost too dark to distinguish forms—followed.

"Well, now, this is sense," said Boone, approvingly; "we may stand a chance to get clear of the red heathen."

Boone felt that the stranger was lifting his corner of the blanket into the air, then he flung it over Boone's head.

"Wrap my head up? Of course; that's a 'cute dodge," and the hunter chuckled to himself. "If any of the pizen Shawnees happen to see me, they won't be able to tell me from one of their own tribe with my head kivered up, 'cos my legs are kivered with buck-skin leggin's, same as their own."

Boone wrapped the blanket carelessly round his head, Indian fashion.

Then the stranger, who seemed to be able to distinguish the movements of the hunter, in spite of the darkness, passed through the hole he had previously cut in the skins that formed the side of the Indian lodge, and gained the open air.

Boone followed.

"Now I kin see who it is," muttered Boone, as he emerged into the air from the confines of the lodge.

But, even as he spoke, a great, black cloud came rapidly over the face of the moon and vailed its silvery rays of light from the earth.

All that Boone could make out in the darkness was, that, by his side, was standing a stalwart form, even overtopping himself in hight, tall as he was. But the form was wrapped so completely in Indian blankets from the head to the feet, that the hunter could distinguish neither feature nor limb.

"Well, dog-gone my persimmons!" said the hunter, in disgust, "I'd like to see what and who the critter is that I'm owing my life to."

The stranger listened, intently, for a moment.

In the position the two were standing, the lodge completely hid them from view of the village. In front of them ran the turbid waters of the Scioto.

The stranger moved, slowly and cautiously, to the bank of the river.

Boone noticed that his footfall gave out no sound, and that, too, he moved with a singular motion, unlike the gait of a human. The hunter could see this despite the darkness that surrounded them.

"Jerusalem, what on yearth is this critter, anyway?" muttered the hunter, in amazement. "He stands on his feet like a man, and he walks with the waddle of a b'ar."

Boone, stout woodman as he was, tried in courage, a man that laughed at danger and faced death coolly and without shrinking, felt a cold shiver come over him as he watched the movements of the mysterious being who was so free in his actions and so sparing of his words.

The old hunter could not understand the peculiar feeling that was so gradually stealing over him. The hair upon his head seemed ready to bristle with fright.

"I feel as if I had jumped into an ice-cold river," muttered Boone, with a half-shiver.

For a moment he took his eyes from the dark form behind him; when he looked again, the form was gone. Naught before him broke the denseness of the gloom.

The hunter rubbed his eyes in wonder.

"Jerusalem!" he muttered, "is it a spook after all?" The hair upon his head rose in fright as the thought crossed his mind.

Then Boone proceeded cautiously onward.

A few paces and he stood upon the river's bank. The waters of the stream, now low—it was in the summer-time—were some feet below the surface of the bank. One walking by the side of the water would be concealed from the view of any one on the level plain above, by the overhanging bank.

Here was an easy solution to the mystery of the strange disappearance of Boone's silent friend. He had stepped from the level down the slope to the side of the stream, and thus hid by the bank had seemed to disappear.

But Boone was loth to adopt this explanation of the riddle; besides, as he stepped down the bank to the water's edge, he could not distinguish the dark form of the stranger anywhere.

"It was a spook, sure," muttered Boone; "but, I may as well be making tracks for the settlement."

Concealed by the bank, Boone proceeded onward until his progress was stopped by an unexpected obstacle.

He had come to the watering-place for the Indian horses. A road had been cut through the bank to the water, and in the road sat a brawny Shawnee warrior.

CHAPTER XIX.

A STRANGE APPEARANCE.

"Durn the critter! he's right in the way!" muttered the old hunter, as his eyes fell upon the figure of the savage, sitting in the pathway leading to the river.

Just then, too, the moon shone out bright and clear.

The position of Boone was one of danger. Although the shelving bank hid him from the view of any one that might be on the level plain above, yet he was in full view of the savage in the horse-path, if that worthy chose to turn his head and look in his direction.

"What in thunder was the use of that terrible critter—whatever he was —a-gettin' me out of the wigwam, if I'm goin' to be captivated ag'in, right on the jump?"

Boone did not dare to move lest the noise might reach the ears of the Indian.

"If the moon would only go under a cloud ag'in, I might be able to skulk round him; but then, the chances are ten to one that some one of the Indians in the village would see me. This is a pesky fix now, for sure."

Boone was in a quandary. To advance was clearly out of the question. To remain where he was would be sure to lead to his discovery and recapture, for the Indian might turn his head at any moment. There was but one course open to him.

"I must take the back track and try to get into the thicket on the upper side of the village. That will be difficult, 'cos the lodges above are nigh the river, and the Injuns may diskiver me a-creepin' along under the bank. It's got to be did, though."

Just as the hunter came to the conclusion to try the desperate chance for escape that was yet open to him, a great black cloud came sailing over the face of the moon.

The silver rays hid by the cloud, darkness again vailed the earth.

Boone could just distinguish the figure of the Indian before him, and that was all.

"By hokey!" muttered the scout, in doubt, "I ought to be able to skulk around that red heathen in this hyar darkness, if it will only last!"

And then the old hunter looked searchingly at the heavens above him.

The cloud was passing slowly along the darkened vault above. In its track came another cloud fully as large and as black as the first.

"I kin do it," muttered Boone, decidedly. "I know I kin do it; I kin get past that critter afore the moon shines out ag'in. I'll risk it, anyway. It will be a narrow shave, but a miss is as good as a mile. So here goes."

Slowly and cautiously, on his hands and knees, the daring woodman crept forward.

He gained the level of the bank, and in his course commenced to describe a semi-circle that would carry him wide of the squatting chief and yet bring him to the bank of the Scioto again.

Many an anxious glance the fugitive scout cast upward to the sky as he proceeded on his way.

The cloud was still over the moon, but was rapidly growing less and less dense, and the silver rays were beginning to struggle feebly through it.

"By jingo!" muttered Boone, in dismay, although he still kept steadily on in his stealthy way, "that confounded moon will be out, 'most as clear as daylight, in a minute. I shall be in a worse fix than I was under the bank. I shall have to lie still and hug the yearth. Then s'pose that heathen takes it into his head to return to the center of the village, or any of the other red devils comes to the river's bank for water? They'll diskiver me, sure. Well, now, I am in a scrape!"

By this time the hunter had completed about half of the semicircle, and was some hundred paces from the Indian. A straight line drawn from the chief to the center of the village would have touched Boone.

Suddenly, almost without warning, the cloud parted and the moonbeams shone brightly over the earth.

Boone crouched to the ground, lying flat upon his face. The back of the savage was toward him, so that, unless the Indian turned around, he was in no danger of being discovered for the present.

The breath of the scout came quick and hard.

Anxiously he looked up to the sky. The remainder of the cloud had broken into fragments, and these, in passing over the face of the "mistress of the night," though somewhat dimming the luster of her smile, yet did not hide the light from the earth.

The second black cloud seemed, also, likely to break into pieces like the first, thus destroying the hope that Boone had of escaping from his present dangerous condition when its mantle should hide the rays of the moon.

"Oh, 'tarnal death!" groaned Boone; "to come so fur, and now to be stopped! If I could only get near enough to give that pesky critter a clean dig—but what am I talking about? I ain't got any we'pon. The 'tarnal heathens took good care of 'em for me. If this ain't a fix, then I never was in one."

Boone looked upward to the heavens, but there could not see any thing that seemed to favor his escape. Then his glance wandered restlessly over the earth around him. He looked to the Indian village; he could just distinguish the forms of the warriors as they passed to and fro in the circle of light thrown out by the blazing fires. Then he looked to the river, and there sat the brawny Shawnee chief.

"Jerusalem! what's that?" muttered Boone. His eyes wandering to the river, caught sight of a dark mass extended on the prairie, a few paces from where the savage sat. The dark object was a little in the rear of the savage, and of course was not in the range of his vision.

Boone was astonished.

"I'll sw'ar!" he muttered, "that air heap of something wasn't thar when I looked afore."

Boone bent a searching gaze upon it. The eyes of the scout, trained from infancy to the life of the woods, were as keen as the eyes of a hawk, yet he could make little of the dark object that broke the level of the plain.

"It looks like a buffler-skin," he said, after a long and careful examination, "but the Injuns wouldn't leave a hide lying round loose like that; 'sides, I'm sure that it wasn't thar when I looked a moment ago. 'Tain't likely that it could have been thar and me not notice it."

Then, to the utter astonishment of Boone, the dark object moved. Little by little it seemed to creep nearer and nearer to the savage, who sat so still in silent meditation.

The hunter rubbed his eyes; he could hardly believe that he had seen aright. But a second look convinced him that his eyes had not deceived him. The dark object that looked so much like the skin of a buffalo had moved a dozen paces or more toward the Shawnee chief.

A horrible suspicion seized upon Boone. For the first time he guessed what the dark form was, and had a suspicion regarding the silent stranger who had freed him from the bonds that bound him in the Indian lodge.

Cold drops of perspiration stood upon the bronzed brow of the old Indian-fighter.

"Jerusalem! to think that *thing* has had its paws on me," he muttered. "I ain't afeard of any human that walks the yearth, but this—well, it's proved a good spirit to me, if it's a bad one to the red heathen."

Slowly the dark form drew near to the savage. Unconscious of danger, the chief sat silent and motionless as a statue.

The Shawnee brave knew not that the dark angel was nigh—that the dread scourge of his nation was about to add him, another victim, to the long list of those who had fallen as his prey.

"If my guess is right, thar'll be a dead Injun round here in about two minutes."

Like one fascinated, Boone gazed upon the scene before him with staring eyes.

The dark form had crept quite close to the savage. It was now hardly a dozen paces from the chief.

A portion of the fleeting cloud passed over the moon; for a single moment the silver light was vailed, and the mantle of darkness cast over the earth.

Hardly had the gloom settled upon the plain, hiding the form of the Indian and the dark, mysterious object that had approached him so stealthily, from the gaze of the scout, when a dull sound, like an ax cutting into a rotten tree, came from the direction of the river; it was followed by a moan of pain.

Boone shivered when the noise fell upon his ears. He guessed only too well what had transpired.

No other sound broke the stillness of the night.

The moon came forth again in its splendor. Again the silver light flooded the prairie, and made the night like unto the day.

Boone, with horror-stricken eyes, looked toward the river.

The Indian chief had disappeared.

Only a dark mass, motionless on the prairie, met the eyes of the hunter.

Earnestly Boone swept his eyes along the horizon. No form was in sight —bird, beast or human.

The scout felt his blood congeal within his veins with horror.

"I can't stand this," he muttered, nervously; "I must see what's been goin' on. If I ain't wrong, my way to the wood is clear now."

Then Boone cast a rapid glance behind him in the direction of the village. He saw nothing there to alarm him.

"Here goes," he muttered.

Slowly and cautiously the old hunter crept near to the dark form lying so still upon the prairie.

Some dozen paces from the shapeless mass the hunter paused.

"By jingo!" he muttered, "I'm almost afear'd to look at it, yet I've seen death a hundred times, but I never seen a human killed by a demon before."

Then again the hunter went on.

The rays of the moon were shining down full upon the earth as Boone crept to the side of the silent form that paid no heed to his approach.

The sight that met the wondering eyes of the scout was strange indeed.

On the prairie, extended on his back, lay a stalwart Shawnee chief.

His head was smoothly shaven, except where the eagle-plumes twined in the scalp-lock.

The blood was gushing freely from a terrible wound in his head.

An awful gash, the work of a muscular arm and a keen-edged tomahawk, told of the manner of his death.

And on the naked breast of the savage were three lines of blood.

The Red Arrow blazed there.
The Wolf Demon had marked his victim!

CHAPTER XX.

VIRGINIA'S GUIDE.

Fruitless was the eager search of Murdock and Bob after traces of the lost girl.

Giving it up at last as hopeless, the two returned to Point Pleasant.

Alarmed at the long absence of his daughter and the young stranger, the old General, with several of the best woodmen of the station, had earnestly searched for her.

The party had penetrated into the ravine where Virginia had been captured and the young man wounded.

The keen eyes of the woodmen quickly detected the marks of blood upon the rocks where the stranger had fallen; then they discovered the footprints of the attacking party. These they followed till they led into the broad trail by the river. There the scouts halted, baffled.

"It's no use, General," said Jake Jackson, who led the scouts, shaking his head sagely. "The trail ends hyer. Thar's too many gone along this path for us to pick out our men."

"What is your opinion of the affair?" asked Treveling, anxiously.

"Well, it's just hyer," said Jackson, slowly. "Your darter and the young feller were in the ravine. They were attacked by the three that we've been tracking. One on 'em wounded—probably the young feller—and then both on 'em carried away by the ones that attacked 'em, 'cos thar's no marks of their footsteps."

"Think you that the attacking party were Indians?" asked Treveling.

"Nary Injun!" responded Jackson, tersely. "They're white as I am."

"What could be the motive of such a daring outrage?" said the old General, whose heart was sorely tried by the loss of his daughter.

"It's hard to say, General," said Jackson, dubiously, "unless you've got some enemies, and this is the way they are taking their revenge."

"I can not understand it," Treveling spoke, sorrowfully, and his brow was heavy with grief. "If my Virginia is lost, it is the second blow of the kind that has fallen upon me."

"The second?" said Jackson, in wonder.

"Yes; my eldest daughter, Augusta, was stolen from me years ago. She wandered forth beyond the borders of the settlement, one bright summer's afternoon, and never returned. Whether she was eaten up by the wild beasts that roamed the forest, or fell beneath the tomahawks of the hostile Indians,

I never was able to discover. And now my second daughter, all that I have left to me in this world, is gone. My lot is hard to bear, indeed."

The old man bent his head in agony. The rough woodmen looked upon him with pity. Fathers themselves, they knew how bitter were the feelings of the old man.

"Well, General, I don't know what to do about this matter," said Jackson, thoughtfully. "I s'pose there's nothin' to be done just at present but to return to the station, and then get up a party to search the country around thoroughly. It's bad that it happened just at this time, too, 'cos we've got an Injun war on our hands, and we ain't got any too many men to fight the red devils; but I guess we kin spare a few to help you out of this difficulty. I'll go for one."

"And I," said another of the woodmen.

"And I, and I!" chimed in the rest of the little party.

And so it was settled that first they should return to the station, make there all the needed preparations, and then set out in search of the girl.

Silently and sorrowfully they took the trail leading to Point Pleasant.

To return to Virginia.

Quietly she remained in the little log-cabin, waiting the return of the stranger who had rescued her from the terrible peril that she had been placed in.

Virginia had but little idea that she had escaped one danger only to encounter another more terrible still.

Innocent and unsuspecting, she readily believed the words of the stranger.

So patiently she waited in the lonely cabin for his return to conduct her to Point Pleasant, and restore her once more to the arms of her father.

One sad recollection was in Virginia's memory—the untimely death of the young stranger to whom she had freely given all the best love of her girlish heart.

Sorrowfully she mourned for his death, as the memory of his handsome face and frank, honest bearing came back to her. He was the first and only man that she had ever loved.

"Oh, my fate seems bitter, indeed!" she murmured. "Why did Providence ever bring us together and implant the germs of love in our hearts, if it was fated that we should be torn apart thus rudely? I thought that we should be so happy together. I looked forward to a bright and blissful future. But now the past is full of dreadful memories, and the future does not show one single ray of sunlight to brighten up the darkness of my life."

If Virginia's thoughts were so dark and gloomy now, with the prospect of being restored to her home and friends before her, what would they have been had she known the truth? Had she guessed that she was in the power of a man more terrible and merciless in his nature than any red savage that roamed the wild woods?

It is, perhaps, a mercy sometimes that we can not guess the future.

Virginia had been in the lonely cabin some five hours, wrapped in these gloomy thoughts. Then the man who had called himself Benton stood again upon the edge of the clearing.

"So far, so good," he muttered to himself, in joy, a smile lighting up his dark face as he spoke. "Now to take the bird from this cage and place it in one more secure; and then, that task done, to visit my foe, let him know the vengeance that has already fallen upon his head, and the more terrible vengeance that is still to come. It has taken years to ripen it, but the fruit will be bitter indeed."

Then he crossed the little clearing and entered the cabin.

Virginia started up with joy as she saw who it was.

To her the dark-browed stranger was as a guardian angel—one destined to protect and save her from the terrible danger that menaced her.

"You have seen my father?" she cried, anxiously.

"Yes."

"And he is coming to save me?"

"No."

"Not coming?" and Virginia looked the surprise she felt.

"No; your father is quite sick, and unable to leave the station."

"My father ill?"

"Yes; the fearful anxiety that your unexplained absence caused him came near resulting fatally; luckily, my timely arrival with the news of your safety gave him hope, and enabled him to fight against the illness that threatened his life."

"Oh, my poor father!" murmured Virginia, sadly.

"Do not be alarmed. The danger is over now," Benton said. "I shall soon restore you to his arms, and your presence will do him more good than all the medicine in the world."

"Then you will take me to him soon?"

"Yes, almost immediately."

"Are my friends near at hand?" asked Virginia, looking anxiously toward the door as she spoke, as though she expected to see the stalwart form of Jackson, or some other friend of her father, filling the doorway.

"No."

"Will they be here soon, then?"

"Your father did not think that it was wise to send a small party after you, and could not send a large one, as the settlement is in danger of being attacked by the Indians at any moment; so it was decided that it was best for me to return alone and conduct you to Point Pleasant. The danger of two being discovered by the savages is less than that attending a large party. And if the Indians should discover us, no party that could be spared from the settlement in this hour of peril would be sufficient to withstand their attack."

This appeared reasonable enough to Virginia.

"I am ready at any moment," she said.

"We will set out at once, then," Benton replied, moving to the door as he spoke.

"The sooner the better," Virginia cried, earnestly. "I wish that I could fly like a bird to the side of my dear father."

"We are not far from the station; it will be only a few hours' travel through the woods. A party from the settlement will meet us at a place fixed upon by your father and myself. If we can only reach that spot without being discovered by the lurking savages, all will be well."

"Let us hasten at once," said Virginia, in a fever of impatience.

The blows of misfortune were falling thick and heavy upon her head. First, her lover struck down lifeless at her feet; then her capture by the hostile red-skins; and now the dangerous illness of her only parent.

"Tread cautiously and lightly," said Benton, in warning, as they passed through the door of the cabin. "We can not tell which bush or tree may conceal a lurking Indian. The very leaves of the grass beneath our feet may hide a foe."

"Oh, I will be very careful!" said Virginia, earnestly.

Then the two set out upon the dangerous journey.

Silently on through the wood they went.

After proceeding for a short time, Virginia began to wonder at the manner in which the stranger led the way. A girl reared on the border, she was somewhat familiar with border ways.

What astonished her was that the man who was guiding her was proceeding straight onward, apparently without caution as if he had no fears of stumbling without warning upon any red foes.

Virginia's thought, however, was that he knew the path so well, and had passed over it so recently, that he did not apprehend danger.

Soon they came to a place where the bank stooped down to meet the river. They had followed the Kanawha in their course.

From the thicket that fringed the stream, the guide drew a "dug-out," and by its aid the two crossed the river. On the opposite bank, Benton again concealed the "dug-out" in the bushes.

And then again they proceeded on their way, following the broad trail that led to Point Pleasant.

But in a half mile or so, Benton left the trail and struck into the woods to the right of the path.

Virginia followed in wonder, for she knew well that they had left the direct road to Point Pleasant and were going away from, instead of approaching the station.

CHAPTER XXI.

IN THE TOILS.

Although wondering at the path that the stranger was pursuing, yet Virginia followed him for a short time in silence.

Deeper and deeper into the thicket went the stranger.

Virginia began to fear that he had mistaken the way. She resolved to speak.

"Have you not made a mistake in the path?" she asked.

"No," he replied, halting.

"But this is not the road leading to the settlement. We should follow the trail running parallel with the river—the trail we just left."

"Yes, I know that that is the *direct* road," he answered; "but we are obliged to make a wide *detour* here to escape the Shawnees. There is a large body of them ambushed by the trail a short distance below here. We are to make a circle to avoid them, and will come upon the trail again in due time. Do not fear; I will guide you safely. I know these wilds well. There is not a foot of ground between here and the Ohio that is not as familiar to me as my own hand. It is many years, though, since I have traversed these woods, but I've a good memory and am not likely to go astray."

"I feared that you might have made a mistake in the path, therefore I spoke," said Virginia, perfectly satisfied with the stranger's reasons.

On went the stranger again, and although he had imposed caution on the girl, he did not seem to use much himself, for he went straight onward as before, without seeming to fear danger.

For a short time only did the guide continue in a straight path, for soon he commenced a zigzag course; first to the right, then to the left, then apparently he retraced the very path that they had come; then turned abruptly to the right again, went on a little way, then bent his course to the left.

Virginia was puzzled; she had been able before to tell the way in which they had been proceeding; but now, after all this turning and twisting, her brain was bewildered, and she could not guess whether she was going straight to Point Pleasant or in the opposite direction.

If the design of Benton had been to bother the girl by the abrupt turns he had made, and to confuse her as to the direction in which they were bending their steps, he had succeeded admirably.

Virginia followed without a word. She was fully trusting the man who was guiding her.

"We will soon be at the meeting-place appointed," said Benton, after an hour's weary tramp through the almost trackless wilderness.

"I am so glad," replied the girl, "for I am getting sadly tired."

"You will have rest enough, soon," said Benton. And it was well that Virginia did not see the dark smile that shone on his features and lit up his evil eyes.

A few steps further on and the two came to a little glade in the forest.

"This is the place," said Benton, stopping in the center of the glade.

Virginia looked around.

The dense forest surrounded them.

No sound broke the stillness of the virgin wood.

The quiet of the grave reigned within the forest glade.

"I do not see any one," said Virginia; and, despite herself, a feeling of apprehension stole over her.

The quiet of the forest seemed ominous of evil.

"They are near at hand," said Benton, with a peculiar smile.

For the first time, Virginia saw the evil look in his face. His words, though apparently harmless, filled her with terror.

"Where are they?" she asked, a heavy weight upon her heart as she spoke.

"Shall I call them?" Benton questioned, surveying the girl with an air of triumph.

"Yes," Virginia said, slowly.

With a mocking smile, Benton turned to where a dense clump of bushes —an outpost of the thicket—had planted itself upon the margin of the glade.

Virginia watched him with earnest eyes.

A dim presentiment of danger filled her soul.

Danger! yet what that danger was, she could not guess.

Two words came from the lips of the man who had acted as Virginia's guide.

Two words that struck a chill of horror to the heart of the girl.

Yet the meaning of those two words she could not understand.

The two words were spoken in the Shawnee tongue.

Then forth from the thicket, in obedience to the summons, came two dark and stalwart forms.

Life *was* in the forest, despite the gloom and silence!

One single glance Virginia gave, and then, with a cry of mournful agony, she fell senseless to the ground.

The shock was too great to bear, and loss of consciousness came like an earnest friend to drive away the terror that was chilling the heart of the hapless maid.

* * * *

And now we will return to the station at Point Pleasant.

The party who had been in search of the girl had returned. They were to set forth again on the following morrow, to try and discover, if it were possible, what had been the fate of the General's daughter.

Treveling himself, bowed down with agony, sought the shelter of his dwelling.

The old man's heart was heavy with woe.

The twilight had come. Treveling, busy in thought, had not noticed the coming darkness, when he was suddenly aroused from his abstraction by the abrupt entrance of a stranger.

Treveling looked at his visitor in astonishment.

The man was a stranger to him. He was a muscular fellow, habited in the usual border fashion of deer-skin.

"You are General Treveling?" the stranger asked.

"Yes," replied the old man, "that is my name."

"My name is James Benton; I am a stranger in these parts, though some years ago I resided hereabouts."

"Your face seems familiar to me," replied Treveling, with a puzzled air, "yet I can not remember to have ever known a man who bore the name you give."

"Your memory may be at fault," said the stranger, coldly.

"It is rarely so, but still it may be as you say," replied the General, who felt sure that he had seen the stranger's face before.

"You and I, General, are old acquaintances," said Benton.

"We are?"

"Yes."

"It is very strange then that I can not remember your name—I mean, that it does not seem familiar to me."

"A man's face is more easily remembered than his name."

"That is very true," replied Treveling. "At what time in the past did I ever meet you?"

"Do you remember Lewis' expedition in Dunmore's time?"

"Yes."

"When he whipped Corn-planter at the head of the Shawnees, Mingoes and Wyandots in the Battle of Point Pleasant?"

"Yes," again replied the old man; "I commanded a division under Lewis in that fight."

"No one knows that better than myself," said the stranger, with a peculiar smile. "I served under you."

"Ah, were you in the battle of Point Pleasant?"

"No."

"How was that?" asked Treveling, in astonishment; "my division was in the hottest of the fight."

"I left your command *before* the battle took place."

"It is strange that I do not remember of ever hearing your name before, but your face certainly is familiar. Well, sir, as an old comrade in arms, I am glad to meet you. You are welcome, sir, to make my house your home while you remain at the station. I can give you an old Virginia welcome, though I am afraid that I can not play the part of the host so well as I ought to, for I am suffering now, sir, under an affliction that has sorely tried me." And the old soldier heaved a deep sigh as he spoke.

"You refer to the loss of your daughter?"

"Yes, sir."

"It is a heavy blow."

"Ah! none but a father's heart can feel how heavy such a blow is. She was my only child, sir; the pride of my old age, and now she is taken from me. I am but an old and withered oak; the support and love that bound me to earth is gone, and I care not how soon I receive the summons that bids me appear before the Great Commander above!" The tone in which the old man spoke would have touched almost any heart and made it sympathize with his sorrow. But, the heart of the dark-faced stranger only thrilled with fierce joy as he listened to the words of the old man.

"Your only child, I think you said?"

"Yes," replied Treveling, in wonder, "my only child!"

"How is that? If my memory does not deceive me, in the old time, when I served under you, you had *two* daughters."

"Yes, you are right," replied Treveling, "but the elder of the two, my bright-eyed Augusta, strayed into the woods one day and never came back. She was but a child then; and now the other, my Virginia, she, too, is gone, and in the self-same manner as her sister. That is what makes the blow more terrible."

"You never discovered any traces of the first?"

"No," Treveling answered, sadly.

"And now no traces of the second?"

"You speak only the cruel truth."

"Cheer up, General; I bring you news of your second daughter!"

"You do?" cried the old man, eagerly.

"Yes; by chance I discovered something in the forest that revealed to me her fate."

"Only give me some clue by which I may find my child and I will go down on my knees and bless you, sir!" exclaimed the old soldier, excitedly.

"Put on your hat and walk with me a short distance. The moon is bright, and I will tell you all I have discovered. It is a terrible affair, and I fear to speak within walls."

Eagerly Treveling followed Benton from the house.

CHAPTER XXII.

CALLING BACK THE PAST.

As Treveling followed the stranger from the cabin he marveled, somewhat, at the odd place chosen by the man, who had called himself Benton, for an interview. But urged onward by the anxious father's heart that beat within his breast, he followed his guide without fear.

Benton led the way through the station, passed the stockade and reached the forest beyond. He followed the trail leading up the Kanawha.

On, through the shadows cast by the tree-tops, the two went.

A good half-mile from the stockade, in a little spot of clear ground, where the flickering light of the moonbeams danced in fantastic rays, Benton halted.

"There," he said, as he wheeled abruptly round and faced the old soldier, "this will do; just the spot for an interview."

The General wondered at the words of the stranger; wondered still more at the peculiar expression that was on his face.

"Do you remember this spot, General?" asked Benton.

"No," replied Treveling, after a glance around him.

"And yet you have been here before."

"That is very likely, but there is nothing in particular that I can remember to fix the spot in my mind," Treveling said.

"Are you sure of that?" asked the other.

"Quite sure." The old General could not understand the meaning of these odd questions in relation to a simple opening in the forest.

"And yet something happened in this very spot that should have fixed it forever in your memory."

"I can not remember," said Treveling, puzzled.

"You were an officer under Lewis when he fought the battle of Point Pleasant and whipped Corn-planter in Dunmore's time?"

"Yes, but you spoke of this before; you said that you served under me in that fight."

"No, not in the fight, but before it," said the stranger. "When I call back the memory of that campaign, do you not remember some event that happened in this very glade?"

"No," Treveling answered, after a moment's pause.

"You do not?" Benton said, with astonishment.

"No," Treveling again replied.

"Let me call back to your mind a scene or two that happened long years ago."

There was an icy tone in the voice of the stranger that struck a sudden chill to the heart of the old man. For the first time he felt a feeling of apprehension regarding the man who was acting so strangely.

"Dunmore is Governor of Virginia," commenced the stranger, "and General Lewis is marching with all the force that can be raised along the border, against Corn-planter at the head of the Shawnees, the Mingoes and the Wyandots. He has halted here, information having reached the ears of the General that the Indians, in great numbers, are at the junction of the Kanawha and the Ohio, ready to give him battle."

As the stranger spoke, Treveling, with a bewildered air, was gazing around him. Slowly, little by little, the memory of the past came back to him.

The little glade now seemed familiar to his eyes. It had been the camping-ground of his own regiment.

"I do remember now!" he exclaimed. "Here I encamped the day before the fight. The glade has changed somewhat, though, since that time. Then, instead of this broad trail, there was naught but an Indian foot-path here."

"Yes, it is some years since Lewis' army eat their hog and hominy under the forest boughs that shadow in this little glade."

"Why do you recall Lewis' campaign?" asked Treveling.

"Wait a little and you shall learn," said Benton, and an ominous light shone in his eyes as he spoke. "Here Lewis' army halted to prepare for the deadly fight that they expected would come on the morrow. In this little opening your division was encamped. Your men had hardly laid aside their arms and begun to prepare their supper, when a blow was given and received. You, the colonel in command, were struck in the face and felled to the earth by a private soldier to whom you had given the lie."

"Yes, I remember the circumstance now that you call it to my memory, although I had forgotten it long since," said Treveling, calmly.

"The man who struck you was a volunteer; a man known far and wide as one of the best scouts in all the Ohio valley. He did not think for a moment that you wore the golden marks of a colonel on your shoulders while his were covered only by the buck-skin hunting-shirt of the borderer. You insulted him, and he struck you to his feet as any man would have done."

"But, on the following morning, he paid dearly for that blow," said Treveling, quickly.

"You never spoke a truer word," returned Benton, bitterly. "When the morning came, the same waving boughs that witnessed you give the lie to the scout, and then saw you kiss the dust, stricken there by his arm, looked down upon the drum-head court-martial. And then beheld the lash cut long welts of blood on the naked shoulders of the borderer, who had dared to forget that he was a soldier and remember that he was a man. And then, degraded, a whipped slave, he was driven forth a dishonored wretch."

"All this happened years ago; why do you recall it?" asked Treveling, impatiently.

"I recall the past that I may speak of the present," replied Benton, a sullen frown upon his face and anger flaming in his eyes. "Did you ever learn the fate of the man whose life you ruined?"

"No," replied Treveling.

"Do you remember what he said to you, after the lash had done its work and they raised the almost helpless man, crimsoned with his own blood?"

"No, except that it was a threat of some sort."

"He said 'your quarters shall swim in blood for this,' and he kept his word. The man whose back was torn by your lash, joined the red-men, became a white Indian, a renegade to his country and his kin. He swore bitter and eternal vengeance against you, and he kept his oath. When your cabin by the Ohio was attacked, he headed the Shawnees. You escaped only by a miracle. Then, when you had taken refuge in the station of Point Pleasant, he thought of another plan to be revenged upon you. You had two daughters once." The stranger paused. There was a fearful meaning in his simple words.

"Can it be possible that this human fiend can have had aught to do with the unaccountable disappearance of my eldest child, Augusta?" cried Treveling, in breathless anxiety.

"She wandered forth one summer's day within the woods and never came back?"

"Yes, yes!" exclaimed the anxious father; "can you tell me aught of her fate?"

"I can," replied Benton, with a look of fearful meaning. "In the wood, like a hawk on the watch, was the man who had sworn such deadly vengeance upon your head. His heart leaped for joy when he beheld the prattling child enter the shadows of the forest. He seized the little girl, your eldest joy, and carried her from the station. In the gloomy recesses of the forest he left her to die."

"Oh! the heartless fiend!" cried the father, in agony.

"And think you that even this glorious vengeance satisfied him? No! He panted for more. Thirsted for it as the hungry wolf thirsts for blood to satisfy the cravings of its savage nature. You still had another daughter left. For years this human bloodhound hung about the station eager to rob you of the sole remaining joy that made your life happy. Time passed on; your daughter grew to womanhood, as fair a flower as ever bloomed on the banks of the Ohio. Patiently your foe waited. Chance at last gave the golden opportunity, and your daughter fell into his hands."

"What?" cried the old man, horror-stricken and hardly able to believe the evidence of his senses.

"Your daughter is now a prisoner in his hands. A captive, helpless, in the Shawnee nation."

"But is there no way to release her?" cried Treveling, in anguish. "I will pay any sum possible for me to procure."

"If you could turn every drop of your blood into a golden guinea and spill them one by one from your veins your foe would laugh at you and bid you remember the hour when in this very glade you scarred his back with a lash," replied Benton, fiercely.

"This man is a demon to seek such a vengeance!" cried Treveling, in despair.

"You are right, he is a demon," replied Benton, bitterly. "Can you wonder at it? Is he not an outcast from all that makes life dear, a savage amid savages?"

"Is there no way to touch this man's heart?"

"He has no heart; in its place is a lump of red clay; is he not a white Indian? What has such as he to do with hearts?"

"Why did not this man strike at my life, if he bears me the hatred that you say he does?"

"Death is not the most cruel vengeance," returned Benton, scornfully. "Can bodily pain cause you greater anguish than that you now suffer?"

"No, no," replied Treveling, slowly.

"He would have you live. Would have you know of the terrible vengeance that he has pulled down upon your head. Can you guess what the fate of your daughter will be?"

A shudder shook the frame of the old man as the question fell upon his ears.

"Oh, the thought is terrible!" he moaned.

"A young and pretty white girl in the Shawnee village will not lack for admirers. Your foe will give her to some brawny red chief to be his slave. A helpless prisoner, the victim of the savages, she will pine away and die. Her death will be a terrible one, for she will die by inches. You now know the fate of both your children. One has already suffered for your acts long years ago, and the other is now paying the penalty."

The stranger turned upon his heel as if to depart.

"Stay!" cried Treveling; "who are you that know all these horrible things?"

"Have you not already guessed?" asked Benton, with a smile of terrible meaning. "If my shoulders were bare, you could tell who I am, for the marks of the lash are still there. If you would know my name, a week hence ask the blazing dwellings along the Ohio that mark the track of the Shawnees; the glowing embers and hissing flames will answer, Simon Girty, the renegade."

Then, with a bound, Girty disappeared in the forest.

Sick at heart, Treveling returned to the station.

CHAPTER XXIII.

BOONE'S ESCAPE.

Almost speechless with horror, the old hunter bent over the body of the murdered Indian.

"One clean cut settled him," the borderer muttered, as his eyes fell upon the terrible gash on the head of the red chief, and from which the red life-blood was slowly ebbing. "I've seen it; thar's no mistake. It's either the devil or a near relation. I owe him something, though, for he's got me out of the tightest place that this old carcass has been in for many a long day."

Then the scout cast a stealthy glance around him. The clouds pushing over the moon still vailed the earth with darkness.

"I must git out of this hyer, quick, ef not quicker. I won't give the red heathen another chance at my top-knot ef I kin help it. I wonder whar Kenton and Lark are? I s'pose they must be nigh the village, somewhar. Well, I've found out all that I wanted to know. The Injuns mean mischief—they're mean enough for any thing—and Point Pleasant will receive the first blow. Now, I'd better be makin' tracks for the settlement. Jerusalem! I hope I won't meet that awful *thing* in the wood. Why, my very blood freezes when I think of it." And the stout borderer shuddered as he spoke. Back to his mind came the likeness of the dark form that had freed him from his bonds in the Indian village; again he felt on his person the light touch of the hairy arm that bore such terrible nails.

"I ain't afeard of any thing human, but I ain't used to the critters from the other world. Now, to gain the shelter of the forest and then to carry the tidings of this attack to the settlement."

Carefully the old scout proceeded on his dangerous path.

Leaving the dead Indian where he had fallen, Boone again sought the shelter of the river's bank.

Fortune favored the adventurer. No hostile Indian barred his way. Unobserved he reached the friendly shadows cast by the forest monarchs.

On the borders of the wood Boone halted for a moment and looked back on the Indian village, that nestled so peacefully by the bank of the rolling Scioto, bathed in the soft moonlight.

"Who could guess that yonder village contained a thousand red-skins thirsting for blood and slaughter?" exclaimed the old hunter, communing with himself; his gaze resting upon the quiet scene before him. The embers of the fires cast a crimson light on the wigwams and played in fantastic shadows along the plain.

"I'd better be moving," muttered Boone; "first for the hollow oak; there I'll probably meet Lark and Kenton. I'll bet a big drink of corn-juice that nary one on 'em has been as fur into the Injun village as I have. I reckon I'm not over anxious to risk it ag'in. How the red devils would have danced around me ef they only got the opportunity to roast me a little." And the old hunter chuckled at the thought. Yet even now he was far from being out of danger, but he thought not of it. In the forest, free, he thought himself a match for all the Shawnee nation.

With noiseless steps the hunter took his way through the wood.

Quickly, but carefully, he went onward. Not a stick cracked beneath his tread. A fox, intent on prey, could hardly have proceeded more noiselessly.

As the shadows of the forest deepened around the path of the woodman, he glanced nervously from side to side as if he expected that some hostile form would spring upon him from the darkness of the thicket; and yet it was no red warrior that he expected to see, no brawny chief, decked with the war-paint and wearing the moccasins of the Shawnee. No, the form he expected was that of a huge gray wolf that walked erect like a man, and carried in his paw the tomahawk of the Indian. A form more terrible than any feathered, tinctured chief; more to be dreaded than any red-skin who claimed the Ohio valley as his own.

On went the hunter, still glaring about him in the darkness; but the terrible Wolf Demon sprung not from the covert of the wood. If he lurked about the pathway of the scout, he kept himself concealed within the fastness of the forest.

Boone reached the hollow oak without seeing aught to make him apprehend danger. The forest was as quiet as if no deed of blood had ever occurred within its bounds. As silent as though the terrible form—the demon of the Indian and the phantom of the white—had never stricken unto death and sent to his long home the stout-limbed Shawnee warrior.

"Hullo! thar's no one about," Boone muttered, as he peered within the hollow of the oak.

"Boone!" cried a voice, low and cautiously from the thicket that fringed the little glade wherein stood the oak.

Then from the darkness, into the circle of light cast by the moonbeams, stepped Kenton.

"Top-knot all right, eh?" questioned Boone, clasping the hand of the other warmly within his own broad palm.

"Yes, but how long it will be all right is a riddle. The Injuns are 'round us thick as bees 'round a honeycomb."

"Then you've seen the red heathen?"

"Yes, I scouted in right to the Injun village. But, as I lay in ambush, there was an awful row kicked up and I was afeard of being caught in a trap by the Injuns, so I jist retreated to safer quarters."

"A row, eh?" said Boone, smiling.

"Yes, a 'tarnal row; they just kicked up Old Scratch for a little while. I reckon it must have been a fight among the Shawnees," Kenton replied.

"You're right, Simon; it were a fight, and in that fight I was captivated."

"Why, you don't say so?" said Kenton, in wonder.

"Gospel truth," replied Boone. "I scouted into the village, and camped down behind a log just as quiet as a mouse, and—would you believe it?—a squaw and her lover came and squatted down right onto the very log ahind which I lay! Then the Injun tried to kiss the gal, she wouldn't let him, and the end of it was that both of 'em tumbled over on me, ker-chunk. I had a lively tussle with the heathen, but the other red devils came up, and thar were too many of 'em for me, and the end was that they took me into one of the wigwams, bound hand and foot."

"But how did you manage to escape?" asked Kenton, in wonder.

"Well, now I'm going to tell you something that will make you open your eyes," said Boone, impressively, and with an air of great mystery. "Mind you, I wouldn't have believed this, if I hadn't seen it. Ke-ne-ha-ha came to me in the wigwam and wanted me to become a white Injun. To gain time I asked till the morning to think over the matter. The chief consented and left me. Then, as I lay bound and helpless in the lodge, the fire burnt down so that I could hardly see, something cut a hole through the side of the wigwam and came in. I could just make out that it was a great black form, all muffled up in blankets. I knew that it was blankets, for a little while arter I had a chance to feel 'em. Well, this thing was a good deal bigger than I am—and thar ain't many men in the Ohio valley that out-top me. This dark form cut the thongs that bound my legs and arms, gave me a blanket, and I followed it from the wigwam. Outside of the lodge this thing, that saved me, either went down into the earth or up into the air, for it vanished just like smoke disappears."

Kenton listened with wonder to the strange tale.

"Then I sneaked along under the bank of the river, making my way to the cover of the wood," continued Boone, "till I came to the hoss-path leading to the river, and thar in the path sat a cussed Shawnee. But as the moon was under a cloud, I thought I'd try to sneak round him on the prairie above. Just as I got about half-way, the moon came out ag'in and I hugged the yearth mighty close, I tell yer. Then I see'd a dark object a-creepin' nigh to the Injun. A cloud came over the moon for a minute, so that I couldn't see; but I heard a groan, though, and the sound of a blow. When the moon came out ag'in, the dark form had disappeared, and the Injun had been killed by a single tomahawk-dig in the skull, and on the breast of the chief were three knife-slashes, making a Red Arrow."

"The Wolf Demon, by hokey!" cried Kenton, in astonishment.

"You're right; but what on yearth is the critter?" said Boone, solemnly.

"I reckon it's the devil," replied Kenton, with a sober face.

"Well, devil or not, it saved me from the hands of the Shawnees," said Boone. "The Injuns meant to roast me in the morning. But if this thing is the devil, thar's some substance to it, 'cos I felt its arm, and it's as hairy as a bear-skin. Besides, it's got claws."

"Of course; it's the devil in the shape of a wolf."

"Yes, but why should he trouble himself to save me from the Shawnees?" asked Boone.

"Well, thar's whar you've got me," replied Kenton, scratching his head, reflectively.

"He's death on the Injuns, anyway," said Boone. "Why, the feller he killed so easy would have given any man a hard tussle, ef he had half a chance."

"It's plain that he don't want white blood, 'cos he wouldn't have saved you."

"Yes, that's true. I don't wonder that the red-skins are afeard of him; why, it makes my blood fairly run cold when I think about it." And the sober look of the old scout told plainly that he spoke the truth.

"Have you seen Lark?" asked Kenton, suddenly.

"No, hain't he come back?"

"Not yet."

"Haven't you seen him since we parted here?"

"No; have you?"

"Nary time," Boone replied, laconically.

"Can he have been captivated by the Shawnees?"

"No, it is not likely," Boone replied. "Ef he had been, I should have heard something of it. The Injuns would have been tickled to death to have been able to have told me that there was another white man to be burnt at my side for their amusement."

"Did you learn anything about the attack?"

"Yes, all about it. The blow will fall on Point Pleasant first. Thar'll be such a blaze along the Ohio that the smoke will almost hide the sun. Let's go into the hollow of the oak, wait for Lark, and while we are waiting, I'll tell you all about it." Then the two sought shelter within the hollow tree.

106

CHAPTER XXIV.

KE-NE-HA-HA AND THE MEDICINE-MAN.

The great chief of the Shawnee nation, Ke-ne-ha-ha, "The-man-that-walks," was pacing slowly to and fro before the door of his wigwam, which was situated in the center of the village.

A cloud was upon the brow of the chief as he paced moodily up and down.

The moonbeams shone upon his stalwart form and glistened in sparkling rays of silvery light upon the blade of the keen-edged scalping-knife thrust so carelessly through the girdle that spanned his sinewy waist.

Care was on the brow and anxiety in the face of the Shawnee chieftain.

His thoughts were of the dreaded Wolf Demon—the terrible scourge that was laying his heavy hand so cruelly upon the warriors of his tribe.

The Shawnee chief had the heart of a lion. No face had ever yet made him turn upon his heel. A thousand bullets had whistled in waked wrath around his head and he had faced the storm undauntedly. The glittering knife of the hostile foe had sought his heart, and even as the point tore his flesh, he had grimly smiled and stricken his enemy to the earth.

Ke-ne-ha-ha feared not mortal man, but now his foe was a fiend from the other world, and the stout-hearted Shawnee chief trembled when he thought of the terrible foe who struck so silently and yet so fearfully.

He would have given all the fame he had acquired on the war-path, all the honor that he had won in the council-chamber, to be put face to face with the demon of his race, so that he might discover who and what the terrible creature was.

At a little distance from the chief stood two of the principal warriors of the nation. One was called the Black Cloud, the other, Noc-a-tah.

"A cloud is on the brow of the chief," said Noc-a-tah, as he watched Ke-ne-ha-ha pacing to and fro, with all the restless, springy motion of the imprisoned tiger.

"Yes," replied the other. "Ke-ne-ha-ha has not smiled since the death of the Red Arrow. She was his eldest daughter and the singing-bird that gladdened his wigwam with her song. The heart of the chief is sad—many moons have passed away, but he can not forget the child that he loved so well."

"Let the chief steep his memory in the blood of the so-cursed white-skins and then he will forget the wrong that they have done him."

"The chief speaks with a straight tongue," said Black Cloud, sagely. "When Ke-ne-ha-ha goes on the war-path he will forget. The sight of this blood and the smoke of their burning dwellings will clear the cloud of sorrow from his brain. Then he will laugh, for he can show the world how the great chief of the Shawnees wipes out the memory of his wrongs."

Ke-ne-ha-ha approaching, the two warriors put a stop to their conversation.

"The white prisoner is securely guarded?" he asked.

"Yes," replied the Black Cloud, "three warriors guard the lodge of the pale-face."

For a moment Ke-ne-ha-ha was silent, apparently lost in thought; then suddenly he spoke again.

"The mind of the chief is not easy—there is a load upon it—as heavy as the house the turtle carries upon his back."

"What troubles the mind of the great chief of the Shawnee nation?" asked Noc-a-tah, respectfully.

"The chief can not tell—the shadows come upon his heart like the clouds over the moon, without warning, without reason. Ke-ne-ha-ha fears for the safety of the white prisoner; he would rather lose one of his ears than have the white foe escape. Let my warriors go with me. We will see the pale-face."

Ke-ne-ha-ha, followed by the two chiefs, sought the lodge where Boone was confined.

As the Indian had said, three braves guarded the door.

In answer to Ke-ne-ha-ha's question they replied that all had been still as death within the wigwam of the prisoner.

Feeling reassured, Ke-ne-ha-ha was about to return to his own wigwam, when a sudden fancy took possession of him to see the white captive and so personally assure himself of the safety of the prisoner.

Taking a brand from the smoldering fire, the chief entered the lodge. The other warriors remained outside.

Ke-ne-ha-ha's tall form had hardly disappeared within the hut, when a cry of surprise broke upon the Indians' startled ears. It came from the lodge and was uttered by the lips of Ke-ne-ha-ha.

Astonished, the Indians rushed into the lodge.

In the center of the wigwam stood the chief.

The lodge was dimly lighted by the burning brand that he carried in his hand.

The prisoner had disappeared.

Great was the astonishment and anger of the Indians.

Soon they discovered the slit in the side of the lodge where the keen-edged knife had opened a passage to the air.

The savages were utterly astounded. Boone had been carefully and thoroughly searched; all his weapons taken from him, and yet it was plain that he had contrived to free himself from his bonds and cut his way out of the lodge.

A moment's examination, however, convinced Ke-ne-ha-ha that the bonds that had bound the hunter had been cut by some other hand than his own.

Then the Indians passed through the hole cut in the wigwam, and outside in the soft earth searched for traces of the prisoner's footsteps.

These they soon found.

The soft earth of the bank of the river was as yielding as wax, and by the clear light of the moonbeams the Indians discovered the mark of two different footprints. The first they came to was evidently made by the broad moccasin of Boone; but the second was a puzzle. It was also the print of a moccasin, but the toes turned inward like the footprint of an Indian.

"The pale-face had some white-hearted Indian, lurking like a snake within the thicket, who has aided him to escape," said Ke-ne-ha-ha, in anger.

A cry of wonder from the Black Cloud attracted the attention of all.

The chief, a little ahead of the rest of the party, had been examining the bank of the river, which, there, from the level of the stream, was about as high as a man's waist.

The others hurried to the side of the Black Cloud, drawn thither by his exclamation.

With wondering eyes the chief was gazing upon some marks on the soft clay bank.

And when the eyes of the other looked upon the strange mark, they wondered, too.

On the soft clay was imprinted an animal's paw.

The impression was perfect; claws, all were there, and the keen-eyed chief, Noc-a-tah, picked out a short, gray hair that had remained stuck in the clay.

Ke-ne-ha-ha's brow grew dark when he looked upon the strange impression.

"It is the mark of a wolf's paw," said the Black Cloud, astonished.

"Yes, and here is one of the hairs of the beast. It is a gray wolf," observed Noc-a-tah.

"Let my warriors look further on, they may find more traces," said Ke-ne-ha-ha, gravely.

The warriors obeyed the instruction.

In the center of the horse-path, cold and dead, they found the Shawnee chief.

On the breast of the slain warrior blazed the fearful token, the Red Arrow.

Ke-ne-ha-ha then knew only too well who it was that had rescued the white hunter from his power, and left the footprint of an Indian and the mark of a wolf's paw as traces behind him. The terrible Wolf Demon had again been in the midst of the Shawnee village. Again had his powerful arm struck the fearful blow that sealed the death of a red warrior.

Mournfully the Indians carried the body of the slain man to his wigwam, and soon the wail of lamentation and despair broke on the stillness of the night.

"What does the chief think?" asked the Black Cloud, as he watched the lowering face of Ke-ne-ha-ha.

"That the Bad Spirit is among us," returned the chief, slowly. "My warriors are falling, one by one, by the hand of this secret foe. I would give my own life to conquer him and save my nation from him."

"Why not seek the Medicine Man? The Wolf Demon is a spirit—the Medicine Man will give the chief a charm so that he can fight the Wolf Demon," said the Black Cloud, sagely.

"My brother speaks well—his counsel is good—the chief will visit the Great Medicine," replied Ke-ne-ha-ha.

And acting instantly on the resolution that he had formed, Ke-ne-ha-ha went at once to the wigwam of the old Indian who was the Great Medicine Man of the Shawnee tribe.

The wigwam of the Great Medicine was far from the others of the village, and half hid itself within the borders of the wood as if it courted solitude.

The Great Medicine of the Shawnees was an aged man. Infirm and old was he, yet gifted with wondrous skill. He knew all the properties of the herbs of the forest, the meadow and the swamp. Could cure by charms and conjurations the most dangerous diseases.

The savages looked upon him with awe and wonder. Even Ke-ne-ha-ha, the great chief as he was of the Shawnee nation, felt a slight sensation of fear creep over him as he entered the wigwam of the Great Medicine.

As usual the Medicine Man sat in a corner of the lodge all wrapped up in blankets, even his head concealed. Only his face was visible, and that painted in streaks of black and white in a horrible fashion.

A little fire burning in the center of the lodge cast a dim light over the scene.

The Medicine Man made a slight motion with his head as the chief entered, as if to acknowledge his presence.

"Let the Great Medicine open his ears while the chief of the Shawnee speaks, and let his words sink into his heart as the soft summer rain sinks into the earth."

Another slight motion of the head answered the words of the chief.

"It is good—let my brother listen," said the chief, gravely.

Again the Medicine Man bowed his head.

"The Shawnees are a great nation—many warriors—brave as the panther—cunning as the fox. The Shawnee braves fear not death, but they wish to meet it face to face. Now it crawls upon them from behind—in the darkness, and strikes them to death before they dream that a foe is near. Can my father tell me of a charm to conquer the Wolf Demon?"

"Does the chief wish to see him?" asked the Great Medicine, in a cracked and wavering voice.

"Yes," answered the chief, eagerly.

"I will bring the Wolf Demon before him at once."

111

CHAPTER XXV.

ON THE TRAIL.

Virginia woke from her swoon to find herself a captive in the hands of the Shawnees.

Three grim and painted chiefs were her guards.

Virginia shuddered when she thought of the terrible fate that was in store for her. No ray of light broke through the darkness of the clouded future. She despaired of ever again seeing home and friends.

The red-men bore her swiftly through the forest, heading toward the Ohio.

The false white man, the treacherous guide, who had led her into the snare, had disappeared.

Crossing the Ohio, the savages conducted their prisoner to the Indian village at Chillicothe.

Great was the rejoicing among the Shawnees, when the hapless girl was brought a prisoner into their midst. It seemed to them like an omen of good fortune.

Virginia was placed in one of the wigwams, and there left in solitude to meditate upon the dreadful misfortune that had come upon her.

Alone, far from home and kindred, there seemed no avenue of escape open to her. Despairing, she prayed to the Great Power above to rescue her from her terrible peril.

Leaving the despairing maid to her own sad thoughts, we will return to the renegade Girty.

After leaving the old General, Girty made his way to the secluded glade in the forest where he had arranged to meet Kendrick.

Girty found his companion waiting for him.

"The Indians have departed with the girl?" Girty asked.

"Yes; by the way, what do you intend to do with her?" said Kendrick.

"Give her to some chief for a wife. I have just had a little talk with Treveling. I told him who I was and of the vengeance that I have taken for the wrong that he did me so many years ago." Girty's face showed plainly his fierce joy as he spoke.

"It was a dangerous attempt to penetrate into yonder settlement," said Kendrick.

"Yes, but my disguise, you see, is perfect. This black wig covers my own hair, and the walnut stain upon my face changes the color of my complexion. But we must return to Chillicothe. The settlers know of Ke-ne-ha-ha's intended attack and are prepared for it. The chief must know it. The design to surprise the station has failed."

"Will he then give up the attack?"

"No; Ke-ne-ha-ha will play the lion if he can not act the part of the fox. The Shawnees and their allies have force enough to drive all the whites from the banks of the Ohio. They will try to do it and I think they will succeed."

"I say, Girty," said Kendrick, suddenly, "why do you give the girl to the Indians? Why not keep her for yourself? She is young and pretty; a prize for any man."

"I have thought of that," replied the other; "perhaps the knowledge that his daughter was mine would give more pain to Treveling than anything else."

"I should think it likely."

"I will think about the matter; but now let us to Chillicothe as fast as our legs will carry us. Soon we will return with brand and steel. Dying men and blazing roof-trees shall mark our path."

Then the two plunged into the thicket, and soon their forms were lost in the mazes of the wood.

For a few minutes the little glade was deserted by all living things, and then again life stood within the forest opening.

Forth from the cover of the wood came the strange girl known as Kanawha Kate. In her hand she carried the long rifle common to the frontier. In her belt was thrust the keen-edged scalping-knife of the Indian.

For a moment she paused in the center of the glade and listened eagerly.

"She is then in the Shawnee village, the prisoner of the renegade," she murmured. "She, the promised wife of the man that I love with all the passion of my nature." Full of agony was the tone in which she spoke.

"Why did I permit this terrible love to take possession of my heart? Why did I not crush it at the moment of its birth? But my rival is in the power of the Indians. This man, Girty, may make her his, then she will be removed from my path forever. Why should I interfere to save her? If Harvey does not see her again he may forget her, and then I may be able to win his love. Oh! how full of bliss is even the thought."

For a moment she stood like one inspired, her eyes flashing and her lips half-opened. And then a change came over her face. Her head sunk down listlessly upon her breast.

"Alas! it is but a dream," she murmured, sorrowfully. "He will never learn to love me even if she is lost to him. I have forgotten the stain that clings to me. Forgotten that I am the daughter of the renegade. One at whom the finger of scorn is pointed. A wretched creature not fit to associate with others whose skins are white like mine. I am an outcast, a child of the forest. What madness then to think that I can ever win the love of a man like Harvey Winthrop. No, it is impossible."

Slowly and mournfully Kate spoke, as the truth forced itself upon her mind.

"I must to the Shawnee village!" she cried, suddenly. "The Indians know me as the daughter of the renegade and will not harm me. On my way through the forest I can decide on what course to pursue. Whether to leave Virginia to her fate, to the cruel mercy of having her life spared by Girty, only to become his wife; or to save her—if it be possible—and give her to the man who has, unknowingly, won my heart. Oh! to leave her to Girty is a terrible temptation; Heaven give me strength to resist it!"

Then through the wood Kate followed on the trail of her father and Girty.

Cautiously she followed on the trail till it led into the Indian village by the bank of the Scioto, known as Chillicothe.

In the thicket that fringed the village, Kate halted.

"Now, what course shall I pursue?" she asked, communing with herself. "Shall I go at once boldly into the village and say that I have come to seek my father? or shall I remain here in concealment and watch my opportunity to enter the village unobserved?"

For a few moments Kate pondered over the difficult question. She could not decide which of the two courses to adopt.

Then from a wigwam, in full view of the thicket that concealed the girl, came Girty and Kendrick.

They bent their steps slowly toward the river.

"I have it!" cried Kale, suddenly; "I will tell my father that I feared to remain alone in my cabin and brave the dangers of the Indian attack, and that I wish to remain here until the war is ended. They will not suspect my purpose."

And having come to this conclusion, she stepped forward from the shelter of the thicket.

The two men started with surprise when they beheld the girl.

"Why, Kate, what brings you here?" asked Kendrick, in astonishment.

"I am in search of you, father," she replied.

"What do you want with me?"

"I have thought over your warning regarding the Indian attack, and have concluded to seek shelter here," she replied.

"It's the best thing you kin do," said Kendrick, approvingly.

Girty's face wore a strange expression as he looked up at the girl.

"Is this your daughter?" he said, in an undertone to Kendrick.

"Yes," the other replied; "don't you remember her?"

"Her face is familiar to me," said Girty, with a puzzled air, "yet I can not remember ever meeting her before."

"She was with me, hyer in the nation, some five years ago; of course she's changed a good deal since that time."

"That is probably the reason why her face seems strange and yet familiar to me. But come this way a moment. I have something to say to you."

Kendrick followed Girty. A few paces on, out of ear-shot of the girl, Girty halted.

"Is your daughter to be trusted?" Girty asked.

"Why what do you mean?" said Kendrick, in wonder.

"I mean is she red at heart, like ourselves? Does she hate the whites?"

"Well, I reckon that she doesn't bear 'em much love. The settlers have allers looked upon her as they would upon a spotted snake; a pretty thing, but dangerous, and not to be trusted, and not to be handled. But why do you ask the question?"

"I'll tell you. I want some one to look after this girl."

"Why not get one of the squaws?"

"I am afraid to trust her with them. Of course I shall have to go with Ke-ne-ha-ha, on his expedition against the whites. If any reverse should happen to the Indians, and the news of it reach the village in my absence, they might take revenge upon the girl."

"Yes, that's very true."

"But if I can get your daughter to take charge of her, why that danger will be avoided."

"Well, you kin ask the gal. I guess she'll be willing to do it," said Kendrick.

"I'll pay her well for the service. The presence, too, of one of her own blood may serve to reconcile the girl to her fate, or, at any rate, it will serve to rob her captivity of half its terrors."

"Better speak to Kate right away."

"I will."

Then the two returned to the girl.

"Kate, my friend hyer wants you to do a little favor for him," said Kendrick.

"What is it?" asked Kate, and even as she spoke the thought came into her mind that the favor had something to do with the captive maid.

"There is a white girl in the village, not exactly a prisoner to the Indians, fur I intend to marry her, but still she is not free. I would like to have you take charge of her; do all you can to make her contented with and accept the fate that is before her. I will pay you well for the service."

"What is her name?" and not a muscle of Kate's face betrayed that she knew what the name would be even before it was spoken.

"Virginia Treveling," replied Girty, after hesitating for a moment, but then an instant's reflection convinced him that it would be folly to attempt to conceal the name of the prisoner.

"Very well, I will do it," said Kate, quietly.

"I told you I thought she would," said Kendrick, with an air of satisfaction.

"She is in yonder wigwam," and Girty pointed to one that stood by the bank of the Scioto, a hundred paces or so from where they were.

"I will take good care of her," Kate said, and neither of the two that stood by her side guessed the double meaning conveyed in her words.

And so Kate was placed to guard the captive Virginia. In her heart two passions struggled for supremacy. The fate of her rival was in her hands. Would she save or crush her?

CHAPTER XXVI.

THE GREAT MEDICINE.

Ke-ne-ha-ha gazed at the old Medicine Man in astonishment, not unmixed with awe.

"Did the great chief hear right? Did my father say that he could show the Wolf Demon to Ke-ne-ha-ha?"

"Yes, the Great Medicine of the Shawnee nation can raise the dead—can bring the evil spirit—the Wolf Demon—from the air, the earth, or from the fire where he has his wigwam," chanted the old Indian.

For a few moments in silence the Shawnee chief looked up on the Great Medicine.

"My father speaks straight," he said, at length, breaking the silence. "His tongue is not forked. Is the wolf Demon an Indian devil?"

"No, white."

"White!" and the chief started.

"Yes, as white as the Ohio waves when the Great Spirit lashes them with his storm-whip, and they bind white plumes around their scalp-locks."

The chief pondered with moody brows. The old Indian from the covert of his blankets watched him with searching eyes.

"Then the Great Medicine can show me the Wolf Demon?"

"Yes."

"When?"

"Does the chief see that green stick?" and the old Indian pointed to the fire.

"Yes."

"When that stick becomes a flaming brand, then turns to a blackened coal, the Wolf Demon will be here."

"In this wigwam?" asked the chief, in wonder.

"Yes."

"Why not before?"

"The Wolf Demon is far down below the earth. His home is in the fire that burns in the mouth of the tortoise that carries the earth on his back. He can not come in an instant. The Great Medicine knew that Ke-ne-ha-ha would seek his counsel before the young moon died. He knew that the chief would wish to see the Wolf Demon, and he summoned him from the land of shadows long ago. But for that, the chief would not be able to have his wish gratified to-night."

"The Wolf Demon will come, then?" and instinctively Ke-ne-ha-ha's hand sought the handle of his tomahawk as he spoke.

"Yes; the chief is wise to prepare, for the Wolf Demon comes to take his life."

"Ah!" and Ke-ne ha-ha's eyes shot lurid fires as he uttered the simple exclamation.

"Does the chief fear?"

"What! the white devil? ugh! Ke-ne-ha-ha's heart is like rock. He does not fear."

"Then the chief will meet and fight the Wolf Demon?" asked the Great Medicine.

"Yes, if the Wolf Demon comes, the chief will fight him. Many great warriors have fallen by the tomahawk of the Wolf Demon. He is a coward. He does not attack the Shawnee braves like a warrior and a man. He creeps behind them in the forest like a cat and strikes them in the back. He will not dare to meet Ke-ne-ha-ha, face to face."

"See, the green stick is burning," and the Medicine Man looked toward the fire as he spoke. "When it is ashes, the chief will stand face to face with the Wolf Demon. He will tremble like a squaw when he sees the white man's devil."

"The Great Medicine is wise, but he lies when he says that Ke-ne-ha-ha will tremble!" cried the Shawnee chief, anger sparkling in his eyes. "The great fighting-man of the Shawnee nation never turned his back to mortal foe, either red or white-skinned warrior. Why should he fear the devil that hides in the wood, and who, like a coward, strikes his foes in the back?" And Ke-ne-ha-ha drew himself up proudly, as he spoke.

"The chief has the heart of a lion; it is a pity that he should die like the snake," said the old Indian, slowly.

"When the chief dies it will be upon the war-path!" exclaimed the Shawnee brave, in defiance; "a hundred scalps will hang at his belt—his hand will be red with the blood of his foe. When he enters the happy hunting-grounds, the chiefs will bow in homage, to him, and say, 'Here is a great warrior; welcome.'"

"The chief is wrong," said the Great Medicine, slowly; "he will not die on the war-path. The Great Medicine sees the future. It is clouded to all other eyes but his. His heart is Shawnee—it is torn with anguish when he reads the future and sees the desolation and dismay that must come upon the Shawnee nation. Before his eyes is a sea of blood, not white blood but red, the blood of the Indian."

Over the brow of the chief came a gloomy cloud as he listened to the prophetic words of the old man.

His heart sunk within him as he heard the prophecy of disaster and death.

"Does the Great Medicine read the future straight?" he asked, anxiously. "Is not the blood that he sees the blood of the white settlers by the banks of the Ohio? the blood of the false-hearted, crooked-tongued chiefs who have stolen the lands of the red-men and whose mouths are full of lies?"

Sorrowfully the old Indian shook his head.

"The blood is the life-current of the Shawnees, the Mingoes, the Wyandots and the Hurons. The heart of the Great Medicine is sad, but he must speak the truth."

"Then the expedition of the Shawnee chief against the whites on the Ohio will be defeated?" asked Ke-ne-ha-ha, with a frown upon his face.

"Yes."

"The chief will go if he had ten thousand lives to lose and knew that by the act he would sacrifice them all," said the Shawnee, proudly, and with an air of dogged defiance.

"The chief has but one life to lose, and he will lose it in the Shawnee village by the banks of the Scioto," said the Great Medicine.

Ke-ne-ha-ha started as the words fell upon his ears, and a look of anger swept over his face.

"Will the chief die by the hand of a spy—a snake who will creep into the Shawnee village to strike him in the back?"

"No, Ke-ne-ha-ha will be killed in a fair and open fight, but he will be killed in the midst of the Shawnees and die in one of the wigwams of his own people."

The chief looked puzzled at the strange words of the old Indian.

"Ke-ne-ha-ha does not understand; will my father speak straighter?"

"The chief does not fear then to learn the future?"

"No," said the Shawnee warrior, proudly.

"Not even when he is to hear of the manner of his death?"

"A warrior must die some time. Ke-ne-ha-ha is ready when the Great Spirit calls him."

"Good; the Great Medicine will speak then. He must speak words that cause him tears of blood, for they tell of the death of the Shawnee chieftain."

"Ke-ne-ha-ha's ears are open—he listens."

"Before the moon dies, a terrible figure will be in the Shawnee village. All fly from its path—the birds of the night, and the insects of the earth—for it is not of human mold. The moonbeams shining in fear will show the figure of a huge gray wolf. The wolf walks on its hind legs like a man. It has the face of a human, and it is striped with war-paint, black and white. In

119

its paw it carries a tomahawk—the edge is crusted with blood that dims the brightness of the steel. The blood comes from the veins of some of the best warriors of the Shawnee nation. The Little Crow hunted the brown deer in the woods of the Scioto. He came not back. His brother found him in the forest dead—the print of a tomahawk in his skull and a Red Arrow graven on his breast. Watega is another great brave of the Shawnee nation. Not two sleeps ago he went with the white red-men—the renegades—on a scout. He has not come back to his wigwam, though the others have returned. His squaw sits in his lodge and wonders where he is. He will never come back. In a little glade on the other side of the Ohio is his body—a tomahawk cut in the skull, and on his breast the totem of the Red Arrow."

Ke-ne-ha-ha started. The death of Watega, who was one of his favorite warriors, startled him.

"Watega dead!" he cried, hardly willing to believe the news.

"The Great Medicine has said that he sleeps the long sleep that knows no waking," chanted the old Indian, his voice coming from beneath the blankets wrapped around his head like a voice from the tomb.

"How can my father know that Watega is dead?" demanded the chief, obstinately refusing to believe.

"Does the Shawnee chief question the power of the Great Medicine, and yet come to him for advice?" said the old Indian, with an accent of scorn in his voice.

"My father is sure?"

"Yes."

"Watega was a great warrior; peace be with him," said the chief, solemnly.

"Little Crow and Watega fell by the tomahawk of the Wolf Demon in the forest, and not an hour ago the Red Leaf met his death by the Scioto, and the Wolf Demon dealt the blow."

"Ke-ne-ha-ha saw the slain brave, the last victim of the white devil," the chief said, sorrowfully.

"No, the chief is wrong; not the last victim, for another Shawnee has felt the keen edge of the tomahawk of the Wolf Demon, since the Red Leaf died by his hand."

"Another of my braves killed!" cried Ke-ne-ha-ha, in wonder and in anger.

"Yes, two have had the totem of the Red Arrow graven on their breasts since the moon rose."

"And who was the other?"

"The Great Medicine can not tell the chief now, but the chief will know when the stick burns to ashes and the Wolf Demon comes."

"But the fate of Ke-ne-ha-ha?"

120

"The red chief will fall by the tomahawk of the Wolf Demon."

There was silence for a few moments in the wigwam.

Over the face of the Shawnee chief came a look of stern resolution. There was no trace of fear in the bearing of the Shawnee.

"Let my father keep his word and bring the white devil," Ke-ne-ha-ha said, breaking the silence. "If the Great Spirit wills that the chief of the Shawnee nation is to die by the hand of the scourge of his race, Ke-ne-ha-ha is content. But he will fight the Wolf Demon before he dies."

CHAPTER XXVII.

THE STORY OF THE WOLF DEMON.

The little fire sputtered as the flame eat into the heart of the green stick.

The light chased and toyed with the dark shadows that lurked, assassin-like, in the corners of the Indian lodge.

Ke-ne-ha-ha, with a resolute but gloomy brow, looked upon the old Indian, who sat like a vampire by the embers.

"My father will keep his word?" the chief said, after a silence of long duration.

"Watch the green stick—when it is ashes the Wolf Demon will stand before the chief."

The Shawnee brave gazed upon the Great Medicine in wonder.

"My father is a Great Medicine, to be able to call the white man's devil."

"The Great Spirit wills that the Wolf Demon should come; the Medicine Man does not bring him. He only knows that he is coming."

"Can my father tell me one thing more?" asked the chief, after thinking for a moment.

"Let the Shawnee brave speak; then the Great Medicine can answer," returned the old Indian, ambiguously.

"The chief will speak," said Ke-ne-ha-ha, decidedly. "The Wolf Demon has slain many a great brave of the Shawnee nation. He is only seen by the banks of the Scioto. He strikes only at the Shawnees. Why does not the white man's devil kill also the Wyandot and Mingo warriors? Why does Shawnee blood alone stain the edge of his tomahawk?"

"The chief is anxious to know why?"

"Yes; can my father tell?"

"The Great Medicine of the Shawnees can tell all things, either in life or death. Let the chief open his ears, and he shall hear."

"Ke-ne-ha-ha listens," said the chief, curtly.

"The Wolf Demon is a white devil, and he hates the Shawnees. He does not hate the Mingo warrior or the Wyandot brave, only the Shawnee."

"But why should he hate the warriors of Ke-ne-ha-ha?"

"Because when the Wolf Demon was on earth they did him wrong."

The chief started.

"The Wolf Demon has lived, then, a human?"

"Yes."

"Will my father tell how that can be?"

"Yes; listen." The Great Medicine paused for a moment, as if to collect his thoughts, then again he spoke:

"Twelve moons ago a song-bird dwelt in the wigwams of the Shawnees, in the village of Chillicothe, by the side of the Scioto. She was as fair as the rosy morn, as gentle as the summer wind, as lithe and graceful as the brown deer. She was called the Red Arrow."

"The Great Medicine speaks with a straight tongue—the Red Arrow was the daughter of the great fighting-man of the Shawnee nation. The chief now mourns for the loss of his flower." Ke-ne-ha-ha spoke sadly, and a gloomy cloud was on his brow as the words came from his lips.

"The Singing Bird was called the Red Arrow—a name fit more for a chief and a warrior than a bounding fawn—because when she was born the Great Spirit marked a red arrow—His totem—on her breast. Over her heart blazoned the mystic sign, yet her nature was as gentle as the pigeon's, though she bore the totem of slaughter."

"What my father says is true," said the chief. "All the Shawnee tribe know of the daughter of Ke-ne-ha-ha and of the mystic totem that she bore on her breast."

"But do all the Shawnee chiefs know of the manner of her death?"

The great chief started at the question and cast a searching glance into the face of the Great Medicine; that is, he would have looked into the face of the old Indian had not the blankets, wrapped around his head, hid it from the gaze of the chief.

"Does not my father know how the daughter of Ke-ne-ha-ha died?" asked the chief, slowly.

"Perhaps the Great Medicine has heard, but his memory is bad—he is an old man. Will the great chief tell him?"

"The Red Arrow left the wigwams of her people to wander in the forest. There she was eaten up by a bear. Ke-ne-ha-ha and a few of his chosen warriors searched for her and discovered her fate."

"The great chief lies to the Medicine Man," said the old Indian, calmly.

Fire flashed from the eyes of the chief, and he advanced a step with a threatening gesture toward the old Indian.

"Does the chief come with lies in his mouth into the sacred wigwam and then dare to raise his hand in violence to the Great Medicine Man because the Great Spirit bids his oracle speak the truth?" said the old Indian, sternly.

With an exclamation of anger, Ke-ne-ha-ha stepped back to his former position.

"The chief forgot himself—he did not mean to offer harm to the Great Medicine Man."

"It is well. Mortal man cannot harm the tongue of the Great Spirit. The Spirit-fires that flash from the storm-cloud would strike unto death the warrior that dares to lift his hand in menace to the Great Medicine of the Shawnee tribe," said the aged oracle, impressively.

With an expression of awe upon his features, the chief listened to the words of the old Indian.

"Let my father forgive and forget," Ke-ne-ha-ha said, slowly.

"The Great Medicine will tell the Shawnee chief the fate of the Red Arrow. She wandered from the wigwams of her people because she had fallen in love with a pale-face—a hunter, whose cabin was by the Ohio and Muskingum. She left home, kindred, all, for the sake of the long-rifle. She became his squaw. Does the Great Medicine speak truth?"

"Yes," Ke-ne-ha-ha answered, slowly and reluctantly.

"It is good. Does the chief see that it is useless to deceive the Great Medicine, who can look into men's hearts and read what is written there?"

"My father is wise."

"The Great Spirit has made him so," answered the old Indian, solemnly.

"The Great Medicine knows the fate of the Red Arrow?" Ke-ne-ha-ha asked.

"Yes; the Shawnees found her in the lodge of the pale-face. They asked her to return to her people. She refused, for she loved the white hunter. Then the red chiefs went away, but when the sky grew dark, covered by Manitou's mantle, again the Shawnee warriors stood by the lodge of the pale-face who had stolen from her home the singing-bird of the Shawnees. The brands were in their hands, the keen-edged scalping-knives in their belts. They gave to the fire the lodge of the pale face, and while the flames roared and crackled, they shot the Red Arrow dead in their midst."

"The Shawnee woman who forsakes her tribe for a pale-face stranger deserves to die," said the chief, sternly.

"The chief speaks straight, for with his own hand he killed his daughter, the Red Arrow."

"And would also kill Le-a-pah, his other singing-bird, if she left the village of her fathers to sing in the wigwam of a white-skin," exclaimed Ke-ne-ha-ha, with stern accents.

"It is good."

"Why has my father told of the death of the bird who flew from her nest to dwell with the stranger?"

"Does not the chief wish to know why the Wolf Demon kills only the Shawnee warriors?"

"Yes; but what has that to do with the dead singing-bird?" Ke-ne-ha-ha said, puzzled.

124

"Does not the Wolf Demon leave as his totem on the breast of his victims a Red Arrow?"

The chief started. For the first time the thought that the mark of the Wolf Demon and the name of his murdered daughter were alike, flashed across his mind.

"Why does the Wolf Demon take for his totem a Red Arrow?" demanded the chief.

"Let the chief open his ears and he shall hear," said the old Indian, gravely. "When the lodge of the white hunter was burnt to the ground, and the body of the singing-bird lay before the warriors disfigured by the flames, they looked for the white hunter, but could not find him."

"He was not in the lodge when my braves attacked it," interrupted the chief.

"Ke-ne-ha-ha is wrong. The white hunter was in the lodge. He saw the singing-bird fly from life to death, and was wounded by the bullets of the Shawnee warriors; then, when the lodge fell, he was buried beneath the ruins. The eyes of the red braves were sharp, but they did not discover the wounded and helpless white-skin under the blackened logs. The red chiefs went away, satisfied with their vengeance. The white brave lay between life and death. A huge gray wolf came from the forest. He found the senseless man under the logs. The forest beast was hungry; he thirsted for human blood. The great gray wolf eat up the wounded white-skin. The body of the white went into the stomach of the wolf; it died, but the soul of the white hunter lived. It did not fly from the body but went with it. The soul of the wolf was small, the soul of the white hunter large, and the large soul eat up the little one. The wolf became a wolf with a human soul. The soul remembered the wrong that the Shawnee warriors had done its body; it burned for revenge. It made the wolf walk erect like a human; it taught him to carry in his paw the tomahawk of the red-man—to steal upon the Shawnee chiefs in the forest—to give their souls to the dark spirit and to graven on their breasts the totem of the Red Arrow. Thus the soul keeps alive the memory of the squaw that the Shawnee warriors killed."

The chief listened with amazement.

"How long will the wolf, who has a human soul, be an avenging angel to give to the death the warriors of my tribe?" the chief asked.

"How many warriors were with Ke-ne-ha-ha when he killed the Red Arrow?"

"Ten."

"Where are they now?"

The chief started. Of the ten warriors not one was living. All were dead, killed by the Wolf Demon. Each one bore the mark of the Red Arrow.

"Only one remains, Ke-ne-ha-ha, the great chief of the Shawnee nation. He will die by the tomahawk of the human wolf, and then the Demon will go to the land of shadows."

With a sharp crack, the green stick snapped in twain. The fire had eaten to the core. The Medicine Man arose.

"Let the chief prepare. The Wolf Demon is near."

CHAPTER XXVIII.

A TERRIBLE ENCOUNTER.

Quietly the Indian chief drew the keen-edged scalping knife from his girdle. Every muscle in his massive frame was nerved for the coming contest.

The little fire, now burnt down to a mass of glowing embers, but faintly lighted up the gloom of the wigwam.

The Medicine Man turned his back to the chief, slowly disengaged himself from the huge blanket wrapped around him, and then held it up in the air.

The blanket concealed the form of the Medicine Man from the eyes of Ke-ne-ha-ha.

Darker and darker grew the gloom.

"Is the chief ready to see the Wolf Demon?" asked the Medicine Man, his voice vibrating with a strange accent.

"Yes," replied the Shawnee warrior, slowly and undauntedly.

"Ere the heart of the warrior can beat ten, the Wolf Demon will stand before him," chanted the solemn voice of the old Indian.

Then all was silent.

In the stillness, the throbbings of the Indian's heart seemed to his excited fancy to make as big a noise as the foot-fall of the brown deer falling upon the forest-glade.

More and more dense grew the gloom.

The blanket that had concealed the figure of the Medicine Man from the chief dropped to the ground.

The old Indian had disappeared.

In his place stood the terrible form that all living things shrunk from.

Face to face with the chief of the Shawnee nation stood the Wolf Demon!

In his paw he held the death-dealing tomahawk, whose edge, even now, was crusted red with Shawnee blood.

The eyeballs of the chief were distended with horror as he looked upon the awful form. But no thought of fear was in the mind of the Shawnee warrior.

For a moment the foemen glared upon each other.

Then, swift as the flash of the lightning, the Wolf Demon leaped upon his destined prey.

The wild war-note of the Shawnee nation burst from the lips of Ke-ne-ha-ha, as he struck desperately at the huge form that sprung so fiercely upon him.

The keen scalping-knife cut deep into the side of the Wolf Demon, but met no flesh in its passage, only hide and hair.

The tomahawk of the unknown being came down upon the head of the chief, but glancing in its course, inflicted only a slight flesh wound.

The two closed together in mortal conflict.

Alarmed by the war-cry of the chief, the Shawnee warriors came pouring into the wigwam.

In the gloom they could only discover that two dark figures were grappling with each other upon the ground that formed the floor of the lodge, in a furious struggle.

Amazed, the warriors paused. In the darkness they could not tell which of the two dark forms—interlaced so snake-like together—was friend or foe.

The combatants paid no heed to the entrance of the warriors, so engrossed were they in their terrible struggle.

For a moment the Indians stood like statues, gazing in bewilderment upon the strange scene before them.

Then, actuated by a sudden thought, one of the Shawnees—wiser than his fellows—dashed from the wigwam to the fire that burned near to the lodge of the Medicine Man.

The chief snatched a flaming brand from the fire, and then re-entered the wigwam.

The struggle between the two upon the ground had ceased. One had conquered the other.

By the light of the burning fagot the amazed Indians looked upon a fearful scene.

In the center of the wigwam, flat upon his back, and with the blood streaming freely from a wound in his temple, lay Ke-ne-ha-ha, the great chief of the Shawnee nation.

Over him, with his foot planted upon his breast, and the blood-stained tomahawk upraised in menace in his hand, was the terrible being that wore the shape of a wolf and the face of a man.

The blood of the warriors congealed within their veins as they looked upon the awful picture.

For a moment the Wolf Demon held his position, with his foot placed in triumph upon the body of the prostrate chief. Then, with a hoarse yell of defiance, he sprung forward upon the warriors gathered in the doorway of the lodge.

With a howl of terror, the Shawnees scattered in fear, tumbling over each other in their fright.

Two quick and powerful strokes of the keen-edged tomahawk, and two more Shawnees were sent to the happy hunting-grounds.

Swift as the hunted deer ran the Wolf Demon through the Indian village.

The warriors, recovering a little from their fright, and with the boldness that the sense of overpowering numbers gives, followed in pursuit.

The yells of the Indians rung out shrill on the still night-air.

Increasing in speed at every stride, the Wolf Demon headed for the thicket.

Far in the rear followed the warriors.

With a hoarse yell of defiance, the terrible figure gained the shelter of the wood, and disappeared within its shadows.

On the borders of the wood the Indians halted. All the village had been aroused by the terrible outcry, and great was the wonder and alarm of the Shawnees when they learned that the terrible Wolf Demon had been in their midst.

After a short consultation, the warriors entered the thicket. But ten paces within the wood all traces of the passage of the Wolf Demon vanished. He had disappeared as utterly as if the earth had opened and swallowed him.

Keen-witted as the Shawnee chiefs were, they never dreamed of examining the oak branches that waved over their heads. They little thought that, even as they paused within the wood, in wonderment and dismay, from his leafy covert in the branches above their heads, the terrible Wolf Demon glared down upon them, and laughed, with fierce joy, when, puzzled and beaten, they took their way in sullen anger back to the Indian village.

The Indians gone, the strange form descended from his perch in the branches of the oak, and, with a rapid but silent tread, stole through the mazes of the forest.

While some of the Indians had been pursuing the phantom form, others had given their attention to the wounded chief.

Ke-ne-ha-ha had suffered but little. Two slight cuts on the head, inflicted by the tomahawk of the Wolf Demon—mere flesh wounds—were all the damage he had received.

To his wondering warriors the chief told the story of the interview with the Great Medicine Man, and the sudden appearance of the terrible scourge of the Shawnee nation, the Wolf Demon.

Then, to the horror of the savages, on examining the wigwam, in one corner, covered by a blanket, they found the Great Medicine Man, *dead*!

The terrible tomahawk-cut on his head, and the totem of the Red Arrow carved upon his breast, told of the manner of his death and the doer of the deed.

The Great Medicine Man of the Shawnees had indeed been slain by the Wolf Demon.

By a miracle Ke-ne-ha-ha had escaped. It was evidently not fated that he was to die so soon.

Carefully they wiped the blood from the face and garments of the chief and bound up his wounds.

Ke-ne-ha-ha at once called a council of his principal warriors.

By the time the council had assembled, the party that had pursued the Wolf Demon returned and told of their failure to trace the terrible being through the forest.

Calmly the chief addressed the council.

He told of the dreadful hand-to-hand encounter that he had had with the white man's devil. Declared that the charm was broken, and that the Wolf Demon no longer was to be feared.

The warriors took heart at the bold address of the great chief.

Then Ke-ne-ha-ha urged the necessity of making an immediate attack upon the white settlements along the Ohio.

In this the chief was supported by every warrior within the council. All were eager for the attack. All thirsted for the blood of the white-skins.

The council broke up, and earnestly the warriors donned their war-paint in readiness for the coming fight.

It was arranged that the expedition was to start on the morrow, and that Point Pleasant should be the first station attacked.

Girty and Kendrick had been in the council, and on its breaking up, walked slowly along together.

"The chief is terribly in earnest," said Kendrick, as they proceeded onward.

"Yes, there'll be a leaden hail rattling around Point Pleasant soon," responded Girty.

"What do you think of this Wolf Demon?" asked Kendrick, suddenly.

"Well, I don't exactly know what to think," said Girty, with a puzzled air.

"The chief had a tussle with him."

"Yes, and the warriors saw him when he fled through the village. A huge gray wolf walking erect on its hind legs like a man and with a human face."

"It ain't a spook, 'cos the Indians wouldn't have been able to have seen it."

"No, but what is it?" asked Girty.

"Now you've got me," said Kendrick, with a dubious shake of the head.

"Man or devil, if he ever comes within range of my rifle I'll wager that I'll drill a hole through him," said Girty, decidedly.

"Well, the chief failed," observed Kendrick. "He said that he struck his knife clean through his side, and yet not a drop of blood was on the blade."

"It's wonderful, to say the least," said Girty.

And then the two entered their wigwam.

CHAPTER XXIX.

A FRIEND IN NEED.

Virginia, in the solitude of the wigwam, full of bitter thoughts, and mourning, silently, over the hard fortune that had befallen her, was surprised by the entrance of a female form.

Looking up in astonishment, she beheld Kate.

A cry of joy came from the lips of the hopeless girl. In Kate she beheld a friend!

A warning gesture from the Kanawha Queen checked Virginia's utterance, and the words of welcome died away upon her lips.

"Be careful, lady," said Kate, warningly; "a loud word to betray to other ears that we know each other, and both of us are lost."

"Oh! it is so hard to keep back the joy that struggles to my lips," murmured Virginia; "your presence here seems like a ray of sunlight beaming full upon the dark pathway through which runs the current of my life. Your face gives me life and hope."

Kate gazed into the upturned face of the fair girl with a mournful smile.

"You are in great danger, lady," she said, slowly.

"Oh, I know that!" cried Virginia, quickly. "I am a prisoner in the hands of the merciless red-men."

"Yes, a prisoner in the hands of one who is more merciless than any painted savage that roams the valley of the Ohio. A man whose skin is white but whose heart is red," said Kate, mournfully.

Virginia gazed at Kate in wonder.

"In Heaven's name, of whom do you speak?" she asked.

"Of one to whom the hungry wolf is a lamb; of one who knows neither fear nor pity. A white Indian; an outcast from his country and his race."

Virginia shuddered at the terrible words.

"A renegade?"

"Yes; you are a prisoner in his hands, not the captive of the Shawnees. Far better were it for you if the red Indians held your fate in their hands," Kate said, impressively.

"And the name of this man?"

"Simon Girty."

Virginia's heart sunk within her as the name of the dreaded renegade fell upon her ears.

"Oh, Heaven help me, then!" she murmured, "for I am in terrible peril."

"Yes, you are right," said Kate, quickly; "you are in peril. A miracle alone can save you."

"Where am I?" Virginia asked.

"In the village of Chillicothe."

"Among the Shawnees!"

"Yes; this is the village of their great chief, Ke-ne-ha-ha."

"I have heard my father speak of him," Virginia said, thoughtfully. "He bears a deadly hatred to the whites."

"Yes; he has sworn to drive the pale-faces back from the Ohio. Even now the savages are arming and preparing for the fight."

"Then my father and friends will be in danger!" cried Virginia.

"What is their danger compared to yours?" asked Kate.

"Yes, that is true," said Virginia, mournfully, "but, for the moment, the thought of their peril made me forget my own helpless situation."

"Have you ever seen this man—Girty?"

"No."

"You do not know, then, why he has selected you for his victim?"

"No," again Virginia replied.

"Strange," said Kate, thoughtfully. "I cannot understand it. He must have some motive in entrapping you from your home and friends and bringing you here."

"I will tell you all the particulars."

Then Virginia told the story of her abduction.

Kate listened attentively.

The story puzzled her. She could not understand the double abduction.

"Have you no suspicion as to who this man is that pretended to rescue you from your first captors, but in reality led you into the hands of the second party?"

"No," Virginia said.

"The false guide was Simon Girty."

Virginia uttered a sharp cry as though she had received a terrible wound.

"For Heaven's sake be silent or it will cost us both our lives!" cried Kate, quickly and with great caution.

"I will not offend again," murmured Virginia, the big tears beginning to well slowly from her lustrous brown eyes. "But I have such a terrible weight pressing upon my heart. I feel that I am utterly lost."

"No, do not despair; there may still be a chance to escape from the toils that surround you."

"Oh! show me some way to escape and I will go down on my knees and thank you!" cried Virginia Treveling, earnestly.

"I do not ask that," said Kate, with a mournful expression in her dark eyes.

"But how is it that you are here in the Indian village? Are you a prisoner, too?" asked Virginia, suddenly.

"No," replied Kate, her eyes seeking the ground.

"I cannot understand," said Virginia, in wonder.

"Do you not remember who and what I am?" asked Kate, a tinge of bitterness perceptible in her tones. "Am I not Kate, the Queen of the Kanawha, the daughter of the pale-faced Indian, David Kendrick, the renegade?"

"Yes, yes, I remember now," said Virginia: "I ask your pardon if my question has given you pain. I did not intend or think to wound you."

"Do not fear. I have heard too many bitter speeches in my short life to be galled now by a chance word. I cannot be wounded by a random shot. I am the daughter of a renegade; all the world knows it. It would be useless to deny the truth. I must bear patiently the stain that my birth and my father's deeds have fixed upon me. I cannot cast aside the shame that clings to me and through no act of mine. All the world despises me. Is it not enough to make me hate all the world?"

"No," said Virginia, softly, "you are not to blame for the deeds of others. Live so that your life shall be a telling reproof to those who would blame you for the acts of your father. I do not think any the worse of you because you are the daughter of David Kendrick, the renegade. No, I rather pity you. I told you so when first we met in the ravine near Point Pleasant, and I repeat the words, now that I am here a captive in the hands of my enemies."

"Oh, lady, you have the heart of an angel!" cried Kate earnestly.

"No, I am only a poor weak girl in deadly peril," said Virginia, simply.

"Lady, I will try and save you from the danger that surrounds you!" cried Kate, impulsively.

"You will?" murmured Virginia, her face lighting up with joy.

"Yes; can you guess why I am here?"

"No," Virginia replied, in wonder.

"I am placed here by Girty to watch you."

"To watch me?"

"Yes, so that you can not escape from the toils that his cunning has drawn around you."

"And you will break faith with him and save me?" asked Virginia, anxiously.

"Yes."

"Heaven will surely bless you for the act!" cried Virginia, quickly.

"Perhaps I may need that blessing," said Kate, earnestly.

"I am sure that you do not!" exclaimed Virginia, impulsively. "I read in your face that your heart is good and noble, and I am sure that your face does not deceive me."

"I will try and keep faith with you. I have promised one who loves you dearly, that, if you were within a hundred miles of the Ohio, neither swamp nor wood, house nor wigwam should hide you from me. I have kept that promise and have found you. But one more task remains for me to do and that is, to save you from the perils that now surround you, and give you safe and unharmed into his arms."

Virginia listened with wonder to this strange speech.

"One who loves me dearly?"

"Yes, better far, I think, than he does his own life."

"I can not understand," said Virginia, bewildered.

"Is there not some one whom you love? One who holds your plighted faith?" asked Kate.

"There *was* one," and as Virginia spoke, the tears came slowly into her eyes. Back to her memory came the scene in the ravine. In imagination she felt again the warm, passionate kiss of the man she loved so well; then, an instant after, saw him stretched bleeding and senseless upon the earth at her feet.

"There *is* one now. You speak of Harvey Winthrop?"

"Yes!" cried Virginia, almost breathlessly.

"He is living."

"*Living?*"

"Yes."

Virginia sprung to her feet, her face flushed with joy.

"Oh! and I have mourned him as one lost to me forever."

"By a happy chance I discovered him in the ravine, helpless. Then I carried him to my cabin and he is there now."

"Is he wounded dangerously?" Virginia asked, the color forsaking her cheeks as she thought of the illness of her lover.

"No, only a flesh wound," Kate answered. "In a few days he will be well again. He told me that you were his plighted wife, and I promised him that I would find you if you were living and upon the earth. But I little expected, though, to find you a captive in the Shawnee village."

"Can you save me from the terrible danger that surrounds me?" Virginia asked, anxiously.

"At least I can try. Heaven alone knows whether the attempt will be successful or not," replied Kate, earnestly.

"Oh, my heart sinks within me when I think of the many miles that intervene between me and my kindred. I fear I shall never see Point Pleasant again. How can we make our way through the trackless wilderness, the home of the wild beast and the red savage?" Virginia asked, in sorrow.

"Do not fear; to me the wilderness is like an open book. Not a path between here and the Ohio that I do not know as well in the darkness as in the light. Trust to me, and if human aid is of avail you shall be saved."

Then, with a gesture of caution, Kate left the lodge.

CHAPTER XXX.

FATHER AND DAUGHTER.

As Kate left the lodge and turned to the right toward the river, she found herself suddenly confronted by her father, David Kendrick.

There was a peculiar grin upon the face of the renegade as he looked upon his daughter.

"Been in to see the little gal, hey?" he asked.

"Yes," Kate replied.

"Been making a neighborly call, hey? Does the critter know you?"

Kate felt that deception would be useless, so she answered truthfully.

"Yes."

"Where did you ever meet her?"

"At Point Pleasant."

"How does she feel?"

"Badly, of course."

"Well, that's nat'ral," said the renegade, with another grin.

"I should think so."

"I s'pose you told her that it would be all right—that the chances were that she would be taken back to the station 'fore long, hey?"

"Yes, I did tell her so," Kate said, puzzled at the odd manner of her father.

"Now, see how good I am at guessing. I ought to set up to onc't for a Great Medicine Man," and the renegade laughed, discordantly.

Kate cast a searching glance into her father's face, but she found nothing there to aid her in guessing the meaning of his strange conduct.

"Have you any thing else to say to me?" and Kate made a movement as if to pass the renegade and proceed on her course.

"Hold on, gal!" cried Kendrick, hastily. "I've got a heap to say to you. Jist foller me off a piece, whar we'll be out of ear-shot of any skulker, and then I'll talk to you like a Dutch uncle," and again the renegade laughed discordantly.

With a mind ill at ease Kate followed her father. His manner boded danger. Yet she could not imagine in what shape that danger would come.

The renegade led the way toward the wood.

On the border of the thicket he paused.

Close to where he stood was a fallen tree—a huge sycamore.

"Sit down, gal!" and he indicated with his hand the tree-trunk, as he spoke.

Kate obeyed the command.

"Now, jist wait quiet a moment, till I scout round and see if thar is anybody in the timber nigh us."

Then into the thicket he went.

Five minutes' search convinced the renegade that there was no one near. Then he returned to the spot where he had left Kate and took a seat on the tree-trunk by her side.

"Thar, gal, we kin talk here without any danger of any pryin' sucker a-hearin' our talk."

"Have you any thing particular to say that you are so afraid of being overheard?" asked Kate.

"Well, yes," replied Kendrick, after a pause. "I would rather a heap sight that only two pair of ears should hear what we're going to say."

"Well, what is it?"

Kate spoke calmly, yet she had a presentiment that a storm was about to burst over her head.

"Gal, you don't play keerds of course, but I guess you understand what I mean when I tell you to play with your keerds on the table and not under it," said the renegade, significantly.

"No," said Kate, calmly, "I do not understand what you mean."

"Oh, you don't," and the tone of the renegade was clearly one of unbelief. "Shall I speak plainer then?"

"Yes, if you wish me to understand," Kate said, quietly.

Kendrick looked at his daughter in wonder. Her calmness staggered him.

"Well, you are a cool hand. If I wasn't certain of my game now, I should think that, like a green dog, I was barking up the wrong tree. But the trail is too clear for me to be throw'd off."

"What do you mean?" Neither Kate's voice or face showed the least sign of alarm or excitement.

"I must spit it right out, hey?"

"Yes."

"If so be, so good. Well, gal, I've got a powerful long pair of ears. I were a-passing back of the wigwam where the little gal is, a few minutes ago, and I heerd something that made me want to hear more."

"Indeed?" Kate's face was as impassible as the face of a statue, and her voice as cold as ice.

"So I listened and heerd a good deal."

"What did you hear?"

"'Bout all you said to the little gal," replied Kendrick, with a grin. "I heerd you tell her 'bout the young feller that you saved in the ravine. I s'pose he's the one I saw in your cabin t'other day, hey?"

"Yes," Kate replied.

"Well, I thought so when you spoke of him. And then it struck me what a funny idea it was for you to be 'tending and fussing over another gal's feller."

"It is strange, isn't it?" said Kate, with a peculiar look. Her father did not notice the odd look.

"Well, I thought it was; but then, you were always a cranky piece, full of odd notions."

"Then you know that I have promised to rescue the girl from her present dangerous situation?"

"Yes, of course I do," replied Kendrick; "don't I tell you that I heard the whole thing as you talked it over?"

"Do you know why I wish to save the girl from Girty?"

"No, unless you've got the milk of human kindness so strong in your breast that it urges you to save the gal, 'cos she's in a tight place," said the renegade, thoughtfully.

"No, it is not that."

"What then?"

"I love the same man that she does."

"Jerusalem!" cried Kendrick, in wonder.

"It is the truth."

"You mean this young feller, Harvey Winthrop?"

"Yes."

"Does he care any thing about you?"

"How can he when he is in love with this girl?"

"Yes, that's true."

"That is the reason that I wish to take her from here."

The renegade looked at Kate in wonder.

"I don't understand," he said, in utter amazement. "You say that you love the feller, and yet you are going to give your rival to him."

"Oh, how dull you are!" cried Kate, impatiently.

"Well I may be," said Kendrick, doggedly. "Anyway, I can't make head nor tail out of your words. If you love the young feller and want him, I should think that giving him the girl that he likes better than he does you, was jist the way *not* to get him."

"What will be the fate of the girl if she stays here in the Indian village?"

"Well, I suppose Girty will make a sort of left-handed wife out of her. I believe that's his idea."

"But is there not a chance that she may escape or be rescued by her friends?" demanded Kate.

"Of course there's the chance. It ain't likely, but still it *might* happen so."

"And if she should escape I could never hope to win the love of Harvey Winthrop."

"Well, I s'pose that's Gospel truth."

"You may be sure that it is the truth!" exclaimed Kate, earnestly. "But if she never returns to the settlement of course he will never see her again. Then he will forget her. I have a double claim to his gratitude if not to his love. Twice have I saved his life."

"But gratitude ain't love."

"No, father; but the space that separates the two sentiments is but a slight one. Once this girl is out of the way he will learn to love me; I am sure of it."

"But you say you are going to give the girl back to him?"

"When you go upon the war-path do you openly tell the foe that you are coming and bid him prepare to meet you?"

"Well, no; not generally, gal," replied the renegade, who began to have a dim perception of his daughter's plan.

"Neither do I. Cunning is my weapon. The girl thinks me her friend. Willingly she will consent to be guided by me. By stealth we will leave the Indian village. Once within the fastness of the thicket, what will prevent me from removing my rival forever from my path?"

Kendrick gazed at his daughter in admiration.

"You're a cute gal, by hookey; but what will Girty say when he discovers that the gal is gone?"

"What can he say, or what do I care what he says?" demanded Kate, spiritedly. "You do not owe Simon Girty many favors, father."

"I don't owe him any," replied the renegade. "It's nothing to me if the gal does get away from him. I sha'n't worry over it."

"I will manage it so carefully that not one in this village—be his skin white or red—will be able to trace us," said Kate, proudly.

"I'll back you ag'in' the whole Shawnee nation for woodcraft," said Kendrick, with evident pride.

"I do not think that you would have cause to regret your confidence."

"Then your plan is to make the gal think that you are taking her back to the station; then, when you get her into the thicket, you'll settle her for this world?"

"Yes," said Kate, coldly; not a tone of her voice trembled as she spoke.

"*Won't* Girty swear when he finds that his little gal has absquatulated and nary sign of her left!" and Kendrick chuckled over the idea.

140

"I care nothing for his anger; besides, he will not be apt to suspect that I had a hand in her escape."

The two then returned to the village.

Girty had little idea that his prey was in danger of slipping from his grasp.

CHAPTER XXXI.

THE VENGEANCE OF THE RENEGADE.

All was bustle in the Indian village, for word had gone forth to make ready for the war-path! Gayly the braves donned the war-paint, and sharpened the scalping-knives and glistening tomahawks.

Girty had been summoned to the lodge of Ke-ne-ha-ha.

The great chief of the Shawnee nation, smarting over his failure to destroy the dreaded Wolf Demon, panted eagerly for the opportunity to lead his warriors against the pale-faces.

Girty recounted to the chief all that he had learned regarding the strength of the settlers—knowledge that he had gained in his recent scout to the other side of the Ohio.

The chief listened with a gloomy brow. His plan to surprise the whites had failed.

"Since we can not creep upon them like the fox, our attack shall be like the swoop of the eagle," Ke-ne-ha-ha said, at length.

"The chief will attack Point Pleasant first?" Girty asked.

"Yes; we will cross the Ohio above the pale-face lodges; then my warriors shall form a circle around the long-knives, reaching from river to river. The circle shall be a line of fire, breathing death to the pale-face that dares to attempt to cross it."

"And the expedition will move to-night?"

"Yes; I have dispatched my fleetest runners to my brothers, the Wyandots and the Mingoes, telling them that the war-hatchet is dug up, and that, like the storm cloud, the red-men are about to burst in arrows of fire upon the pale-faces, and drive them from the land that the Great Spirit gave to the Indian."

"I will prepare at once for the expedition," Girty said, in savage glee, his soul gloating over the prospect of slaughter. Then he withdrew from the wigwam.

As Girty proceeded in the direction of his own lodge he met Kendrick.

"Blood ahead, hey?" Kendrick said, as they met.

"Yes; to-night we take up the line of march."

"And where are you going now?"

"To see my captive."

"What are you going to do with the gal?"

"Make her my prey," Girty said, and a look of savage triumph came over his dark face as he spoke.

"That's your vengeance, hey?"

"Yes. What wrong can rankle more keenly in the breast of General Treveling than the knowledge that his cherished daughter is my slave, the creature of my will?" said Girty, fiercely.

"You're a good hater," Kendrick said, with a grin.

"Yes, or my hate would not have lasted all these years. Why, man, I hate this Treveling as bitterly now as I did years ago when the lashes cut into my back. I swore once that I would have his life, but that is poor and paltry vengeance compared to that I have heaped upon his head. First I stole his eldest daughter—then a mere child—and left her to perish in the forest, and now I have taken his other daughter from him. The second blow is worse than the first, for death is far better than the fate that is in store for Virginia."

"I s'pose you'll let him know in some way of what you've done?" Kendrick said.

"He already knows that the death of his eldest daughter lies at my door; knows, too, that I have carried off this one, but he does not yet know the fate that I have marked out for her," Girty replied.

For a moment Kendrick was silent; then he suddenly broke into a loud laugh.

"Why do you laugh?" asked Girty, in astonishment.

"You've fixed this matter out all straight, hain't you?"

"Yes, I think so."

"S'pose a bullet from one of the settlers' long rifles should interfere with this hyer cunning plan, hey?"

"The bullet is not yet run that is to kill me," rejoined Girty, sternly.

"Not afeard, hey?"

"Not a whit."

"Got a 'big medicine?' as the Injuns say."

"I do not fear death; that is my 'medicine,'" Girty replied, carelessly.

"Well, I wish I was as sure of not going under as you are," Kendrick observed, with a grin.

"By the way, where is your daughter?" Girty asked.

"Inside the wigwam with the little gal," Kendrick answered.

"I think I'll visit the girl and let her know the fate that is in store for her."

"You'll find my gal inside," Kendrick said.

"I'll be out in a few minutes; wait for me."

Then Girty entered the wigwam that held Virginia a prisoner.

As Kendrick had said, Kate was there in attendance on the captive.

143

"Leave us for a little while, girl; I want to speak to the lady alone," Girty said.

Without a word, Kate left the wigwam.

Captor and captive were face to face.

The loathing that swelled in the heart of the girl was plainly visible in her face as she looked upon the man who had betrayed her into the hands of the savages.

"Do you know who I am, girl?" Girty asked.

"You are Girty, the renegade," Virginia answered, calmly, though every vein was throbbing with indignation.

"You are right. I am Girty, and the settlers call me the renegade."

"Yet I can hardly believe that you are that dreadful man."

"Why not?"

"Because you have the face of a human, and his should be the face of a wolf."

Girty scowled, ominously, at the words.

"Keep your tongue within bounds, or it may be the worse for you. Do you know where you are?"

"Yes, a prisoner in your hands," Virginia answered, with a look of settled despair.

"Do you know what your fate is going to be?"

"Death by some dreadful torture, I suppose."

"No, your guess is wrong; you are not fated to die yet. Were you the captive of the Shawnees it is probable that you would die at the torture-stake; but you are my prisoner; no red brave holds your fate in his hands."

"If report speaks true, I am the prisoner, then, of a man whose nature is more cruel than that of the Indian," said Virginia, with spirit.

"I am merciless to those that brave my anger," retorted Girty, with a lowering frown.

"And how have I ever wronged you?" asked Virginia, in wonder.

"You have never wronged me."

"Why then have you torn me from home and friends?"

"You are the daughter of General Treveling?"

"Yes."

"I hate your father. Through you I strike at him. You are dearer to him than even life itself. A blow dealt at you also wounds him. That is the reason why I have lured you from the settlement." Fierce was the tone in which Girty uttered the words, and a demon look of triumph gleamed in his dark eyes.

Virginia listened in wonder. She had often heard her father speak of the renegade, but always as a stranger.

"How has my father ever injured you?" she asked.

144

"How?" demanded Girty, in rising wrath. "The cut of his lash has scarred my back. It happened long years ago, but the memory is as fresh in my brain as though it were but yesterday. I swore a bitter oath of vengeance. Years have come and gone, but at last I strike, and the blow must reach him through you."

"This is a manly vengeance!" exclaimed Virginia, while her lip curled in scorn. "If my father has wronged you, why not seek him? Why select a helpless woman as your victim? Is it because you are too cowardly to face my father?"

"Taunt on; you will repent these words in scalding tears ere long," said Girty, calmly.

"They speak truth in the settlement when they say that you are like the wolf, both cruel and cowardly."

"And before another week is gone, they will say, too, that like the wolf, I love blood, for I will have rivers of it!" cried Girty, savagely.

Virginia's heart sunk within her as she looked upon the angry face of the renegade.

"And now your fate; can you guess what it is to be?" he asked.

"No," Virginia answered.

"You're to be mine—my slave. This is the vengeance that will scar your father's heart and make him curse the hour when he dared to wrong me!" Triumph swelled in the voice of the renegade as he spoke.

Virginia—hapless maid—felt that she was lost indeed.

"Oh! why can I not die at once?" she murmured, in despair.

The renegade gazed upon his victim with a smile of triumph.

"First my vengeance, and then death can come to your aid as soon as fate pleases. It will be rare joy for me to tell your father of the shame that has come upon you. It is almost worth waiting for all these years."

"You are a wolf, indeed," Virginia murmured, slowly.

"And who has made me so?" demanded the renegade, fiercely. "Your father! His act drove me from the white cabins to the wigwams of the savage; made me an outcast from my race; a white Indian. May the lightning of the Eternal strike me dead if I ever forget or forgive the injury that he has done me. Even now—after all these years—the memory of my wrong is as fresh in my brain as though it happened but yesterday."

In a torrent of passion came the words from the lips of the angry man.

Virginia shuddered at his manner.

"You have no pity?" she cried.

"Pity? No!" he said, with fierce accent. "Can pity dwell in the heart of the wolf? Your father has made me what I now am. Let him blame himself if the wolf he has created rends his child."

"I am entirely lost," Virginia murmured, faintly.

"And now I go to take the war-path against the settlement—to crimson with blood the waters of the Ohio. I will give to the flames the cabins of the whites; the smoke of the burning dwellings shall mark my course and attest my vengeance. When I return, then—Well, my revenge will be made complete. Let no vain thought of escape cross your mind, for I shall leave you doubly guarded. There is no power on this earth that can save you from me. Prepare, then, to meet your fate with resignation. For the present, farewell."

Then the miscreant left the lodge.

CHAPTER XXXII.

A STRANGE STORY.

In a tangled mass of bushes, near to the hollow oak that the three scouts had selected as a meeting-place, Boone and Kenton lay concealed.

They were waiting for the return of Lark.

"Strange, what can keep him?" muttered Boone, impatiently.

"Haven't you seen him at all?" Kenton asked.

"No, not since we parted."

"It must be past twelve."

"Perhaps he's been captivated by the red heathens," Boone suggested.

"That is possible," Kenton replied.

"Shall we wait any longer?"

"Just as you say."

"Hello! what's that?" cried Boone, suddenly.

The scout's attention had been attracted by a slight noise in the wood beyond the little glade.

Eagerly the two listened.

Then, through the wood, with stealthy steps, came a dark form.

It passed close to where the two whites lay in ambush.

Cold drops of sweat stood, bead-like, upon the foreheads of the two scouts as they looked upon the dark form.

It was the Wolf Demon that was stealing so stealthily through the wood.

"Jerusalem! did you see it?" muttered Boone, with a shiver, after the terrible form had disappeared in the shadows of the wood.

"Yes," replied Kenton, in a solemn tone.

"What do you think it is?"

"It's a spook, and no mistake," Kenton said, with a shake of the head.

"Well, it does look like it, don't it?" Boone rejoined, sagely.

"Yes. Why, they wouldn't believe this if we were to tell it in the station."

"That's truth; but seein' is believin', you know."

"I think we may as well be going," said Kenton, with a nervous shiver, and a stealthy look around, as though he expected to see a demon form in every bush.

"And not wait for Lark?"

"What's the use? It will be morning soon. Ten to one he has missed us and taken the back track to the station."

"Yes, that is likely. Let's be going, then," coincided Boone.

The two, carefully emerging from their covert in the bushes, crossed the little glade and passed in front of the hollow oak.

As they passed the tree, Kenton, who was a little in the advance, halted suddenly and placed his hand in alarm upon the arm of Boone.

"What's the matter?" asked Boone, quickly, in a cautious whisper.

"Look there," Kenton said, in the same low, guarded tone, and, as he spoke, he pointed to the ground before him.

Boone, with straining eyes, looked in the direction indicated by the out-stretched hand of his companion.

On the earth before them was stretched a dark form.

Carefully, rigid as two statues, the two scouts examined it.

"What do you think?" said Kenton, in a whisper.

"It's a man, I think."

"Can it be another victim of the Wolf Demon?"

"P'haps so; let's examine it," said Boone.

Then the two, stealing forward with stealthy steps, knelt by the side of the senseless form. It was a man attired in the forest garb of deer-skin. He was lying with his face downward.

The scouts turned him over, and then a cry of surprise broke from their lips.

The man was Abe Lark.

"Lark, by hookey!" exclaimed Boone, in wonder.

"And hurt, too!" cried Kenton.

"It 'pears so."

Then carefully they searched for the wound.

The search was fruitless. Lark was unhurt.

The two scouts looked at each other in wonder.

"Nary wound," said Boone, tersely.

"What on yearth is the meaning of it?" questioned Kenton.

Boone shook his head in doubt.

Lark's face was as white as the face of the dead, excepting that part where the crimson scar traversed it.

Large drops of sweat stood upon the forehead of the senseless man, and he breathed heavily, as if in pain. The veins, too, of the forehead were swollen out like whipcords. All gave evidence of great agony.

"What shall we do?" asked Kenton, puzzled.

"First, get him out of this faint," replied Boone.

"What do you suppose is the matter with him?"

"It looks like a fit," Boone said, thoughtfully. "P'haps he's seen that awful figure, and the spook cast a spell upon him."

To the superstitious minds of the borderers this seemed a reasonable explanation.

"If I only had a little water now," said Boone, looking around him as if in search of some friendly spring.

"I've got a little flask of whisky," and Kenton produced it from an inside pocket of his hunting-shirt as he spoke.

"That will do fust-rate, but it's kinder of a shame to waste good liquor," said Boone, with a comical grin, as he proceeded to bathe the forehead of the senseless man with the whisky.

In a few moments a low groan came from the lips of Lark. Then a convulsive shudder shook his massive frame.

"He's coming to," said Kenton, who was anxiously watching the face of Lark.

"I knew the whisky would fetch him," Boone remarked.

Lark's eyes opened slowly, and with a bewildered expression, like one in a maze, he gazed into the faces of the men who knelt by his side.

"What the deuce is the matter with my head?" he muttered.

It was evident that his senses were still in a maze.

"He don't know you," said Kenton, in a whisper, to Boone.

"No," replied the other, in the same guarded tone; "he hain't fully recovered yet; hain't got his mind right."

Then again Lark, whose eyes had wandered off listlessly in the forest, looked into the face of the man who bent so earnestly over him.

A gleam of recognition came over Lark's features. Feebly he raised his hand to his head and passed it across his forehead, as if by the act to call back his scattered senses.

"Kurnel Boone," he murmured.

"Yours to command," replied Boone, with a hearty press of Lark's hand that lay by his side.

"And Kenton, too," Lark continued.

"Right to an iota," returned the borderer.

"What on yearth has been the matter with me?" and Lark, with the assistance of Boone, rose to a sitting posture as he spoke.

"That is what bothers us," Boone said. "We have been waiting for you to come for some time, as agreed upon; and at last, growing tired of waiting, we concluded either that you had been taken prisoner by the Shawnees, or else that you had returned to the station, having missed us in the forest in some way."

A puzzled look appeared upon Lark's face.

"I can't understand it," he muttered, in doubt.

"Understand what?" Boone asked.

"Why, how I came to be here."

149

Both Boone and Kenton looked at Lark in amazement.

"Don't you know?" Boone asked.

"No," Lark replied.

"Ain't you hurt in some way?"

"Not as I knows on."

"Have you seen any thing terrible for to skeer you?" and the old hunter glanced nervously around as he spoke, as though he expected to see the dreaded wood demon by his side.

"No," again replied Lark.

"Well, where have you been?"

"I don't know."

Again the two scouts stared at their companion in amazement.

"You don't know?" Boone questioned, in wonder.

"No; I can't remember any thing about it."

"What have you been doing since we parted?"

"I can't tell you that, either," replied Lark, evidently as greatly puzzled as the other two.

"Can't tell?"

"No. I can remember parting with you here some hours ago, and making the agreement to meet you here again. Then I struck off into the forest, intending to scout into the Indian village."

"Yes."

"And that is all I can remember."

"You don't remember what you did after that?"

"Not a thing about it," Lark replied, decidedly.

"Why, that was hours ago. I've been a prisoner in the hands of the Shawnees, and escaped from them, too, in that time," Boone said.

"I can not explain; it is all a blank to me," Lark replied.

"Perhaps you were taken with a fit?" suggested Kenton.

"Perhaps so."

"But where have you kept yourself?—for I'll swear that you wasn't hyer thirty minutes ago," Boone said, decidedly.

"I can't understand it in the least," Lark replied, rising to his feet as he spoke.

"Well, it's the most mysterious affair that I ever heerd of," Boone added, with a doubtful shake of the head. "How do you feel—weak?"

"No, as strong and as well as I ever was."

"It sounds just like one of the old hobgoblin stories that my father used to tell by the fire on a winter's night," Boone said, thoughtfully. "I allers thought that they were all lies, but this story of yours is as strange as any of them."

"It beats me," Kenton observed.

"Well, let's be going."
And following Boone's lead, they proceeded on their way.

CHAPTER XXXIII.

A STRANGE ATTACK.

For a few minutes in silence the three proceeded on through the forest. Boone was in the advance, Kenton followed, and Lark brought up the rear.

Suddenly, Lark spoke.

"Hold on a minute, kurnel."

Astonished, both Boone and Kenton halted.

The party were just crossing a little glade, whereon the moonbeams brightly fell.

As the two turned to Lark, they noticed that his face was deadly pale—even whiter and more corpse-like than when he was stretched senseless upon the sward. His lips were moving convulsively.

"What's the matter, Abe?" asked Boone, in alarm.

"I don't know," said Lark, in guttural tones, and speaking with evident difficulty.

Boone and Kenton exchanged glances of astonishment.

"Don't you feel well?" Boone asked.

"No. I—I am deathly sick," and, as the words came from his lips, Lark sunk heavily to the earth.

Alarmed, his two companions knelt by his side.

"Jerusalem! You're tuck bad," said Boone, bending over the fallen man.

"My strength is all leaving me," murmured Lark, in anguish.

"And hain't you been hurt at all?" asked Kenton, who could not understand this strange sickness.

"No," murmured Lark, speaking with great difficulty.

"Have you ever had one of these spells before?" said Boone, fully as much puzzled as his brother scout to account for Lark's strange illness.

"Yes," replied Lark, feebly.

"Oh, you have?"

"Yes."

"Well, what shall we do for you?" Boone felt a little relieved in his mind by Lark's words.

"Take me and bind me to the trunk of the largest tree that there is near here."

"Why?" cried Boone, in astonishment at the strange request.

"Bind you to a tree!" exclaimed Kenton, in amazement.

"Yes," replied Lark.

"Jerusalem! That's odd treatment for a sick man," said Boone.

"It is the only way to treat my sickness," replied Lark, in a husky voice.

"You ar'n't in earnest?"

"Yes."

Boone could hardly believe his hearing.

"Tie you to a tree?"

"Yes, and it must be a stout one," murmured Lark.

"A stout one?"

"Yes, one that I can not pull up."

"Pull up!" exclaimed both Boone and Kenton, in a breath.

"Yes," replied Lark, his breath coming thick and hard, like the breath of a hunted animal.

"Pull up a tree! Why, you ain't got strength enough now to pull up a blackberry bush," said Boone.

"That is true," murmured Lark, hoarsely; "but in a few minutes I shall have the strength of a giant."

Again Boone and Kenton looked at each other in wonder.

"This is a riddle!" cried Boone.

"Do not waste time in trying to guess it," gasped Lark, hoarsely, "but, if you are friends of mine, do as I wish before it is too late."

"Too late!"

"Yes, a few minutes more and it will be too late. I have had these attacks before, but never until this one did I guess what the result of the attack would be. But, now, Heaven has permitted me to have a knowledge of the truth." Lark spoke with great difficulty, and white froth began to gather at the corners of his mouth.

The two scouts looked upon the pain-distorted face of their companion in horror.

"What on yearth is the matter with you?" exclaimed Boone.

"Can't you guess? Don't you see it in my face?" Lark gasped, in torture. "I am going mad."

"Mad!" cried both the scouts, and they recoiled a step or two in horror.

"Yes mad," moaned Lark, in agony. "I can feel the madness creeping over me; tie me to a tree, else I may injure you or myself."

"I'll do it!" cried Boone, impulsively. "Come, Kenton, give me a hand!"

Then the two carried the helpless man to the foot of a stout oak that grew by the side of the clearing.

With thongs cut from Lark's hunting-shirt they bound him securely to the tree. They placed him in an upright position against the trunk of the oak.

"There, can we do any thing else for you?" asked Boone, after the tying had been completed.

"No, except to remain near at hand and watch me. The attack will not last long," Lark replied. It was with great difficulty that he spoke at all.

The scouts withdrew a short distance, and sitting down in the bushes, watched their friend that they had bound so securely.

The moonbeams came down full on the head of the bound man—upon the massive head that drooped so listlessly upon the shoulder.

For fully ten minutes Boone and Kenton watched, and Lark gave no sign of life.

Face and figure seemed alike a part of the tree.

"I say, kurnel," said Kenton, in a cautious whisper, "what do you think of it?"

"Well, I don't know," replied Boone, slowly; "it's a most wonderful affair. That a critter should be able to tell aforehand that he was going to have a mad spell and want himself tied up. Why, I never heerd of any thing like it."

"He ain't moved yet," said Kenton, still watching Lark, intently.

"P'haps he ain't going mad after all?" suggested Boone.

"Or, it may be that he ain't quite right in his mind now, and the idea of his going mad is only one of the strange fancies that sick people have sometimes?" queried Kenton.

"That's sound sense," rejoined Boone, thoughtfully.

Then a slight movement of Lark's head put a stop to the conversation of the two scouts, and eagerly they watched the man bound so tightly to the tree-trunk.

Lark raised his head slowly. By the light of the moonbeams the two watchers could plainly see that it was deathly pale. But they also noted a change in the face. The eyes, which before had been lusterless and half-closed, were now opened wide, and, seemingly, strained to their fullest extent. They glared like eyes of fire—shone more like the eyes of a wild beast than the orbs of a human.

"Look at his eyes!" said Boone, in a cautious whisper.

"They look as if they would pierce through a fellow!" observed Kenton, in a tone of awe.

Carefully and searchingly Lark glared around him as if to discover whether he was watched or not.

Then he essayed to move from the tree, but the bonds that bound his hands and feet to the tree-trunk restrained him.

In amazement Lark looked down upon the fetters that impeded his action.

"His memory's clean gone," said Boone, in Kenton's ear.

"I do believe he is mad now," observed Kenton, in a tone of conviction.

"Yes, but look at him."

Lark was carefully surveying the bonds that bound him to the tree.

A moment or two his eyes glared upon the leathern fetters, and then, with a desperate effort, he essayed to break them.

The veins on his forehead knotted and swelled as he tugged with almost superhuman strength, but the effort was useless. He could not free himself.

"Jerusalem! ain't that strength thar!" muttered Boone, as he watched the tension of the thongs.

"They're going to hold him, though," replied Kenton, eagerly watching the strange scene.

Again Lark glared around him, and again he tried to burst the bonds that bound him.

The thongs cut into the flesh of the wrists, but he seemed not to heed the pain. Every muscle in his huge frame was brought into play.

Another mighty effort and the leathern thong burst as if it had only been a band of straw!

"Talk about a giant—did you see that thong go?" exclaimed Boone, in a guarded tone to Kenton.

"He snapped it like a pipe-stem."

No look of triumph appeared upon Lark's face as he felt that his hands were free—only the look of fierce, settled determination.

Again he glanced around the little opening as if in search of watchers; then he proceeded to untie the lashings that bound his feet to the tree.

In a few minutes the thongs dropped to the ground, and Lark was at liberty.

He stepped from the side of the oak and drew himself up proudly to the moonbeams, as if rejoicing that he was free. All traces of his former feebleness had disappeared.

The two scouts watched his movements with anxiety.

Lark, pausing in the center of the little opening, fumbled for a moment at his girdle.

"He's looking for a we'pon," said Boone, in a whisper.

"Yes, it looks like it," replied Kenton.

Then from his girdle Lark drew a keen-edged scalping-knife. He tried the edge of the blade and the point, carefully, upon his finger; then, with a grim smile of satisfaction, he replaced the knife in his girdle.

Slowly, with cautious steps, Lark stole across the glade, but on the borders of the wood he halted—paused for a moment, irresolute, and then his strength seemed to fail him. A deep groan of anguish came from his lips.

He tottered for a moment, as though striving by the mere force of his will to keep his feet; then, with another groan, deeper and more agonizing than the first, he fell heavily to the ground.

Quickly Boone and Kenton left their covert in the thicket, and hastened to his side.

Again he lay in a swoon, senseless, as before; the swollen veins marked the white forehead, and the waxy drops of perspiration formed a strange contrast.

CHAPTER XXXIV.

THE RETURN TO POINT PLEASANT.

"Now I know what was the matter with him before!" cried Boone, as he knelt by Lark's side.

"One of these fits, eh?"

"Yes."

Slowly Lark's scattered senses came back to him. With a vacant look he gazed into the faces of the two men who knelt by his side.

"By hookey, you've had a rough time of it," said Boone.

"I have been out of my head, then?"

"Yes, mad as a March hare," replied the borderer.

"Just look at the strips of deer-skin," said Kenton, pointing to the severed pieces lying at the foot of the oak. "You bu'st 'em just as if they had been paper."

"I feel weak enough now," said Lark, sadly.

"No wonder!" exclaimed Boone, "you've used up all your strength. Jerusalem! I thought you'd pull the oak over. I shouldn't like to have a tussle with you when you're in one of them queer fits like you had just now."

Aided by his companions, Lark rose slowly to his feet.

"I say, Abe, have you any idea what it is that makes you act so queer?" Kenton asked.

"Yes; do you see this scar?" and Lark pointed to the terrible, livid mark that disfigured his face.

"Of course," Kenton replied.

"The wound that made that scar is the cause of it; that is, I think it is. The wound affected my head. I have never been the same man since."

"It's a mighty strange thing," said Boone, wonderingly.

"Yes; I've had these spells before. I can always tell when they are coming on. I have a strange, burning sensation in my head; everything before my eyes is tinged with red; the blood races like wildfire through my veins, then all my senses leave me. I can remember nothing."

"How did you receive the wound?" Boone asked.

"In an Indian fight. After it was given me I lay for days between life and death. I escaped death, but the dark cloud of madness follows me."

"Well, it's the queerest story that I ever did hear tell of," said Boone, sagely.

"How do you feel now?" asked Kenton.

157

"Oh, much better," replied Lark.

"Strong enough for to go on?"

"Yes."

"Let's be making tracks, then."

Carefully and cautiously the three proceeded through the thicket.

No hostile Indians barred their course, and by the time the sun reached the meridian, the three entered the stockade that fenced Point Pleasant.

Warm was the greeting that they received from the settlers, but many a sun-bronzed cheek grew pale, and many a stout heart beat quick when the scouts told the story of Ke-ne-ha-ha's expedition.

It was sad news indeed to the hardy borderers when they learned that the great Shawnee chieftain had dug up the war-hatchet, and would soon bring his painted warriors—hot for slaughter—to the banks of the Ohio.

Then, too, for the first time, Boone heard the story of the strange disappearance of General Treveling's daughter, Virginia.

The rage of the old Indian-fighter knew no bounds when he heard that the renegade, Girty, had abducted the girl.

"The eternal villain!" he cried, in wrath, "let me draw 'bead' on him once, and he'll never carry off any other white gal to give to the painted devils that he calls his brothers."

The party headed by Jake Jackson, who had been in search of traces of the missing girl, had returned to Point Pleasant just before the arrival of the three scouts. Their search had been fruitless; no traces of the missing girl had they discovered.

"I'll tell you what it is, General," said Boone to the aged father, whose sad countenance showed plainly his deep grief, "thar ain't any use of looking for the gal, or that 'tarnal villain either, in the timber 'bout hyer. He's made tracks long ago for the Injun settlement by the banks of the Scioto, Chillicothe, as the red heathens call it."

"But, colonel, can nothing be done to rescue her?" asked the aged father, in despair.

"Why, General, you see it's a bad time for to do any thing. Within twenty-four hours the Injuns will be around us thick as bees round a hive. We'll have our hands full to attend to the savages and keep their paws off our top-knots. I feel right bad for you, General, but you know our first duty is to the helpless she-critters and young 'uns hyer. We can't let 'em be massacred right afore our eyes, you know. We've got to whip the red devils fust; then we'll do what we can toward saving your little gal."

"You are right, Boone," said the old soldier, sadly; "the safety of the whole settlement can not be put in peril for the sake of my private grief. I must bow in submission to the will of Heaven, though my affliction is sore."

"General, I feel for you, but duty you know is duty," said Boone, slowly.

"Heaven forbid that I should say a single word to swerve you from the path of duty. I am too old a soldier to counsel you to do wrong," said the old man, quickly.

"Besides, General, I think about the best blow that we can strike for your daughter's rescue is to whip the red heathens that are coming ag'in' us. When we drive 'em back, then we can follow them up, and perhaps be able to snake the little gal out of their hands." Boone was trying by his words to lift the weight of sorrow that pressed so heavily upon the heart of the old soldier.

The father shook his head sorrowfully. He had little hope of ever seeing his daughter again.

He knew the nature of the red-men well. If defeated in their attack on the station, they would be apt in their rage to avenge their defeat by giving any helpless prisoner that might be in their hands to the fiery torture of death at the stake. No wonder that the father's heart was sad.

"How many men have come in, Jake?" questioned the old hunter.

"We've got nigh onto two hundred, all told," replied the sturdy Indian-fighter.

"Well, we ought to be able to whip a thousand of the red-skins, easy," said Boone, in a confident tone. "Do you expect any more, Jake?"

"Not above half a dozen, kurnel; we've drawn 'bout all our men in now," Jackson replied.

"Set the women to running bullets, and get plenty of water inside the stockade. The red heathens may make a siege of it," said Boone.

"Everything has been fixed, kurnel."

"That's pert. Now, Jake, I guess we three had better take a little rest. We've been everlastingly tramping through the timber. Throw out some scouts up the river to watch for the red devils. After I've had an hour's nap I'll take to the woods myself."

Then Boone went to his cabin; he was followed by Kenton and Lark.

"I wonder what's the matter with the stranger; did you notice how pale he looked?" Jackson said, referring to Lark.

"Wal—yes, I did," replied one of the settlers, who stood by Jackson's side. "I reckon they've had a putty tough tramp onto it. Maybe, though, some on us will look white afore we git through with Ke-ne-ha-ha and his Shawnees."

Many an anxious face in the little group of men that surrounded Jackson testified to the truth of the speaker's guess.

In the cabin the three scouts stretched themselves upon the bear-skins spread upon the floor, and soon were in the land of dreams.

The hour's nap of Boone had lasted some four hours, and the shades of evening were beginning to gather thick about the settlement when the old borderer awoke.

Boone rubbed his eyes and indulged in a prolonged yawn.

"Jerusalem! my eyes feel as if they were full of sticks," he muttered.

Then Boone cast his eyes through the little window that lit up the cabin, to the sky.

"It's late, too, by hookey!" he cried. "It's time for us to be on the look-out, for the red devils will probably try to cross the Ohio some time after dark."

Then Boone laid his hand upon Kenton's shoulder.

The scout awoke instantly. His slumber was like the sleep of a cat.

"Time for our scout, Kenton," Boone said.

"All right; I'm on hand, kurnel. Shall I wake Lark?" Kenton asked.

The third one of the scouts was still buried in heavy slumbers.

"Yes; he'll be mad if we go without him, or at least, I know I would be," said Boone, with a chuckle. The stout hearted borderer welcomed danger as he would an early friend.

"All right; I'll wake him, then."

Kenton laid his hand upon Lark's shoulder, but the sleeper stirred not.

"Shake him a little," suggested Boone.

Kenton did so, but the sleeping man never stirred.

"He's laying himself right down to it, ain't he?" said Boone, with a dry humor in his voice.

"Hadn't we better go without him?" asked Kenton.

"Try once more. He's the soundest sleeper that I ever did see," Boone said.

Again Kenton shook the sleeping man, and this time violently, but the effort was useless; Lark never moved.

Kenton bent over and examined him.

"He ain't a-breathin' right," the scout said, in some little alarm.

"Has he got another fit?" asked Boone, quickly.

"Well, it looks like it. His teeth are clenched together, and he's breathing like a quarter-horse."

Boone knelt by Kenton's side and bent over Lark.

A moment's examination convinced Boone that there was something the matter with his companion.

Lark's breath came thick and hard.

"Another spell, by thunder!" muttered Boone, as, with Kenton, he bent over the unconscious man.

Then, suddenly, as though moved by some secret spring, Lark's eyes opened. He stared into the faces of the two that bent over him, but his eyes were like eyes of glass; there was no life therein.

Like men in a trance, Boone and Kenton gazed into the white face and the great, staring eyes.

There was something in the face that seemed to chill the very blood coursing in their veins.

For a moment Lark stared with meaningless eyes at the two, and they, fixed as statues, horrified, they knew not at what, returned the look.

Then, with a sudden start, and apparently with the strength of a giant playing in his muscles, Lark sprung to his feet.

As he rose, he came in violent contact with Boone and Kenton, and the sudden shock hurled them to the floor as though they had been two children.

When he had gained his feet, Lark cast a rapid glance around him, passed his hand mechanically across his forehead, and then, with a stealthy step, like unto a wild beast crawling in upon its prey, he left the cabin.

For a moment Boone and Kenton, seated upon the floor where they had fallen, looked at each other in speechless astonishment.

"If he ain't mad, I'm a catfish!" cried Kenton.

"Let's foller him; he may do some one a mischief!" exclaimed Boone. Then, with eager haste, they followed Lark.

CHAPTER XXXV.

THE PRICE OF LE-A-PAH'S HAND.

The shades of night descended upon the village of Chillicothe, yet the plumed and painted warriors headed by Ke-ne-ha-ha went not forth upon their expedition against the whites on the banks of the Ohio.

The red chieftain fumed and chafed like a caged lion. His allies, the Wyandots and the Mingoes, had sent word that they could not move their forces for three days, and so, despite his desire for war, he was compelled to remain inactive.

The wily sachem knew full well that he could accomplish nothing unless he came down upon his foes in overwhelming numbers.

Ke-ne-ha-ha had faced the deadly fire of the white rifles on many a bloody field. He had felt the prowess of the hardy bordermen, and had learned to respect it. No hot-headed boy was he, to rashly dare the power of the white-skins, without a force far superior to their own.

And so he waited, and while he waited—furious as the angry bear cheated of his prey—he called down the curses of the Great Spirit upon the heads of the slow-moving chiefs, his allies.

He paced restlessly up and down the narrow confines of his wigwam.

"The chiefs of the Wyandots and the Mingoes are like turtles; they should have houses on their backs. A warrior should be like the eagle or the hawk—swift as the forked light of the Great Spirit. The white-skins must know that the red-men will soon take the war-path against them. The great chief, Boone, has long ears. Like a fox he crept into the Shawnee village; he will carry back to his people the news that the red warriors are arming for the fight."

The meditations of the chief were interrupted by the entrance of his daughter, Le-a-pah.

The features of the chieftain softened as he looked upon the handsome face of his only child.

"May Le-a-pah speak with her father, the great chief?" asked the girl, with a timid smile.

"The heart of the father is always open to the words of his child," replied the chief, drawing the little form of the girl to him as he spoke, and smoothing back the dark masses of ebon hair from her low forehead.

"Will my father be angry if Le-a-pah speaks straight?" and the girl looked shyly into her father's face as she spoke.

"Let my daughter speak; the chief will not be angry at his singing-bird, because her tongue is not forked," said Ke-ne-ha-ha, tenderly.

"My father is the great chief of the Shawnee nation; will my father be angry if his child has looked upon a young brave with loving eyes?"

An earnest look the chief cast into his daughter's face.

"The singing-bird wishes to leave her father, then?"

"Did not the mother of the singing-bird leave her father when she came to sing in the lodge of the great chief?" the maiden asked, shyly.

"My daughter speaks straight. It is the course of nature. The leaf falls from the tree and seeks the embrace of the earth. What is the name of the chief in whose wigwam Le-a-pah would sing?"

"He is only a young brave," began the girl, timidly.

"Youth is not a crime," interrupted the chief; "nor would I give my child to a brave whose hairs are like the snow in color. Spring should not sit in the lap of Winter, else her blood will be chilled into ice—it is bad."

"The young brave is not yet a great warrior, but he has a heart as big as a bear, and no white plume is bound up in his scalp-locks. He will be a great chief when years come heavy upon his head," said the girl, cheered by the encouraging words of the great chief.

"Let my daughter speak his name, and then Ke-ne-ha-ha will know how to answer," said the father.

"He is called the White Dog," and then the girl gazed anxiously into her father's face, but the face of the chief was like a face of marble; not a muscle moved as the name of his daughter's lover fell upon his ears. Even the keen womanly instinct of Le-a-pah, now made doubly keen by the fires of love burning so intensely in her bosom, could not detect whether her father was pleased or displeased.

"The young warrior that captured the great white fighting-man, Boone?" said the chief, slowly.

The heart of the girl leaped for joy; she thought the speech of her father an omen of good.

"Yes," she replied, joyously, and the warm blood leaped freely into her cheeks.

"The young brave is very young," said the chief, gravely. But the heart of the girl could not be deceived. Her heart had told her that her father approved of her choice.

"Le-a-pah is young, too," replied the girl.

"The chief is new on the war-path."

"Yet, alone he grappled with the great white hunter, and brought him to the earth. What other red warrior has ever done the like?"

A grim smile crept over the stern features of the chief as he listened to the unanswerable words of the girl.

163

"My daughter is as wise as the fox—she speaks for her lover as stoutly as the she-wolf fights for her young."

"The great chief is not angry at Le-a-pah because she speaks for the man she loves?"

"No; it is the blood of Ke-ne-ha-ha running in the veins of Le-a-pah that bids her speak."

"My father will then give his consent that the young chief shall claim Le-a-pah as his own?"

"Ke-ne-ha-ha will then be alone in the world. The Red Arrow, his eldest joy, lies beneath the big oaks that sway their leafy branches in the woods of the Scioto valley. It is the will of the Great Spirit—the chief will not murmur at it."

"Then Le-a-pah may go and sing in the lodge of the young warrior, and make glad his heart?" asked the girl, her heart swelling with joy.

"Yes—on one condition," replied the chief.

"And what is that?" asked the girl, puzzled.

"The chief must first know. If he accepts the condition and performs the service asked, then Le-a-pah shall be his wife, and Ke-ne-ha-ha will himself give her into his hands."

The look of joy upon the face of the girl amply repaid the father for his kindly words.

"Ke-ne-ha-ha too is growing old. In years to come he will be too old to lead the Shawnee warriors to battle. His feet will be feeble upon the warpath and his sight will be dim. The Shawnees will select a new chief to lead them. Who so fit as the son-in-law of their old sachem, if Ke-ne-ha-ha lifts up his voice in his favor?"

The heart of the girl beat high with pride as she listened to the words of her father and thought of the future that looked so bright before her.

"Le-a-pah can not speak as she would, for her heart is too full."

"Let my daughter send the young chief to me. Ke-ne-ha-ha will tell him of the service that he must attempt in order to win the flower of the Shawnee tribe."

"It is a service of danger?" and a look of anxious fear swept over her dark face.

"If the flower is not worth the winning, no chieftain's hand shall ever pluck it from the parent stem," replied the father.

"The young brave will face a thousand deaths, Le-a-pah will pledge her life for it," said the girl, promptly, and then she left the wigwam.

In a few minutes the young warrior who aspired to the hand of the great chieftain's daughter stood within the lodge of the great chief.

Ke-ne-ha-ha cast a searching glance into the frank and open face of the young Indian. Therein he saw written both courage and skill.

"The young brave would have the daughter of Ke-ne-ha-ha to sing in his wigwam?"

"The chief speaks straight," replied the young warrior, firmly.

"The love of a pure girl is priceless; no treasure like it on the earth; it is the greatest blessing that Manitou ever gave to his red children. What will the young warrior give or do to win the singing bird?"

"He will give his life for Le-a-pah; do all possible things. Let the chief speak—tell of the service that he wishes the young warrior to do," said the Shawnee, promptly.

For a moment Ke-ne-ha-ha looked into the face of the young brave as though pondering upon the words that he was about to speak.

The warrior waited anxiously, impatient to know of the deed that he must do to win the girl that he loved so fondly.

"The chief has heard of the Wolf Demon?" asked Ke-ne-ha-ha.

"Yes," replied the warrior, and a look of dread crept over his face as he heard the name of the terrible scourge of the Shawnee nation.

"The paws of the Wolf Demon are red with the blood of my people. Many Shawnee warriors have fallen by the tomahawk of this terrible being. On their breasts he cuts his totem—a Red Arrow. Does the chief know why the totem of the Demon is a Red Arrow?"

"No," the warrior replied.

"The Red Arrow was the eldest daughter of Ke-ne-ha-ha—the sister of Le-a-pah. She left her tribe to dwell in the wigwam of a white stranger. Ke-ne-ha-ha followed and struck to the death the false girl who forsook her tribe. He killed also the white skin. The dead white was eaten up by a wolf, but the soul of the white-skin lived. It eat up the soul of the animal, and the beast became the Wolf Demon—a wolf with a human soul. The Wolf Demon can be killed. Ke-ne-ha-ha has grappled with him. He did not clutch air but substance. The human wolf can be struck to the death if the blow be given rightly."

The words of the great chief opened the eyes of the young brave. He guessed what the service was that the Shawnee chieftain wished at his hands.

"Let the great chief speak of the deed that must be done to win the hand of Le-a-pah."

"The human wolf can be killed—"

"Yes."

"Let my young brave try to kill the Wolf Demon. If he draws one drop of blood from the scourge of the Shawnees, he shall have the daughter of Ke-ne-ha-ha."

A look of fierce determination settled upon the face of the young warrior.

"The Shawnee warrior accepts the offer," he said, firmly. "He will seek for the Wolf Demon in the wood. He will search for him as the panther searches for the red chief that steals its cub. If mortal hands can take the life of the Shawnee terror, then he shall fall by the knife of the White Dog."

"It is good!" cried Ke-ne-ha-ha, and a look of satisfaction came over his face. "Let the young warrior perform the service and the great chief of the Shawnee nation will give him his child."

"The White Dog will seek the Wolf Demon at once."

Then the warrior turned upon his heel and left the wigwam.

CHAPTER XXXVI.

DEATH OR FREEDOM.

While the great Shawnee chieftain was stating to the anxious lover the condition that covered the gift of his daughter's hand, another strange life drama was being enacted in the Indian village.

Kendrick—the renegade—and his daughter—the Kanawha Queen—stood together by the wigwam that held in its confines the helpless prisoner, Virginia Treveling.

Before the door of the lodge sat a brawny Shawnee brave, placed there by Girty to watch the prisoner.

The dark-browed renegade had taken ample measures to hold his victim, securely, in his power.

First, Kate guarded the prisoner; second, the Indian warrior kept ward and watch.

No thought of the prisoner's escape ever crossed the mind of Girty. He, too, like the Shawnee chieftain, Ke-ne-ha-ha, chafed at the delay of the expedition against the whites.

The renegade was fully as eager as his red brother for the banquet of blood. He longed to see the smoke of the burning dwellings cloud the face of the sky, and to wet his knife in the warm life-blood.

Kendrick had just explained to his daughter the reasons that led to the delay of the expedition.

Kate listened attentively, her brain busy in thought.

"And when will the expedition move?" she asked.

"That's duberous, gal," he answered. "It all depends upon the Wyandots and the Mingoes. When they send their warriors, then we kin go ahead, but not till then."

"And my plan, father, to remove this girl from my path?"

"You had better carry it out right away," said the renegade, after thinking for a moment. "Thar'll be no better chance than at the present. I owe Girty a little balance, which I reckon this affair will settle. Instead of staying with his own tribe, the Wyandots, he's been sneakin' round hyer with the Shawnee. If it goes on, he'll have more influence hyer than I have, and I ain't a-goin' to stand that, nohow. So, gal, if you want any help to snake the gal out of his clutches, I'm the critter for to give it to you, and no mistake."

"I may need your aid, father," said the girl, thoughtfully.

"All right, you kin have it. I'd do most any thing to spite him."

"I think that it will be better to carry the girl off to-night. He may place her in some safer place to-morrow."

"Jest so; thar's no tellin'; he's as suspicious as a crow. It will worry him some to lose the gal," said Kendrick, with a grin.

"But the Indian sentry before the door of the wigwam?" and, with her eyes, Kate indicated the brawny warrior, who, seated before the lodge-door, was smoking a rude pipe, fashioned from a corn-stalk, with great satisfaction.

"Oh, I kin fix him easy 'nough," replied Kendrick.

"Then I will make the attempt at once," said Kate, decidedly.

"I'll fix the Injun. You go into the lodge. I'll talk to the chief and get him to leave his post for a moment. When he's gone, I'll cough; then, you slip out of the lodge with the gal and take to the timber. It ain't likely that they will be apt to discover that the gal is gone till morning."

"And by that time it will make very little difference whether it is discovered or not," said Kate, meaningly.

"Are you going to kill the gal?" asked Kendrick, speaking as coolly and as unconcerned as though it was the killing of some worthless beast that he referred to.

"Why should I let her live?" asked Kate, fiercely. "Is she not loved by the man whom I love better than I do any one else in this world?"

"But if you leave her hyer with Girty—"

"May she not escape from him?"

"That's true; but dead—"

"She can not return."

"That's true; ag'in."

"Once in the forest, dead, a prey to the wolves, she never more will rival me."

"Wal, I don't know but what I like it better that way myself. It'll worry Girty, and that will jest suit me," said Kendrick, thoughtfully.

"I'll enter the wigwam at once and prepare the girl."

"And arter you go in I'll tackle the Injun. I've got an idea for to git shet of him. When I cough, you'll know that he's out of the way, and that you kin fetch the little gal out."

So without further words, Kate left her father and entered the lodge. Kendrick waited until she was fairly inside, and then he walked, leisurely, to the Indian on guard and sat down by his side.

The brawny chief acknowledged the approach of the renegade with a nod of recognition.

"Ain't this kinder dull work for my brother?" asked the renegade.

"Ugh!" and the Indian gave vent to a grunt of dissatisfaction.

"You'd rather be on the war-path ag'in' the white-skins along the Ohio than to be hyer, a-keepin' watch over a squaw?"

"My brother speaks straight," said the Indian, in a surly tone, taking the pipe from his lips for a moment.

"Pity we can't go on the war-trail, hey?"

"Big pity," replied the chief, sententiously.

"My brother thinks much of his Wyandot brother, Girty?" said Kendrick, in a tone of question.

"His Wyandot brother is a great warrior," replied the chief, evidently not willing to commit himself by a decided answer.

"Wal, I judged that you thought a heap of him by being willing to do his watching, hyer," said Kendrick, suggestively.

"Girty is a great Wyandot chief, but the Shawnee brave is not his watch dog for love. The chief does a service, but the chief will be paid for it."

"Oho!" muttered Kendrick, to himself, "I reckon I know how the chief is a-going to be paid."

"My brother knows now that the Shawnee chief is to be paid for his service," said the Indian.

"No more than right," said Kendrick, heartily. "I heerd the other day that Girty got some corn-juice from a flat-boat that he captivated on the Ohio."

"Wah! it is good. The Shawnee brave is to have corn-juice in payment for his service."

"Wal, corn-juice ain't bad to take when it's good," said Kendrick, reflectively.

"It is good!" replied the warrior, decidedly.

"I wish my wigwam wasn't so far off," said Kendrick, with a sly look into the Indian's bronzed features as he spoke.

"Why does my brother wish that?" asked the chief.

"Wal I feel thirsty, and I've got some of the best corn-juice that you ever see'd in my wigwam, and I'm too 'tarnal lazy to go after it."

"It is bad," said the warrior, slowly, looking askance at the renegade.

"If my brother did not have to watch the wigwam he could go for the corn-juice and we would drink it together."

"My brother speaks straight."

"I'm sorry the chief can not go—"

"Why can not the chief go?" asked the Indian, within whose breast there had sprung up a desire to taste the precious fire-water of the renegade.

"Is he not watching the wigwam for his Wyandot brother Girty?"

"Can not the Shawnee chief go for the fire-water, and leave his Shawnee brother to watch the lodge?" asked the Indian.

Of course this was exactly what the shrewd renegade wished.

"My brother is as wise as the fox."

The Indian bowed at the compliment.

"Will my Shawnee brother go for the fire-water and leave me to watch the lodge?"

"My brother speaks good. The chief will go," and the Indian rose to his feet.

"The chief will find the corn-juice under a blanket near the door of the lodge."

The Indian bowed gravely, and departed.

"He'd smell it out, anyway," muttered Kendrick; "leave a red-skin alone for finding whisky, if thar's any around. They go for it quick es a coon does for a tall tree when the dogs are arter him. Now I'll jest warn Kate, so that she will know that the coast is clear. I reckon Girty will swear some when he finds that the gal has broke for tall timber," and the renegade chuckled in glee.

His fit of laughter over, he looked about him carefully. No one was in sight; so he cautiously gave the signal agreed upon between Kate and himself.

A few moments after the sound of the cough died away on the night air, Kate came cautiously from the wigwam, followed by Virginia.

"All right, gal," said the renegade, quickly. "The Injun's out of the way, but don't let grass grow under your feet between hyer and the Ohio. They may diskiver that you've cut your stick any moment."

"Do not worry, father; I know every foot of the ground between here and the river," replied the girl, a strange nervousness patent in her voice. "Come, lady; do not fear; before this night is over, you shall be free from danger."

"Thar ain't much danger in the grave," muttered the renegade between his teeth.

Then Kate led the way into the wood, and Virginia followed without a word.

The renegade watched them until the dark shadows of the forest closed around them and they were hid from his view.

"I reckon my little gal will fix her," muttered the renegade, in a tone of satisfaction.

Then a thought flushed suddenly across his mind. With a sudden spring he leaped to his feet.

"By all the imps below, I never thought of that before!" he cried, excitedly. "Shall I foller and stop 'em?" and he took a few steps toward the wood, as if to execute the purpose. "But no, why should I?" and he halted. "One don't know it, and the other don't either. It can't be a crime if she don't know what she's doing in killing this gal." And then another thought came into his mind. The dull-witted renegade was getting strangely bright.

"The gal has fooled me! I remember now that she once told me that Miss Treveling was the only woman in the world that had ever spoken a kind word to her, and that she would willingly lay down her life for her sake. The truth on't is, that she has sneaked the gal out of our hands to save her. The lover story was all moonshine. Wal, let the gal do it, if she kin. She little knows what she is doing when she saves this she-critter."

Then the renegade resumed his place by the lodge.

In a short time the Shawnee returned with the gourd bottle of whisky.

It only took a few minutes for the renegade and the chief to empty the gourd.

Hardly had they finished the whisky when from the darkness came Girty.

Girty said but a few words to the two and then entered the lodge.

"There'll be a hurricane 'fore long," muttered Kendrick.

The renegade was right, for Girty rushed from the wigwam, furious as the panther cheated of its prey.

"Curses on you, the gal is gone!" he cried.

The Indian looked the astonishment he felt, while on Kendrick's face was a look of amazement, of course assumed for the occasion.

"You have left your post," Girty cried to the Indian.

The chief did not attempt to deny it, but strove to excuse himself by stating that Kendrick had watched in his place.

Girty guessed the scheme at once.

"You eternal villain!" he cried, addressing Kendrick; "it was all contrived between you and your daughter to rescue the girl from my hands, you lying hound!"

Enraged, Kendrick rose to his feet, drew his knife and made a dash at Girty, but his opponent was quicker far than he, for, as Kendrick advanced, Girty dealt him a terrific blow with his tomahawk that felled him like a log to the earth.

"Lie there and rot!" cried Girty, contemptuously. "And now summon the warriors; we must follow our birds at once. As for this affair, you can bear witness, chief, that I struck him in self-defense."

Within five minutes, a dozen painted warriors, headed by Girty, were on the trail of the fugitives.

CHAPTER XXXVII.

FOLLOWING A MADMAN.

With eager haste, Boone and Kenton followed in the footsteps of Lark.

On through the station, without turning to the right or left, but heading straight toward the forest, Lark went.

Amazed at his strange action, they strove to overtake him, but the madman—for the two borderers had but little doubt that Lark had been attacked by sudden madness—entered the shadows of the wood before the others could overtake him.

The two paused on the edge of the timber and looked at each other for a moment in astonishment.

"Well, dern my old hide, ef I know what to make of this!" exclaimed Boone, breaking the silence.

"Shall we follow him?" asked Kenton.

"Yes," replied Boone, decidedly. "I never see'd anything like this hyer afore, and I feel a nat'ral curiosity to see the end onto it. We were a-goin' to make a scout, and ef we foller him, why, it's pretty much the same thing."

So, without further conversation, the two plunged into the wood.

They tracked Lark easily, for he crashed through the wood without caution, making fully as much noise as a huge bear.

Lark was heading straight for the Ohio; in fact, retracing the course the three had taken in coming from the Indian village of Chillicothe.

"Ef we should happen to run into a war-party of Shawnees, they'd make mince-meat out of us afore you could say Jack Robingson," growled Kenton to Boone, as they raced through the tangled mazes of the thicket, in their endeavor to keep up with the madman's headlong course.

"Yes, it's lucky that thar ain't any chance of meetin' the red heathens this side of the big drink." Boone was referring to the Ohio.

"Derned ef I ain't gitting short-winded," said his companion, breathing heavily.

"Well, I ain't got any more wind than I want myself," Boone replied.

Still onward through the forest Lark went, never slacking his headlong speed, stopping not for bush nor brier.

At last he reached the river's bank.

The shades of night were descending fast upon the earth, covering forest and river with a mantle of inky blackness. Afar off in the eastern sky, the moon, like a sword of fire, was rising above the forest's dark line.

Calmly on rolled the great river, its turbid waves lashing the banks that bound its pathway with many a dull and sullen moan as though impatient of restraint.

When Boone and Kenton reached the river's side, Lark had just drawn a canoe from its hiding-place in the bushes that ringed the bank. The canoe was the same that the three had used before when they had crossed the stream.

Lark dragged the canoe to the river and launched the frail bark on the dark and sullen waters.

The two scouts, profiting by the delay, overtook Lark just as he gave the canoe to the embrace of the dark stream.

"Hallo, man! what on yearth has got into yer?" cried Boone.

For the first time, Lark turned and looked upon his pursuers.

One look the hardy bordermen took at the face of their companion, and then they felt that the warm life current in their veins was congealing with horror.

They looked not upon the face of a man, but rather on the face of a corpse, newly risen from its grave.

White as the stainless marble was the face of Lark, and his large eyes glared with demoniac fires.

Like men inspired with sudden fear, the stout-hearted borderers recoiled.

Then, to their amazement, Lark raised his hand and pointed to the canoe, that rocked and danced like a thing of life upon the turbid waters.

"He wants us for to git in and cross the 'drink' with him," said Boone, in a voice that showed plainly the feeling of horror that had taken possession of the old Indian-fighter.

"Shall we go?" asked Kenton, scarcely speaking above his breath.

"Yes; it's our duty as Christian men to see that this madman comes to no harm. I'm afeard that we are a-goin' to see something terrible," Boone answered.

Again, and with a gesture of command, Lark pointed to the frail boat, that was dancing like an eggshell on the bosom of the surging tide.

The two obeyed the gesture and entered the canoe.

Then Lark seized the paddle, and the little craft, with its human freight, sped rapidly across the river.

The white-capped billows—the children of the wind—surged and dashed against the sides of the canoe as if eager to tear from their frail shelter the mortals that dared to risk their lives amid the turbid waves of the Ohio.

The rising wind whistled and surged through the frail forest trees; the waves were turbid and angry; the moon, a ray of lurid light, was darting lambent fires through the dark cloud-banks.

The scouts looked around them and shuddered. A terrible depression was upon their feelings. The very air they breathed seemed full of evil.

The bow of the canoe touched the bank.

With a sweep of the broad paddle, Lark brought the canoe sideways to shore. Boone and Kenton at once gained the bank. Lark followed slowly.

On the bank Lark halted. In his hand he held the "painter" of the canoe, a sprig of grapevine.

A moment he looked at the trail bark and then deliberately drove his foot through the bottom and cast it adrift to the mercy of the swollen waters.

Eagerly, like living things, the sullen waves leaped over and around the canoe as it sunk from mortal sight in their chill embraces.

"Jerusalem! how on yearth are we a-goin' to git across the drink ag'in?" muttered Boone, in dismay.

Kenton did not reply, for he was watching Lark eagerly.

The stalwart borderer, who was acting so strangely, watched the canoe until the dark waters hid it from his sight. Then, without paying any more attention to the two who stood by his side on the bank, than if they had been sticks or stones, he plunged into the thicket that fringed the river's side.

Utterly dumbfounded at his unaccountable actions, Boone and Kenton again followed on his track.

This time, however, Lark did not proceed carelessly and without caution, as before, but, on the contrary, crept through the tangled underwood with all the care of a wild beast stealing upon its prey.

The two woodmen had but little difficulty in following their strange companion.

Seconds lengthened into minutes, minutes into hours. The great moon, rising slowly up, no longer flecked the sky with swords of fire, but beamed a flood of soft, silvery light, save when the flying clouds crossed her path, and, like agents of evil, hid her rays from sight.

"We must be near Ke-ne-ha-ha's village," muttered Kenton to Boone, after a weary tramp through the pathless wilderness, trailing Lark's erratic course.

"Putty near," replied Boone.

Hardly had the words left the lips of the old woodman when, as suddenly as if he had sunk into the earth Lark disappeared from sight.

The woodmen stood aghast. They had followed Lark easily. He had not seemed to notice that the two were near him, and had not attempted to evade them.

"Where on yearth *has* he gone to?" muttered Boone, in astonishment, and rubbing his eyes as if he doubted the evidence of his own senses.

"Down into the yearth or up into the air," answered Kenton, who was as much astonished as his companion at the sudden and mysterious disappearance.

Then the two advanced to the spot whereon Lark had stood when they had seen him last.

It was too dark for them to attempt to follow his trail, if he had left one, and so, defeated in their pursuit, they halted to counsel what their next move should be.

"Let's go on a little way; maybe we'll find some trace of him ahead," said Boone, thoughtfully.

Then the two proceeded onward till they came to a little open glade, whereon the moonbeams shone.

As the two reached the glade and stood within the timber that fringed its edge, a slight noise fell upon their ears.

"Hush!" cried Boone, in a cautious whisper, and he laid his hand lightly upon Kenton's arm as he spoke.

Stout Sim hardly needed the caution, for his quick ear had caught the sound.

"It's some one coming through the forest," said Kenton, in a whisper.

"Yes," replied Boone, listening intently.

"Can it be Lark?"

"No, I think not," said the old woodman; "it's more likely to be an Injun. We must be mighty nigh to the Injun village."

"Maybe we've run into a hornet's nest," said Kenton, coolly.

"We'll have to git out, then," observed Boone, nothing terrified.

"Whoever it is, he don't seem to be afeard of any thing, for he's marching right along as if he owned the hull wood."

"Let's to timber," said Boone, curtly.

A second more and the stalwart forms of the two scouts had disappeared. Like snakes they nestled in the grass and waited for the man who walked through the wood so carelessly.

The two did not have long to wait, for the sound of the steps grew louder and louder, and then an Indian warrior, decked in the gaudy war-paint and prepared for battle, stepped into the little glade whereon the moonbeams shone.

In his hand the warrior carried a tomahawk. The moonbeams danced upon the edge of the steel.

The warrior paused in the center of the glade and looked around him as though expecting some one. Then he spoke, defiantly:

"I am the White Dog, a great brave of the Shawnee nation. I seek the Wolf Demon in the forest. If he has a heart as big as a weasel's, he will come from his lair and face me."

CHAPTER XXXVIII.

A JOYOUS MEETING.

Virginia followed Kate without fear.

Once within the wood, Kate enjoined caution upon her companion.

"It is a long and weary way from here to Point Pleasant," she said.

"I have traversed it once already, then a prisoner. It will not seem so long now, for I know that each step is taking me nearer to my dear home and those I love," Virginia replied, cheerfully.

Kate looked at the fair girl, a mournful smile upon her olive-tinged features.

"And you trust yourself fearlessly in my hands?" Kate asked.

"Yes, why should I fear?" Virginia said, in a tone of wonder.

"Am I not the daughter of a renegade?" Kate asked, a world of bitterness in her tone.

"You are not answerable for the faults of others," Virginia said, gently. "I freely trust my life in your hands and I have no fear."

They were proceeding rapidly through the wood as they spoke.

Kate did not reply aloud to Virginia's speech, but to herself she murmured:

"Would this girl trust me if she knew how deeply I loved the man that possesses her heart?"

Kate led the way at a swift pace—not that she feared pursuit, for she did not dream that Virginia's escape, and her own treachery toward the renegade Girty, would be discovered until the morning.

Virginia, both in her face and dress, showed visible traces of the peril that she had passed through.

Well was it for her that her gown was of stout homespun stuff, for many a thorn-bush laid hold of it in her quick passage through the wilderness.

"Where will you go first, to the station of Point Pleasant or to my cabin, where Harvey Winthrop is?" Kate asked.

"Is not your cabin some miles beyond the station?"

"Yes, but from the route I am obliged to take, my cabin is but a short distance further than the station."

"Let us go there first, then," said Virginia, eagerly. "Oh! the anguish I have suffered, thinking him dead," and a cloud came over the fair face of the girl as she spoke.

Every word that Virginia spoke in reference to Winthrop, touched Kate to the quick, for she saw how deeply and truthfully she loved him. Then she realized, too, how hopeless was the passion that burned so fiercely in her own bosom. But, neither by word or sign, did she betray that love to Virginia.

Steadily Kate pursued her course, heading direct for the Ohio; and, without a murmur at the toilsome way, cheered by the thought that a few hours would give her to the arms of both lover and father, Virginia followed.

Leaving the two girls, so strangely unlike in station and in nature, to pursue their tedious journey through the wilderness, they little thinking that the fierce renegade, Girty, had discovered their escape, and with a chosen band of Shawnees was following hard upon their track, we will return to the man whom Girty had stricken to the earth, Dave Kendrick, the renegade.

The Indians bore the wounded man to his lodge, and examined his wound.

The blow had been a fearful one, and Kendrick's time on earth was short.

When the renegade recovered from his faint, it did not take him long to discover that he had not many minutes to live.

"The skunk has finished me," he muttered, with a deep groan of pain. "I haven't got many minutes more of life, but I'd give 'em all to have a single chance at him," and then the stricken man ground his teeth together fiercely.

"My brother is hurt much?" said one of the warriors, bending over him.

"The happy hunting-grounds for me, chief, afore I'm an hour older," replied Kendrick, with a gasp of pain. "The cursed skunk—to use his tomahawk ag'in' my knife," he muttered.

"Can Noc-a-tah do any thing for his brother?" said one of the Indians, a tall chief who was one of the principal men among the Shawnees.

For a few moments Kendrick was silent, apparently overcome by pain; then, with a great effort, he rallied his scattered senses.

"Yes, chief, you kin do something for me. I want to make a 'totem.' Bring me two pieces of bark and a pointed twig."

One of the Indians departed and speedily returned with two pieces of white birch-bark and a pointed twig.

"That'll do," muttered Kendrick, faintly. "I reckon I'll get even with the skunk now."

Then, the renegade dipped the pointed twig in the blood that was flowing freely from the terrible wound in his head, and with great difficulty— for Dave Kendrick had little of the scholar about him—he traced some half a dozen lines on the smooth surface of the two pieces of birch-bark. On both pieces he wrote the same words, and then sunk back, exhausted.

The breath of the renegade came thick and hard. The icy fingers of Death already were closing upon and chilling their victim.

"Chief," he muttered with a gasp, "one of these totems to the man who wounded me, Girty; the other to the white-haired chief, General Treveling, at Point Pleasant—you know him?"

The savage bowed assent.

"Tell him the totem is true—a dying man swears to it—how cursed dark it is; I—" and then, with a stifled groan, Dave Kendrick, the renegade, sunk back, dead.

Noc-a-tah, the Shawnee chieftain, carefully rolled up the two pieces of bark that bore on their smooth surface the "totems," thrust them into his pouch, and then departed to fulfill the mission of the renegade.

We will now return to the fugitives.

Kate and Virginia paused not, either for food or sleep, but through the darkness of the night steadily pursued their way.

To Kate, the forest—although to strange eyes a trackless wilderness—was as familiar as her own little garden. She knew the way as well in the darkness as in the light. She was, in very truth, a child of the wilderness, and from infancy she had traversed freely the brown paths of the wild woods.

The first light of the morn was lining the eastern skies with leaden and white purple rays when Kate and her companion came within sight of the little cabin that was the home of the Kanawha Queen.

A weary march it had been through the live-long night, and Virginia, her garments wet with dew, and torn in many places by the rough grasp of the brambles, that had sought to stay her progress through the thicket, presented but a sorry sight.

Her hair, too, escaped from the simple knot that usually held it in its place, streamed down over her shoulders in wild confusion. Her face was pale, save where a hectic spot burned in either cheek. Her eyes, though, shone with a determined light, for Virginia, weak woman as she was, held within her veins the stern soldier blood of her father. That blood had nerved her to face the peril that she had encountered.

"There, lady, is refuge at last," said Kate, pointing to the humble cabin.

"A palace could not be more welcome than your cabin," said Virginia, gratefully, and a joyous light sparkled in her eyes as she spoke.

The two advanced to the house. The door sprung open as if by magic, and on the threshold stood Harvey Winthrop.

With a cry of joy, Virginia rushed into his arms and sunk almost fainting upon his breast. She was in the arms of the man she loved; she thought only of that and of naught else.

Winthrop folded the slender form of the girl to his heart, and tenderly brushed the damp dew from her shining locks.

Kate turned her head aside. She could not bear to look upon the meeting of the lovers. Their joy tore her heart and made the life-blood in her veins run chill with agony.

"Oh, Heaven! give thy poor handmaiden strength to bear her cross," she murmured, in despair. And as she spoke, a sudden faintness came over her; all things swam before her eyes, and but for the support of the rude fence by which she stood, she would have fallen.

The lovers wrapped up in the joy of each other's presence, did not notice her agitation.

"Again I hold you in my arms," the young man said, softly, as he strained the loved form of the maiden to his heart.

"And I thought you dead," Virginia said.

"To Kate I owe my life!" And as he spoke, both he and Virginia turned their eyes toward the Kanawha Queen.

By this time Kate had recovered her composure, except that her cheek was paler than it was wont to be.

"To Heaven your thanks, not to me, its humble instrument," replied Kate, modestly.

Then the three entered the cabin.

A cheerful fire blazed in the broad fire-place. By the fire, the three sat.

Kate, clad in buck-skin, Indian fashion, showed few traces of the terrible night-journey, but Virginia, although clad in stout homespun garments, had many a mark of bramble and brier; yet, to the eyes of Winthrop, she looked prettier than ever.

"And your wound?" asked Virginia, suddenly remembering her lover's hurt.

"I scarcely feel it now," Winthrop replied; "a few hours has worked wonders. The thought of your danger troubled me more than the pain of my wound."

"And from that danger, Kate has saved me, although at the risk of her own life," and Virginia cast a glance full of love and thankfulness toward the daughter of the renegade.

"I did what was but my duty to do. I promised to save you if I could. I kept that promise—"

"At the risk of your own life," Virginia said, quickly.

"The life of the outcast is worth but little," Kate replied, sadly.

"The life of my sister is as precious as my own!" Virginia exclaimed, earnestly, and rising, she knelt by Kate's side and folded her arms around her.

"Your sister!" said Kate, in wonder.

"Yes; for henceforth you shall be my sister. Kate, you must forsake this wild life and make your home with me. Will you not do so?"

Virginia looked, pleadingly, in the face of Kate, and wondered to see her brown cheek pale and her great eyes fill with tears.

"Oh, you do not know what you ask!" cried Kate, in agony, "and I can not tell you."

Virginia heard the strange words in amazement.

"Can you not be my sister?"

"No, no, it is impossible," Kate murmured, sadly.

"Impossible, why?"

"Because—"

The wild war-whoop of the Shawnees, pealing forth on the still morning air, and ringing in the ears of the three like a signal of doom, cut short Kate's words.

Then the door yielded to a heavy blow, and a score of dark forms rushed into the room.

181

CHAPTER XXXIX.

THE TOTEM OF THE RENEGADE.

A single glance at the dark forms that filled the doorway, and the hearts of the three sunk within them.

They were prisoners to the Shawnees!

At the head of the painted warriors was Simon Girty, the renegade.

Girty's eyes lit up with fiend-like joy as he gazed upon his captives.

"A keen she-devil you are, to snatch the game out of my hands; but did you think that you could escape from me so easily?" he cried, addressing Kate.

The warm blood flushed the face of the "Queen," as she listened to the insolent words of the white Indian.

"You are in my power; no human force can snatch you from me," he continued, exultingly. "A nice trick it was, to pretend to watch my prisoner for me, and then aid her to escape in the darkness! But I tracked you, though, cunning as you are. A fit daughter of a worthy father; but, maybe, my turn will come now, Chiefs," and he turned to the warriors that filled the doorway, "which of you want this dainty brown maid for a squaw? I'll give her to one, for her fate is in my hands now."

All the fire in Kate's nature shone in the lurid flash of her dark eyes.

"Take care, Simon Girty!" she cried, in anger. "If my father is not man enough to protect me from insult, my rifle will."

"Your father is dead, girl, or mighty near it," returned Girty, scornfully. "When I discovered the trick that you and he played upon me, I sunk my tomahawk in his skull and let out his fool's brains."

"My father slain!" cried Kate, in horror.

"I reckon that there isn't much life left in him by this time. He dared to cross my will, the hound that he was, and I struck him to his death," said Girty, fiercely.

Kate felt that she was indeed at Girty's mercy.

"And for you, my pretty white bird," and the renegade turned to Virginia as he spoke, "did you fancy that you could escape the fate that I marked out for you? You will learn in time that my blows seldom fail."

"Oh, have you no mercy!" cried Virginia, in despair.

"What mercy did your father have when his lashes tore my back, long years ago?" demanded the renegade, fiercely. "The mercy that he showed to me I will show to him and his. I'll tear his heart as his punishment tore my flesh. When he learns your shameful fate, then, and not till then, will the debt of vengeance be canceled. How he will curse his evil fortune when he learns that his dainty daughter—the apple of his eye, the pride of his old age—is the victim of the renegade, Simon Girty!" and then he laughed loud and long.

"Accursed villain!" cried Winthrop, suddenly, unable to restrain his fury; and quick as thought, he flung himself upon the renegade, regardless of the overpowering number of foes that surrounded him.

With a single heavy blow between the eyes, he beat the renegade, like a log, to the ground; but ere he could pursue his advantage further, the Shawnee warriors dashed themselves upon him. Ten to one, Winthrop was speedily overcome and securely bound.

The renegade rose to his feet, his eyes gleaming like a demon's, and a livid mark upon his face, where the knuckles of the young man had bruised the skin.

"You shall pay dearly for that blow!" Girty cried, between his clenched teeth. "You shall die at the torture-stake, a thousand deaths all in one. The tomahawks of the Indians will cut your flesh from your bones, even while you are a living man. You will cry aloud for death to come to end your misery. And in your last moments the thought will come that this fair girl—whom I guess you love—will be wholly in my power—a helpless victim to my caprices. And as you die in lingering torments, I will stand by your side and taunt you till death releases you from my power."

Words can but feebly describe the waked wrath of the renegade.

Winthrop faced him undauntedly.

"It suits your cowardly nature better to taunt a helpless prisoner than to face a free man. I do love this girl, and the thought that she is helpless in your power, demon that you are, gives me greater pain than can all the fire and torture of the red devils with whom you claim kindred. I am your captive. Look well to me; see that I do not escape from you, for it would cost you your life if I should ever again regain my freedom."

Every muscle in the young man's form swelled with indignation as he spoke.

"When you cease to be my captive, death will claim you," replied Girty, grimly.

Kate looked around her. She saw no avenue of escape. She felt that they were hopelessly lost.

"Come," said Girty; "but first bind the wrists of these two squaws."

The Indians obeyed his order.

"Now for your future home, the Shawnee village!" Girty cried, in triumph.

The Indians and their prisoners, led by the renegade, passed through the door of the cabin and stood within the little clearing that surrounded the house.

Then forth from the timber came the Shawnee brave, Noc-a-tah.

He came straight to Girty.

"Well, chief, what is it?" asked the renegade. He conjectured from the Indian's manner that he was the bearer of some important tidings.

"Your white brother has gone to the land of shadows—he sends this totem to you." Then the Indian drew from his pocket the piece of birch bark whereon Kendrick had, with his blood and the pointed twig, traced his dying words.

"Dead, eh?" said Girty, with a sneer. "A totem to me? What can it be?"

Then the renegade took the piece of bark and endeavored to read the lines.

Rudely were the letters formed, for Dave Kendrick could boast of but little scholarship.

The renegade puzzled over the writing. Suddenly the meaning flashed upon him. A gleam of fierce joy swept over his dark face.

"By all the fiends, this is double vengeance!" he cried in glee. "Chief, in Chillicothe, thou shalt have the best scalping-knife that I own, in payment for this precious totem."

Noc-a-tah gravely nodded, and then disappeared within the thicket.

Girty turned to where the two girls stood, side by side.

The maidens wondered at his searching look.

"What a blind idiot I have been not to have noticed it before," he muttered, "and yet I remember, now, the face of the girl did look familiar to me when I first saw her in the Shawnee village. To think of my vengeance slipping through my fingers, and then, after long years, being put again within my hands! There's fate in this. And Kendrick, too—he thought, by this dying declaration, to strike a blow at me, even from the grave. He thought both the girls were safely out of my hands. He little dreamed when I should read his 'totem'—as the savage termed it—that the two he referred to in it would be helpless prisoners in my power. Could he have foreseen that, he would have cut off his hand rather than divulge to me what he has here written."

Then the renegade laughed long and silently. His captives wondered at his glee.

"You risked your life to save this girl; why did you do it?" he asked of Kate, suddenly.

"Because she was helpless in the power of a cruel monster. My heart told me to save her, even at the risk of my own life," replied Kate, promptly.

"And you, girl—are you not grateful to this maiden, who has tried so hard to save you from me?" he said to Virginia.

"Yes, I am *very* grateful," replied the girl, wondering at the question.

"Their hearts don't tell 'em," muttered the renegade. "The old adage is a fable; blood is *not* thicker than water. Virginia, years ago I stole your eldest sister, and left her to perish in the forest. This was the first blow that I aimed at your father. Now see how strangely fate sometimes disposes of things in this world. The child that I left to die did not die, but was saved, and has grown to womanhood, and I all the time thinking her dead. Girls, can't you guess the truth? The man that saved and reared the child was Dave Kendrick, the renegade!"

The truth flashed upon the maidens in an instant.

"Sister!" cried Virginia, warmly; but the bonds upon their wrists forbade further greeting.

"Yes, she is your sister. Kate, you are Augusta Treveling, the eldest daughter of the old General," said Girty, and a triumphant smile was upon his face.

The smile made the two girls tremble.

"The hound that I gave to the worms never told the secret to me, but, dying, he wrote it here on this piece of bark. This was his vengeance," and Girty laughed loudly. "It will be pleasant news to the old General, your father, when he hears that both of his daughters are living, and both are in my power."

"Oh, man, have you no mercy?" plead Kate.

"Mercy?" cried the renegade, fiercely. "Ask it of the hungry wolf, the angry bear, or the red savage, when his knife is raised to slay! Expect mercy from all these, but expect none from the man whose skin is white but whose heart is red. Come; in Chillicothe you will meet your fate."

A broad sheet of flame, springing from the woods to the north of the little clearing, followed by the sharp report of a dozen rifles, answered the boast of the renegade.

Of the ten savages who had followed Girty's lead, seven lay wounded or dead upon the earth.

From the timber came the ringing shout of the borderers, and a score or more of the settlers, headed by General Treveling and stout Jake Jackson, came with a rush into the clearing.

Girty, though badly wounded, and the unhurt savages, had fled at once.

Jake and fully one-half of the borderers followed in pursuit.

The captives were speedily released from their bonds.

"Let me give thanks to that Heaven that in its bounty has seen fit to give me back both my daughters to gladden the last years of an old man's life!" cried Treveling, in joy, as he folded his children to his heart.

The timely arrival of the settlers was easily explained. Noc-a-tah, the Shawnee chief, had faithfully kept the promise made to the dying renegade, and had first sought Point Pleasant and given the "totem" into the hands of the General.

The father's joy on learning that his eldest daughter lived can easily be imagined.

Jackson, who had seen the Indian depart, instantly counseled that he should be tracked, that the whereabouts of the rest of the Shawnees might be discovered.

The advice of the stout Indian-fighter had been followed, and the happy result was, the rescuing of Girty's victims.

Well might the aged father lift up his voice in joy.

CHAPTER XL.

THE WHITE DOG AND THE WOLF DEMON.

"He's a plucky young cuss, ain't he?" said Boone, in a whisper to Kenton, when he heard the bold defiance of the Indian warrior.

"The Wolf Demon will make mince-meat out of him ef he puts his claws onto him," replied Kenton, in the same cautious whisper that Boone had used.

"I wonder if the spook will come?" said Boone.

"I reckon not; them things never come when they're expected. They alers take their own time," returned Kenton.

"How easy we could 'rub' him out now, eh?" Boone observed, suggestively.

"I'm afeard it would bring a hull grist of his relations down on top of us, thick as skeeters in a swamp," said Kenton.

"That's so."

A movement on the part of the Indian put a stop to their conversation, and eagerly they bent their eyes upon him.

After pronouncing his war-like defiance, the warrior, with his tomahawk in one hand and his keen-edged scalping-knife in the other, remained motionless as a bronze statue.

Full five minutes he waited.

His eager eye, quick and piercing as the eye of a hawk, surveyed the forest before him.

He heard each rustling leaf that stirred in obedience to the soft night-wind's commands; the noise of the pinions of the owl, winging its nocturnal flight through the dim aisles of the great, green wood; the cry of the tree-toad; the chirrup of the cricket, deep down in the earth. But, none of these stirred the senses of the Indian. He knew the voices of the night full well, for he was a child of the forest and had slept many an hour beneath the shadows of the spreading boughs.

He listened for a sound that he heard not—the tread of the great gray wolf, who wore the face of a man.

Impatient, the warrior uttered a guttural exclamation.

Again he addressed the silence and the gloom, called for the dread being to appear, at whose approach all living things of the earth or air fled.

"The warrior is weary of waiting. If the Wolf Demon is in the thicket let him come forth. The White Dog will strip off his hide, or else the Wolf De-

187

mon shall take his scalp and mark the totem of the Red Arrow on his breast."

But the silence and the gloom replied not to the bold defiance.

After a pause of a few moments the warrior uttered a contemptuous exclamation.

"The Wolf Demon should wear the skin of the muskrat; he skulks in the dark and fears to meet his foe face to face."

The chief turned upon his heel and thrust his scalping-knife into his girdle as if to depart.

One single step he made, and then a sound fell upon his ears that made him pause; made him draw the keen-edged knife again from his belt; made him prepare for battle.

The quick ear of the Indian—trained from infancy to note the noises of the forest, the plain and river—heard a stealthy step prowling through the thicket.

The noise came from behind him. Quick as thought the warrior turned and faced the point from whence the noise proceeded.

No form stepped from the timber into the little glade, whereon the soft moonbeams fell, but the Indian still heard the sound of the stealthy steps.

The steps seemed to come no nearer, and yet the sound grew no fainter.

Whoever was within the wood was circling around the Indian as if to attack him in the rear, and by surprise.

The chief guessed the truth, and as the unknown foe moved, he moved. Slowly he turned, keeping his face always in the direction from whence came the sound of the steps.

The two borderers, concealed in the thicket, watched the movements of the Indian with astonishment.

When he assumed the attitude of defense and drew again the knife, Boone nudged Kenton.

"He hears something," he whispered.

"'Pears like it," Kenton replied.

And as they watched the Shawnee, they, too, heard the sound of stealthy steps approaching them.

They noted that, as the steps approached, the face of the chief seemed to follow the direction of the steps.

At once the Indian-fighters guessed the truth; guessed that the terrible Wolf Demon, lurking in the thicket, was circling around the chief, eager to spring upon him unawares.

The stealthy steps came nearer and nearer to the concealed men.

Boone, stretched out so near to Kenton that he touched him, felt that the stout borderer was trembling like an aspen leaf; and, to speak the truth, the blood in Boone's veins was running cold with horror.

There, not a dozen paces from them, within the thicket, they saw the terrible form of the Wolf Demon.

With stealthy step he moved through the wood, his eyes glaring, like coals of fire, upon the Indian warrior. In his paw he carried the fatal tomahawk that had brained so many Shawnee chieftains.

The terrible form was moving in a circle around the warrior. But the Indian was on his guard, and, guided by the sound of the stealthy steps, kept his front always to his foe.

The Wolf Demon completed the circle, and then, as if fully satisfied that he could not take the warrior by surprise, came slowly from the thicket and stood within the open space; not, though, in the soft light of the moonbeams, but half hid by the shadows thrown by the forest monarchs that hemmed in the little glade.

The keen eyes of the Indian detected the appearance of the terrible form.

The light of fierce determination shone upon the face of the Shawnee warrior, and firmly he grasped his weapons and waited for the onset of the foe.

Boone and Kenton, in breathless suspense, watched from their leafy covert, eager to see the issue of the contest that was, apparently, so near at hand.

A few seconds only the Wolf Demon paused within the friendly shadows of the wood; then, with the swiftness of forked lightning, he leaped upon the Shawnee warrior.

Bravely the Indian met the assault. With his tomahawk he parried the blow aimed at his head, and, at the same moment, drove his long knife, up to its haft, in the side of the phantom foe; but, the glittering blade met no flesh in its passage, and not a single drop of blood dimmed the brightness of the steel.

The thrust of the Shawnee chieftain cost him dear, for, ere he could withdraw his knife again, the tomahawk of the Wolf Demon descended upon his head. By a quick motion of his own ax he partly parried the blow, but the force of the stroke bore him over backward to the earth.

With a howl of triumph the Wolf Demon planted his foot upon the warrior's breast, and the glittering tomahawk gleamed before his eyes, raised to give the death-blow.

The warrior felt that he was lost.

The death-note of his nation broke from his lips.

Then, forth from the timber, from the direction in which the Indian village lay, came the Shawnee girl, Le-a-pah.

She had arrived upon the scene of conflict just in time to witness the discomfiture of her lover.

With outstretched arms and a cry of horror—regardless of her own life —she rushed forward to save her lover from the edge of the fatal tomahawk, which was raised to drink his blood.

The paw of the Wolf Demon which clutched the tomahawk remained poised in the air as the girl advanced. The blow descended not upon the unprotected head of the prostrate man.

The phantom form, motionless as one of the forest oaks, glared upon the Indian girl with its eyes of fire as if struck dumb with horror.

It was a startling tableau.

The scouts looked on with awe-struck eyes. They expect each instant to see the tomahawk descend, and the Indian girl fall lifeless at the blow.

Steadily for a few moments the Demon form glared at the girl, and then, taking its foot from the breast of the down-trodden chief, it retreated backward with slow steps, toward the forest, still, however, keeping its eyes upon the face of the girl as though under the influence of some terrible enchantment.

The Indian chief, hardly able to realize that he was saved from the death that but a moment before seemed so certain, made no effort to rise, but appeared transfixed with horror.

The Wolf Demon gained the shadow of the thicket, and then—as if the spell that had bound him had been broken—with a terrible cry, that rung through the forest like the wail of a lost soul, doomed forever to eternal fires, he vanished amid the darkness.

The cry of the Wolf Demon froze the blood of his hearers with horror.

The girl, with a sob of terror, sunk down by the side of the young chieftain.

Rising, the Shawnee warrior tenderly lifted the light form of Le-a-pah from the greensward.

"Light of my heart, thou hast saved the life of the red chief!" cried the warrior.

"Le-a-pah could not bear the thought that her lover should seek the terrible Wolf Demon in the wood; she followed in his track to urge him to return," said the maiden.

"The White Dog has tried to win Le-a-pah. If he has failed to kill the Wolf Demon, it is because the Great Spirit wills that he shall not die by the hand of a red-man."

"Let us seek my father. I will beg him to release you from the cruel task."

Then the chief and the maiden left the glade.

After a few minutes Boone and Kenton came from their hiding-place.

"Now, let's look for Lark," said Boone. "I've a thought that he has met this terrible Wolf Demon when he was hyer afore, and that the sight has made him mad."

The two left the glade, and to their surprise found they stood before the hollow oak which had served them as a rendezvous when in the wood before.

At the foot of the oak they found Lark's cap. As Boone picked it up, it felt moist.

He looked at his hand.

It was stained with blood.

"By heaven!" he cried, in horror. "Lark has been killed, and perhaps by the Wolf Demon!"

CHAPTER XLI.

THE FIGHT UNTO THE DEATH.

The two scouts looked upon the blood-stained cap with horror.

"The blood is fresh, too!" cried Boone. "Lark must have been killed by this monster immediately after we missed him in the thicket."

"It looks like it," said Kenton, solemnly.

"Let us look for the body."

But as they were about to commence their search, the sound of footfalls approaching through the wood fell upon their ears.

"Hush!" cried Boone, grasping Kenton by the arm as he spoke; "do you hear that?"

"It's some one coming through the wood."

"Yes, and hyer all comers are enemies and not friends; let's to cover," said Boone.

A second after the two woodmen were snugly concealed in the bushes.

The steps came nearer and nearer, and then, through the gloom of the night, the watching eyes of the two saw the fearful form of the terrible Wolf Demon approaching.

He walked not now with stealthy tread but his step was heavy and slow. His head was bent down, low upon his breast. Slowly he came on, passed by the ambush of the scouts, then crossed the moonlit glade and entered the thicket on the opposite side. He was bending his steps in the direction of the Indian village of Chillicothe.

Hardly had the awful form disappeared within the gloom of the forest when Boone grasped Kenton nervously by the shoulder.

"Kenton," he said, in a hoarse whisper, "let us not search for the body of our friend, whom this awful thing has killed, but revenge his death."

"I'm with you, tooth and nail," replied Kenton, firmly.

"Let's follow this thing then."

"Go it," said Kenton, tersely.

Then the woodmen, with caution, followed in the path of the Wolf Demon.

The Demon proceeded direct to the Indian village.

The woodmen were guided in their course by the noise of his footsteps.

Suddenly the sound of the steps ceased.

Boone and Kenton crept forward with increased caution.

A few rods on and they found themselves on the edge of the timber, and in full view of the Indian village.

The Wolf Demon was not to be seen!

The scouts then guessed the reason why the sounds of the Wolf Demon's tread had ceased so suddenly. The Demon had entered the village in search of prey.

The path that the two had followed entered the village close by the river's bank.

It was plain to Boone that the Wolf Demon had selected the same road into the Indian village that he, Boone, had taken in escaping from it.

"We're treed," said Boone, as they reached the edge of the timber and perceived that they could proceed no further in their pursuit without danger of their being discovered by the red-skins.

"A full stop hyer," said Boone, thoughtfully.

"Yes, it 'pears like it," Kenton replied.

"S'pose we wait hyer for the varmint? Ef he went into the village this way, it's likely that he'll come out the same path."

"That's true."

"Yes, as preachin'. I don't know as we kin damage the critter," said Boone, thoughtfully. "We hain't got no silver bullets, and I've heerd say that it takes a silver bullet to stop a spook."

"We kin try," said Kenton, decidedly.

"Right again, by hookey! Give us your paw, Sim; we'll stick by each other in this."

"Yes, to death," answered Kenton.

A firm grip of hands sealed the compact.

Then the two again concealed themselves in the bushes.

They watched and they waited.

* * * *

In the Indian village, Ke-ne-ha-ha, the great Shawnee chieftain, sat in the gloom of his wigwam.

The little fire that burned in the center of the lodge cast a baleful light over the dusky face of the warrior.

Dark and full of sorrow were the thoughts of the chieftain.

He saw again the death-scene of the Red Arrow; heard her shriek for mercy, and then beheld the warm life-blood gushing, free, from her young veins. Amid the smoke and flames, she died. Like the Roman father, he had given to the death his own flesh and blood. And that deed had brought upon his nation the terrible scourge of the Wolf Demon.

Well might the brow of Ke-ne-ha-ha look dark as the thunder-cloud when he thought of the past. And in the future he saw no ray of light. He had little hope that the White Dog would succeed in his mission and kill the terrible foe.

As he was brooding over these gloomy thoughts, his daughter, Le-a-pah, entered the wigwam.

"May the White Dog speak with the chief?" the girl asked.

"Let the brave enter," Ke-ne-ha-ha replied. A gleam of light flashed over his clouded face. Why should the young warrior seek him, save to tell of the death of the Wolf Demon?

A second more and the warrior stood before him. The girl remained, discreetly, at the door of the lodge.

"Well?" questioned the chief.

"The White Dog sought the Wolf Demon in the forest, fought him hand to hand, but the Shawnee brave fell beneath his foot; the tomahawk was raised to strike, when Le-a-pah bounded from the wood and the Wolf Demon held his arm and fled from her like the night flies from the dawn."

Ke-ne-ha-ha listened, in amazement.

"The warrior has failed," he said, slowly.

"Manitou did not will that he should kill the Wolf Demon," replied the young brave.

"The brave has tried, and the Shawnee chief will keep his word. Le-a-pah!"

The maiden came at his call.

The chief gave her to the embrace of the young warrior.

"You are both my children—go." But no gleam of joy lighted up Ke-ne-ha-ha's stern face as he gave his daughter into the arms of her lover. The living Wolf Demon cast a mantle of gloom over his brain.

The brave and the girl withdrew from the lodge. The manner of the chieftain forbade further words.

Left alone, Ke-ne-ha-ha strode up and down the narrow confines of the wigwam in sullen thought.

"Oh, that my life might save my people from this terrible scourge!" he murmured, with clenched teeth. "For the two lives, he has taken twelve. How many more of my nation must fall by the tomahawk of the Wolf Demon ere his taste for Shawnee blood will be satisfied?"

"One!" responded a deep voice.

Ke-ne-ha-ha turned, his blood chilled to ice with horror.

His eyes looked upon the terrible form of the Wolf Demon standing in the doorway of the wigwam. In the hand of the Demon shone the deadly tomahawk.

Ke-ne-ha-ha gazed with staring eyes upon the terrible figure.

"Let the chief prepare to die. He is the last Shawnee that will feel the edge of the tomahawk of the avenger," cried the deep voice.

With an effort, Ke-ne-ha-ha roused himself from the spell of terror that the appearance of the dreaded Wolf Demon had cast around him.

With a sudden bound, he seized his tomahawk, that had been carelessly cast upon the floor of the wigwam.

The Wolf Demon made no effort to prevent the chief from possessing himself of the weapon.

Tomahawk in hand, the foes faced each other.

Slowly they moved around the narrow circle of the wigwam, watching each other with wary eyes, each seeking an unguarded opening for an attack.

Thrice they made the circle of the lodge, the little fire, with its glimmering light, revealing their movements to each other.

Then with a spring, like unto the panther's in quickness, and in force, the Wolf Demon leaped upon the Shawnee chief.

Ke-ne-ha-ha did not seek to parry the attack, but nimbly he evaded it by springing to one side.

The tomahawk of the Wolf Demon spent its force upon the air; and as he passed, the wily Indian dealt him a terrible stroke upon the head, that cut in deep through the wolf-skin, and felled him heavily to the earth.

A hoarse note of triumph came from the lips of the chief as he beheld the downfall of his foe. But his joy was of short duration, for, like the ancient god of the fable that gathered strength from being cast to earth, the Wolf Demon rose to his feet. The shock of the fall had torn the tomahawk from his hand, but he did not attempt to recover the weapon.

With naked hands—weaponless—he faced the Shawnee chief. The blood streaming down freely over his face—over the black and white pigments with which it was painted in horrid fashion—made him look like an evil spirit fresh from the fires below.

His eyes shot lurid flames as he glared upon the Shawnee warrior.

Ke-ne-ha-ha grasped his tomahawk with desperate energy and waited for the attack of the unarmed foe.

The Shawnee chieftain did not have long to wait.

With the spring of a tiger the Wolf Demon leaped upon the Indian.

Desperately Ke-ne-ha-ha struck at him with the tomahawk, but the Wolf Demon warded off the blows with his arm, and despite the efforts of the chief to prevent it, he closed in with him.

Sinewy and supple was the Shawnee warrior, yet he was but as a child in the powerful grasp of his terrible foe.

The Wolf Demon held him in a grip of iron. His arms, linked round the Indian like bands of steel, were crushing the life out of him little by little.

Vainly Ke-ne-ha-ha struggled to free himself from the anaconda coil.

Like the serpent of far-off India, wreathing its huge length around its prey, the Wolf Demon held the Shawnee chieftain in his grip.

The breath of the Indian came thick and hard.

Up and down in the narrow confines of the wigwam swayed the contending foes, like two venomous snakes coiled together.

Exerting all his strength, the Indian tried to break the grasp of the Wolf Demon. Vainly he struggled—vainly he tried. He felt that his strength was going fast.

Tight and tighter grew the grip of steel.

The Indian turned black in the face. The blood gushed from his mouth. He ceased to struggle. The grip relaxed and Ke-ne-ha-ha fell to the ground, dead.

CHAPTER XLII.

THE LAST OF THE DEMON.

A look of triumph swept over the blood-stained face of the Wolf Demon as he looked upon the lifeless form of the Shawnee warrior.

From the cut in the head of the Wolf the blood was slowly trickling, but he did not seem to mind the hurt.

With a hoarse cry of joy he knelt by the side of the man whom he had strangled to death with his powerful arms.

He tore the hunting-shirt from the breast of the dead chieftain; then he drew the dead man's knife from his girdle.

Three rapid dashes and the Red Arrow, graven in the flesh, was blazoned on the breast of the Shawnee warrior.

"Inhuman dog, more like the wolf in heart than I, thus do I mark you," the Wolf Demon cried in a voice hoarse with passion. "Eleven red demons slew the Red Arrow, eleven Shawnee warriors have I slain. Not one of the murdering band has escaped my steel. She fell in the blazing cabin amid the great green wood, near where the Muskingum waters laugh and play. The assassins have fallen in the glade and in the woodland, by the banks of the Scioto and the Ohio, in the paths of the Shawnee village and by the lodge-fires of the Chillicothe. I have struck them down by night and by day. And on each breast, in memory of the Indian maid that I once loved so well, have I stamped the Red Arrow. Now, at last, the chief of the red band of slayers has felt the edge of the scalping-knife. My work is done—my mission ended, and now, death, take me for thine own." The Wolf Demon rose to his feet and glared wildly around him. His eyes were starting from their sockets and gleamed like balls of fire.

"What is this I see?" he cried, suddenly; "a river of blood! It is the blood of the red warriors that have fallen by my hand, and she the loved and lost is in its center. She beckons me to her. I see her as plainly as I did an hour ago when she sprung from the earth in the woodland glade by the hollow oak, to save the young Indian warrior from my vengeance. I know that he was not one of the assassin band that took thy life, but in his veins ran the blood of the accursed Shawnees, and I had doomed him to the death. But I spared him. Did you not come from thy spirit home among the blest and lift up thy hand to stay my arm? Go on, I'll follow thee! Death is near. It is welcome, for it brings me to thee, my love. I hear the song of angels in mine ears! I am coming."

Slowly, with his eyes fixed vacantly on the air, the Wolf Demon came from the lodge, descended the bank, and hid by it from sight, left the Shawnee village.

Boone and Kenton from their ambush perceived him approach.

Boone touched Kenton on the arm as if to call his attention, but Kenton had already perceived the terrible figure.

"Shall we fire at him?" questioned Kenton, in a whisper, and the usually firm hand of the borderer trembled as he fumbled with the lock of his gun.

"No, no!" cried Boone, quickly, and in a cautious whisper; "the report would bring the hull of the Shawnee village down upon as, jist like stirring up a nest of hornets."

"What shall we do, then?"

"We'll follow and attack him in the forest," answered Boone.

The Wolf Demon came slowly on, his eyes staring full upon the air before him. He passed by the ambush of the two woodmen and entered the thicket.

As he passed, the two noted the signs of a conflict so apparent upon him.

"Jist look at his face! it's kivered all over with blood!" exclaimed Boone, in wonder.

"He's fixed another Shawnee, I reckon," said Kenton, seriously.

"Sim, it's a terrible thing to attack this awful critter," said Boone, with a grave look upon his honest face.

"But the death of poor Lark—"

"Must be avenged!" exclaimed the old hunter, compressing his lips together, firmly.

"That's so, said Kenton, with a pale face and a throbbing heart, yet with undaunted courage.

"I didn't see as he had any we'pons, but ef he's the devil, he don't need any. Come on, we'll give him a tussle, anyway. Lord, I wish I could remember a prayer or two," said Boone, seriously.

Then with cautious steps they followed on the trail of the Wolf Demon.

The singular being pursued the same path returning that he had taken when coming through the wood.

He moved so slow that the two in pursuit followed him without difficulty.

Every now and then he halted for a moment and then again went on.

His steps became irregular. The hunters, following close behind, noticed that he was reeling like a drunken man.

From side to side he swayed as he made his way through the forest.

He reached the little glade by the side of which stood the hollow oak.

"Let's attack him in the glade!" cried Boone, as he and Kenton reached the edge of the opening and beheld the Wolf Demon standing motionless, as if irresolute, in the center of it.

"Come on, then."

Clubbing their rifles—they did not dare to fire for fear of the report arousing the Indian village—the two scouts dashed into the opening.

Hearing the noise of their footsteps, the Wolf Demon turned, extended his arms as if to stay their progress, and then, with a heavy groan, fell sideways to the ground. The sudden shock burst the wolf-head from its fastenings to the body, and it rolled away from the prostrate figure.

The scouts halted in astonishment.

The wolf-head gone, the head of a man, covered with light, clustering curls, was revealed to their gaze.

Quickly they knelt by the side of the Wolf Demon and wiped the blood and war-paint from his face.

The superstitious fear of the woodmen was all gone now, for they knew that it was a human form that lay extended on the earth before them.

The terrible Wolf Demon was dying. The tomahawk of the Shawnee had given him his death-wound. The strong limbs, once so powerful, were now made feeble by the near approach of that terrible mystery that human mind never yet has solved.

The two scouts lifted up the head of the dying man. His eyes opened slowly and, with a vacant look, he gazed around him.

"Oh, what a terrible dream!" he murmured, faintly.

The woodmen bent their heads, eagerly, to listen.

"It seems as if I have waded through a river of blood—fresh, warm blood, gushing, freely, from terrible wounds. I dreamed that I had been changed into a wolf, a beast with a human soul, and in that soul one thought only, vengeance on the Shawnee nation. In the light and in the darkness I sought that vengeance. The red braves fell around my path as the wheat falls around the reaper, yet I staid not my hand, for the cry went up for blood, rivers of it. On each victim I cut my mark, a Red Arrow, in remembrance of the wife that the red demons tore from me a year ago by the Muskingum. I was gifted with the cunning of a maniac, for at times I am mad. The wound on my head, that I received from a falling rafter on that fearful night when my wife was killed, affected my brain. In my madness I must have dreamed all these terrible things. Dreamed that I fashioned myself a wolf-skin like a wolf, and then struck down my foes. A hollow oak in the forest was my home; there I concealed my wolf-skin when my mad fit was over. Oh! it was a terrible dream."

Boone and Kenton exchanged glances; they knew that the dream was a reality.

Then the eyes of the stricken man, glaring around him, fell upon the strange disguise that covered his person.

"What is this?" he cried, in horror; "the skin of a wolf! Then it is not a dream! No, no, I see all clearly now; the near approach of death has cleared my eyes unto the truth. In my madness I have been like an avenging angel to the Shawnee nation. I see their tall forms around me now—masculine warriors—the tomahawk cut is on their skulls, and on their breast is graven in lines of warm blood the emblem of vengeance, the Red Arrow!"

Exhausted by the outburst, his head sunk back upon the knee of Boone.

"Heaven have mercy on his soul," said the rough old Indian-fighter, solemnly.

Kenton turned his head aside to brush away a tear. He had seen many a death-scene, but none like this.

Again the dying man raised his head. A soft light now gleamed in his blood-shot eyes.

"I see you," and he extended his hand feebly toward the thicket. Kenton and Boone looked in amazement, but they beheld nothing. The sight was visible to the eyes of the stricken man, alone.

"See, she beckons me to come—no more blood, but peace—peace and love eternal. I will come—see! she is there amid the cloud, I come—wait."

With a stifled gasp his head sunk back.

Boone could not repress a shudder, for he felt that he held a corpse in his arms.

No more would the Wolf Demon carry terror to the hearts of the Shawnee warriors.

With their hunting-knives the two scouts scooped a shallow grave beneath the boughs of the hollow oak, and there, by the pale light of the dying moon, they placed the mortal remains of Abe Lark, the terrible Wolf Demon, the white husband of the Indian girl—Ke-ne-ha-ha's daughter—"The Red Arrow."

The blood on Lark's cap was easily accounted for by the woodmen when they noticed a slight wound on the forehead of the body, made by some bramble in the madman's rapid flight through the forest.

Boone and Kenton returned to Point Pleasant, and great was the wonder of all when they learned who the Wolf Demon was.

The Indian expedition was abandoned. The death of the Shawnee chieftain broke up the proposed confederacy.

Winthrop and Virginia were married in due time, much to the disgust of Clement Murdock, who, shortly after, with Bob Tierson, emigrated to Kentucky, and there met his death at the hands of the Regulators for horse-stealing. Tierson, less guilty, escaped with a sound thrashing.

Kate bore her cross with resignation, and none guessed the love that was in her heart.

Our task is ended. The strange legend of the Wolf Demon is ended. It is some six years since—with fishing-rod in hand—the writer explored the pleasant tract of country bounded by the Scioto, the Ohio, and the Muskingum; and he little dreamed then, when, in a rude log-hut, an aged hunter told the strange old Indian legend, that he should ever give to the world the story of the Red Arrow and the Wolf Demon.

THE END.

* * * *

www.ingramcontent.com/pod-product-compliance
Lightning Source LLC
Chambersburg PA
CBHW012151260626
47155CB00020B/3562